Dear Reader,

As a teenager, I would stay up well into the night reading sweeping family sagas, thousand-page melodramas filled with dark secrets and surprise deathbed revelations. My own happy, well-adjusted family, alas, was never as dramatic. But over the years, as I learned more about my grandparents and other relatives, I found that even the most ordinary lives contain extraordinary moments. *The Letter* was inspired by this realization. My main characters, Lydia and Henry, may appear unremarkable to their granddaughter, Cassie. But once she starts digging into their past, she finds they have lived through more than she ever imagined—and that decisions they made long ago can still affect her life today.

I like to think that great love stories are all around us, lurking just beneath the surface of otherwise average lives. By following Lydia and Henry's story, I hope I inspire readers to appreciate the smaller, everyday dramas of their own families.

Thanks for reading!

Elizabeth Blackwell

ABOUT THE AUTHOR

As a magazine writer and editor, Elizabeth Blackwell has written about everything from designing a dream kitchen to fighting a duel. She lives outside Chicago with her husband, three children and a vast collection of long underwear. She is the author of *The Letter, The House of Secrets* and the upcoming *While Beauty Slept,* a retelling of the Sleeping Beauty legend. For more on her books and work, visit www.elizabethblackwellbooks.com.

Books by Elizabeth Blackwell

HARLEQUIN EVERLASTING LOVE
11—THE LETTER

HARLEQUIN SUPERROMANCE
1559—THE HOUSE OF SECRETS

Other titles by this author available in ebook format.

The Letter

—

ELIZABETH BLACKWELL

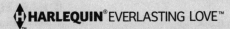

HARLEQUIN® EVERLASTING LOVE™

Recycling programs
for this product may
not exist in your area.

ISBN-13: 978-0-373-22968-0

THE LETTER

Copyright © 2007 by Elizabeth Blackwell

Printed in U.S.A.

The Letter

To Mom, Dad and Rachel
For always listening

Chapter 1

Cassie

Dearest Lydia, my darling,
This is my last hope, because I am desperate. Desperately in love with you and desperate to understand what happened. You won't see me, won't write. Why? I thought you loved me and I loved you and that would be enough. Instead you keep secrets, you keep things hidden even from the people who love you. But whatever mistakes you made and whatever mistakes I made, none of it matters. I don't care. All that matters is that I love

you. I love you so much my heart aches whenever I think of you. My arms miss holding you, and my lips miss the feel of your soft skin.

I wonder if you know the depth of my love for you. Perhaps I never told you what you needed to hear. So consider this my last stand. I love you, I always will, and I would do anything to make you happy. If you want a new life for yourself, I will try to understand, because your happiness means more to me than my own. What happens next is your choice. If you no longer want me, I need to hear it from you, otherwise I'll keep hoping. I'll keep looking for you, because without you I'm lost.
I will always be yours,
F.B.

Cassie fingered the pale yellow paper, softened by age to the consistency of tissue. No envelope, no date, no signature. Just those mysterious initials at the bottom, and a passion that still burst from the page—despite the years that had obviously passed since it was written.

Dearest Lydia…

The letter had been well hidden, tucked away between layers of cloth in a box marked Quilting Supplies. A box Cassie had walked by countless times in the twenty years she'd lived in her grandparents' house. A box that, before now, she'd never touched.

Cassie had always found Lydia's quilting slightly embarrassing. The fact that her grandmother's main accomplishment in life involved sewing together mismatched fabric remnants symbolized the gap between her and Cassie, the distance between Cassie's professional ambition and Lydia's old-fashioned housewife ways. At seventy-three, Lydia was a full decade younger than the grandparents of Cassie's friends. But Lydia had always struck Cassie as old before her time, a woman who'd married her high school sweetheart and settled down by the age of twenty-one. A woman who was content to help out with her husband's landscaping business but never had a life of her own. Other than college and one year studying abroad, she'd never traveled or experienced the world. She lived quietly with her quilts in the same house she'd grown up in, making no mark.

I wonder if you even know the depth of my love for you.

Cassie hastily refolded the letter into thirds and tucked it between the layers of cloth inside the box. She noticed her hand shaking as she hurriedly smoothed the fabric over the paper. Cassie had grown up believing that her grandfather was the only man Lydia had ever loved, her first and only boyfriend. But Henry Armstrong's initials weren't F.B.

Then there was the handwriting—words strung together frantically, with barely a space between, as if the letter had been written in one furious burst of energy. Henry took his time writing, meticulously tracing the shape of each letter, lifting his pen off the paper after each word before starting the next. His handwriting was as careful and measured as his speech, a far cry from the messy scrawl on the mysterious letter.

But the words were the real tipoff. Henry Armstrong—while he certainly loved his wife—didn't talk like this. Cassie had never heard Henry tell Lydia he loved her. He acknowledged Lydia's birthday with generic drugstore birthday cards, signing his name beneath the poem inside. He had to be nagged to add even the shortest greeting to Lydia's annual Christmas letters. Henry didn't express himself with words; he showed his love through action, whether it was stroking the head of his lonely young granddaughter or nurturing a tender plant in his beloved greenhouse.

This letter had been written by someone in pain. Someone literally sick with love for Lydia.

The Armstrongs weren't ones for exchanging family stories over the dinner table; the past was only revisited occasionally, filled as it was with echoes of tragedy and regret. Cassie learned at an early age what was off limits. Her grandparents would talk willingly enough about their first dates, or what life used to be like in Knox Junction before the interstate highway arrived. Once in a while, Lydia would reminisce about the early days of her marriage, and Cassie would get a brief, precious glimpse of her father as a baby or young boy. But questions about Cassie's parents—who had died when she was five years old, before she'd time to form anything more than impressions of them—were met with awkward silence. The past, she learned, meant pain. And the last thing Cassie wanted was to cause her grandparents any more heartbreak. They'd had enough.

The only safe memories, the only ones Cassie could ask about and get a smile, were the stories of Lydia and Henry's courtship and marriage. By now, it had taken on the aura of a fairy tale in Cassie's mind. They'd first met as children, when Lydia's family moved to town, had their first date at a high school dance and married right after college. Henry, the quiet, steadfast farmer's son, and Lydia, the artistic doctor's daughter, might have been an unexpected match; Lydia had hinted that her parents didn't approve of Henry at first. But love had triumphed in the end, and Lydia and Henry had eloped in France, where Lydia was taking college art courses. Paul, Cassie's father, was born while they were traveling in Europe, and the young family returned home soon after.

Their brief European adventure over, they settled into their average, all-American lives. For the next fifty years, they had built a thriving business together, established a network of close friends with whom they organized bridge nights and potluck dinners, raised a son and later, a granddaughter. Now, in their seventies, they were local fixtures in town, a much-lauded example of a happy and long-lasting marriage.

Henry and Lydia's story had made a powerful impact on the young Cassie, who grew up believing in the power of first love. But as she made her way unhappily through high school—where being smart disqualified her from popularity, and her frizzy hair and acne-prone skin only reinforced her brainy image—Cassie began to wonder whether her grandparents' story was a fairy tale after all, the kind of thing that rarely ever happens in real life.

It wasn't until college that she met her savior: Cooper Lynch, someone just as socially awkward and grade-obsessed as she was. Cooper's home life couldn't have been more different than hers—the middle child of three boys and two girls, he'd been raised in a large, raucous family—but like Cassie, he approached life as an outsider. The only way to stand out from his siblings, he'd decided at an early age, was to be smarter than them, and he'd concentrated on school to the exclusion of almost everything else. Cooper and Cassie had started out as "study buddies," cramming for finals together late at night in the university library. They'd applied to law schools together and somehow both decided that the University of Chicago was their first choice. And when law school began and they were busier than ever, it seemed natural to find comfort in each other. Cooper understood Cassie's drive, and he didn't embarrass her with public displays of affection.

Together, they'd blossomed into a confident, focused couple. Cassie transformed herself from an awkward bookworm into a polished woman, her unruly hair smoothed into sleek ponytails and chignons, and Cooper's shy silences gradually faded as he became an ever more powerful force during law-class debates. Entering a world where intelligence wasn't a liability, they had emerged as winners. Ten years after they first met, they decided to take the next logical step: marriage.

It was a wonder they found time to get engaged at all. The subject had first been broached in the most unromantic way possible—which was par for the course in their relationship. It happened as Cassie was in the final stages of buying a condo in the heart of downtown Chicago, on the top floor of a modern high-rise.

"What do you think?" she asked Cooper during her final walkthrough.

He paused in front of the floor-to-ceiling windows overlooking the Chicago skyline and Lake Michigan. "I could get lost in this view."

As Cassie watched him, standing in the place she pictured herself living for years to come, she realized Cooper was one of the few constants in her life. Friends who didn't understand her nonstop work schedule had drifted away. Her social life outside the office was nonexistent. Cooper was the only person who understood her ambition. Not only did he understand it, he encouraged it. It was the perfect partnership; they each pushed each other to be the best.

"So, you like it?" Cassie asked.

Cooper looked at her, then back out the window with a perplexed expression. "The view?"

"The apartment," she said.

"Oh, yeah."

"Could you see yourself living here?" she asked.

"With you?" His eyes widened with surprise, then pleasure.

"Yeah. Move in, get married, the whole deal." She'd thrown it out so casually, without thinking. Emotionally, she felt as if they were already married. All that was missing was some paperwork.

Cooper smiled, that gradual widening of his mouth and quick blinking she'd found so endearing when they first met. That cautious smile was the only hint of the shy boy hidden beneath the high-powered-lawyer facade.

"Sure," he said. "The whole deal."

And that was it. A quick hug and kiss, but no declaration of eternal love. For a moment, Cassie wondered if such a monumental decision should have been marked with something more. But Cooper wasn't one for grand romantic gestures. Raised in a family that valued light-hearted teasing over deep emotional discussions, Cooper had never been comfortable talking about his feelings. Within a week, he'd moved in with her, although she refused to acknowledge the new living arrangement to her grandparents. "They're really old-fashioned," she cautioned Cooper.

So Cooper had made it official a few weeks

later, whisking Cassie off to an expensive Italian restaurant and arranging to have a diamond ring perched atop her chocolate torte. Lydia's relief over Cassie's engagement was amusingly obvious and Cassie wondered if she'd figured out that she and Cooper were already living in sin. To Lydia, Cassie's impending marriage became a grand creative project, filled with opportunities for sewing and baking and girl talk. Lydia had once had vague artistic aspirations; now, all her pent-up creativity was channeled into household projects. Cassie was worried she'd offer to make the wedding dress herself.

Henry seemed to approve of Cooper, but the approaching wedding didn't dent his Midwestern reserve. Whenever the talk turned to reception venues and flowers, he would escape to his greenhouse in the backyard. He'd built it when he first started his landscaping business; now that he was mostly retired, the space had become his personal retreat. Cassie loved to watch him stroke tender new shoots as they first erupted from the dirt in tiny pots. It was the same way he used to stroke her hair when she was little, on the evenings she would lie in bed crying, missing her mother.

His tall, big-boned body would twist awkwardly to sit on her bed as his hands carefully brushed the tears from her cheeks. She knew, even through the pain and grief, that she was loved. That she was safe.

This gratitude was what kept Cassie coming back to her grandparents' house every Sunday for lunch, despite the long drive from downtown Chicago. Normally, Cassie would have had no reason to visit the basement during the few hours she spent there. But that Sunday was the day Lydia announced she'd be making Cassie a quilt as a wedding present.

"The traditional style would be the Wedding Band," Lydia had explained as she cleared the lunch dishes off the table. "A pattern of overlapping circles, to symbolize a continuing union."

"Um, I guess," Cassie said. She couldn't tell her grandmother that a bright, homemade quilt would never fit with the modern, minimalist furniture she and Cooper preferred. It would be the sort of thing that sat in a closet, whipped out only when Lydia came to visit.

"Do you have your colors picked out yet?" Lydia asked.

"Colors?"

"You know, your linens and towels. I want to make sure the quilt matches."

"Grammy, we don't even know where we're going to register." Or where they were going to get married. Or when. Or anything else that newly engaged couples usually talked about.

"Too busy with work again?"

Cassie nodded. "Cooper and I only had time for one dinner together this week," she said. "The planning is going to take a while."

Lydia shook her head and gave Cassie a pitying look. She didn't understand the life of a corporate attorney. Didn't know that you could complain about the hours, and whine about never seeing your boyfriend, but still love your job so much that the adrenaline got you through all the late nights and canceled vacations.

"Well, you won't get out of picking fabric," Lydia said. "I'd hate to put together something you don't like. Why don't you take a quick look downstairs while I finish with the dishes?"

The basement was Lydia's workroom, the place she designed quilts with the methodical intensity of a military maneuver. A large table in the center of the room was usually strewn with scraps, and rolls of material were lined up along the walls, sorted by color. Lydia did her sewing throughout the house—while watching TV or on the back porch on warm summer mornings—but the basement was her mission control.

"Stop by the greenhouse when you're done," Henry told Cassie. "I'll show you those new pansies I was talking about."

So Cassie reluctantly headed downstairs by herself. She quickly scanned the colors along the wall, all of them bright and eye-catching and utterly wrong for her sleek apartment. Cassie and Cooper wanted their home to be a tranquil retreat from work and stress; there were no colors anywhere, merely shades of white and cream and gray. Lydia's cheery bandana-red cottons and bold royal blues would have no place there.

Cassie knew Lydia stored smaller fabric scraps in a series of boxes along the floor. She could see stripes of color through the translucent plastic. Maybe a pale green or understated taupe was tucked away in there. She took the top off a box and began riffling through neatly folded piles of cloth. And that was when she found the letter.

I will always be yours.
F.B.

F.B. Her only clue to the writer's identity. She scanned her memory for the names of her grandparents' friends, but couldn't come up with anyone who had those initials. Besides, it was unlikely that the person who wrote this letter would still be a friendly acquaintance. This person had been desperately in love with Lydia. Given that she'd been married to Henry for fifty years, the mystery man must have long since been disappointed. But for some reason, Lydia had kept the letter.

Some people, Cassie had always believed, don't have the capacity for soul-baring, earth-scorching romance. In that way, she felt a certain bond with her grandmother—they were both women who valued comfort over passion. Not the type of women to get swept off their feet by whispered words and grand gestures.

Now Cassie wondered if that was true. Because it seemed that Lydia had once had something more. Why had she run from it? Had something terrible happened to send her back to Henry and the safety he offered? Or had this letter been sent after Lydia was already married?

"Did you find it?"

Cassie jumped at the sound of Lydia's voice. Find it? How did she know?

Lydia stepped off the bottom of the stairs and walked over to Cassie. "So, what do you think?"

The cloth. Lydia was talking about her quilt, not the letter. Cassie realized her hands were still pressed against the top of the plastic storage container.

"Um…" Cassie stammered.

Lydia's eyes narrowed when she saw where Cassie was standing.

"What are you doing?" she asked quickly.

"Uh, well, I thought there might be some more fabric samples inside." Cassie stared at Lydia, waiting for her grandmother to ask the question.

Lydia briskly pushed the box to the side of the table, her eyes focused downward. "There's nothing in there to interest you."

This was it. Her opening. All Cassie had to do was ask, but she knew it was pointless. If she couldn't get a straight answer about her own parents' death, how could she expect Lydia to confess a long-ago love affair?

Lydia walked over to the bolts of cloth leaning against the wall and pulled out a pale pink floral. It was classic Lydia behavior—move right on through an awkward moment and refuse to acknowledge it ever happened. The brief opportunity to ask about the letter had passed.

"This is nice, don't you think?" Lydia murmured.

Maybe for a six-year-old girl's room, thought Cassie. "Whatever you think works best," she said. "I really don't care."

She saw the hurt flit across Lydia's face, saw her shoulders slump inside her hand-knit sweater. Cassie was used to being direct, both in the office and in court. She didn't have time for subtlety. But she sometimes forgot that Lydia was her grandmother, not a plaintiff.

"I mean, the pink is fine," Cassie said. "Just keep it light and soothing—nothing too bright."

Lydia nodded and fingered the fabric. "Understated."

"Yeah."

"I can do understated, believe it or not." Lydia smiled, and Cassie started to laugh. Understated was not exactly Lydia's specialty. The quilts that adorned the beds and walls of her house were riotous mixtures of clashing colors and swirling patterns. Some paintings Lydia had done years ago hung in the front hallway, landscapes filled with bright red trees and vibrant purple grass. Lydia's life might have been drab, but her artwork certainly wasn't.

As Lydia pulled out the pink fabric and spread it out on her worktable, Cassie's eyes wandered back to the box that had been pushed aside. The letter itself might be hidden, but its contents had been released. The words still floated through her mind, imprinted on her memory.

Without you I'm lost.

Cassie knew the letter would haunt her until she found out the truth. Lydia—out of loyalty to Henry—would never tell her. But someone else might. Her aunt Nell, Lydia's sister, had grown up with Lydia and Henry. Nell had witnessed their early years together. Maybe she'd know what had happened to the man who had loved Lydia so deeply.

Chapter 2

Lydia

Lydia Prescott couldn't remember the first time she met Henry Armstrong. He seemed to have always been there, in the background, waiting for her to notice him. All her life she would wonder how a connection so strong could have started so unremarkably, how their first encounter could have passed without a foreshadowing of the bond that was to come.

Then again, Lydia had blocked out many things during those first months in Knox Junction. The move had passed in a blur. Packing up the house in a flurry of boxes.

Mother's tears as she whispered rebukes to Father about disgracing the family. Father telling Lydia she couldn't go back to school to say goodbye. Filing behind her parents through cavernous Union Station in Chicago on the way to the train south. Something had gone wrong with Father's job, something shameful, and now they were starting over. Lydia was eleven, old enough to know not to ask questions. Faced with a family teetering on the edge of disaster, she was determined to help her parents maintain a pretense of happiness. Lydia's younger sister, Nell, then only eight, didn't yet possess the mental sensors to pick up their parents' simmering tension.

"What's our new house like?" Nell asked, after Mother had settled them in their private train compartment. Lydia took this as a good sign; surely the money couldn't all be gone if they were still able to travel like this.

"I don't know," Mother said in the clipped tone that had become her normal speech pattern. "I haven't seen it."

"It's very nice," said Father. "It looks like a farmhouse. Lots of room to play outside."

"Is there a beach?" Nell asked.

"No," Mother said.

"It's in the middle of cornfields," Lydia explained. "Nowhere near Lake Michigan."

Nell's eyes began to water. "But I like the beach," she whined.

Their old house—the place Lydia still thought of as home, although she knew it would have to be sold—had been only two blocks from the beach. Lydia and Nell had spent the summer digging with shovels, searching for buried treasure. They'd walked the tree-lined streets of Winnetka, the tranquil Chicago suburb that felt like a small town, albeit one where all the residents could afford sprawling brick or wood-frame homes with wraparound porches and separate entrances for the staff in back. Winnetka was where couples moved when they wanted to raise their families somewhere safe and idyllic. Not a place where families suddenly left in disgrace. Lydia's friends had told her they'd write, but she knew they wouldn't. Nell was having a harder time realizing that their life there was over.

"Does the house have an attic?" A favorite winter activity had been to rummage through Mother's old trunks of clothes, playing dress-up.

"I don't know," said Mother, staring out the window.

"I don't think so," Father said. "But there's a pretty room I think you'll like. With pink flowered wallpaper."

"I don't want pink!" Nell began to wail. "I want blue!"

Lydia reached around her sister's shoulders and squeezed tight. "I'll take the pink room if you want," she said. She watched her parents for their reaction. True to form, Mother hardly paid attention and Father gave her an approving smile.

Still, brave as Lydia tried to be, she couldn't hide her disappointment when the train pulled into Knox Junction, her new hometown. It was a creation of the railroads, a small gathering of buildings that sprang up at the intersection of the lines running north to Chicago and west to Des Moines. It had begun with a hotel, expanded to a few shops and houses, but never developed into anything more than a minor transportation center in the midst of farmland. Knox Junction might call itself a town, but there was only one paved road, and tractors outnumbered cars.

Lydia watched Mother's face crumple with

disappointment as they slowed down at the station. She forced the muscles around her mouth to prop up her lips in an approximation of a smile.

"We're home, aren't we, Father?" Lydia said.

Father rubbed his hand over the top of her head. If hiding her fear and anger would keep her family together, if pretending happiness could somehow erase the shame hovering over them like a fog, Lydia was determined to put up a brave front.

"Yes," said Father. "Home."

The house, while smaller than the one they'd had in Winnetka, wasn't nearly as bad as Lydia had feared. For Knox Junction, it was positively palatial: four bedrooms, a deep porch lined with white columns, an enormous kitchen with walk-in pantry. Even Mother nodded approvingly. Living in such a home seemed to bode well. Surely the family of the town's new doctor, living in one of the finest houses in town, would be greeted with excitement and respect?

Lydia's hopes of being embraced by Knox Junction were soon shattered. On her first day of school, she could feel the eyes of her class-mates focus on her with confusion rather than welcome. Had Henry been the only one to look at her as more than a suspicious outsider? He must have been there, in that room, but she couldn't remember him. To Lydia, all those faces blended together, a blank wall she could never penetrate. Cheery Nell had an easier time of it. Within a few weeks she was walk-ing home from school chattering about the funny rag dolls she'd played with at recess.

But for Lydia, school was a disaster. In her first school year at Knox Junction, she made exactly one friend, Melanie Dixon, whose parents ran the town's hotel. Being raised among travelers had broadened Melanie's out-look. She was the only classmate who treated Lydia as a normal person, rather than an in-terloper.

Lydia had developed a habit of reading dur-ing recess, a routine that shielded her from the fact that the other girls ignored her, while si-multaneously insuring a reputation as stuck-up and proud.

The book that day was *Little Women*. Lydia had only gotten through the second chapter when she saw Melanie's face peering at her over the top.

"Do you like to sew?" she asked.

The question was so unexpected, Lydia didn't know how to respond. Was Melanie trying to make some connection between sewing and the book? Was this a test, something she'd be teased about later?

Lydia shrugged. "I'm not very good," she said.

"I could teach you if you want," Melanie said. "But, you see, I thought I'd make something for the social, and if you want some help with your dress…"

"The social?" Lydia asked.

"Don't you know? We always have one on a Friday afternoon in June, to celebrate the end of the school year. We don't have dates, exactly, but there's dancing with the boys." Melanie smiled in anticipation, and her round cheeks and kind dark eyes were such a welcome sight that Lydia smiled back.

"Oh, I don't know if that's the sort of thing I'd do…." she began, then stopped herself. She heard how her own words sounded the second they flew out of her mouth—"not the sort of thing *I'd* do"—and she realized that distancing herself to be protected from rejection could only lead to more rejection.

"That is, I'm not a very good dancer," Lydia said. "But I'd be happy to help you with your dress, if you want."

"Can you do embroidery? There's a darling pattern I'd like to put along the bodice."

Lydia nodded. "That sounds like fun. Could you show me how?" Lydia's previous sewing experience had been strictly practical—mending holes and finishing hems—and Mother never failed to criticize her crooked seams and uneven stitches. But Lydia was willing to risk bloody fingers if it meant having a friend.

The friendship that blossomed between the two girls was rooted in pity (on Melanie's part) and gratitude (on Lydia's). But lasting friendships have been built on shakier ground, and gradually Melanie softened Lydia's wariness. Lydia absorbed Melanie's passion for sewing, and Melanie marveled over her ability to sketch a dress pattern. Lydia had never thought much about her talent for art. She'd been drawing and painting as long as she could remember. But through Melanie's admiring eyes she began to see her way with shapes and color as something special. Her own particular gift.

But encouraging Lydia's love of art was only one of the ways Melanie changed Lydia's life. The other had to do with Henry Armstrong.

It was a week or so before the social, an event Lydia had grudgingly agreed to attend. The future had seemed especially precarious then, in the spring of 1942. Adults talked worriedly about Pearl Harbor and France and the draft. A sense of unease had penetrated even isolated Knox Junction, as boys from the surrounding farms talked about joining up and the men gathered at the general store talked ominously of gasoline rations. The glares between Mother and Father continued to make Lydia's home a battlefront.

The social would at least be a distraction from Lydia's daily routine, although she dreaded spending the afternoon as a wallflower. She'd secretly experimented with different hairstyles in the bathroom mirror at home, taking out her pigtails and attempting to brush her thick, chestnut-brown hair into glamorous waves. But once she'd achieved the desired effect—her dark brown eyes, framed by long lashes, peeking around the swirls of hair—she could tell it wasn't enough. Her thin lips and narrow nose accentuated the suspicious gaze with which she greeted the world. She would never be pretty enough to make boys overlook her schoolmarm reputation.

"Of course someone will ask you to dance!" Melanie declared when Lydia threatened once again not to go.

"Who? Lyle Shea?" Lydia threw out the name of a boy who was best known for bragging about his hogs. Lydia doubted he'd ever read anything other than the *Farmers' Almanac*.

"Oh, I know someone who's sweet on you," said Melanie with a teasing grin.

"Who?"

"Henry Armstrong."

Lydia knew who he was by then, but not much more. Henry. Slim, wiry, with lightly freckled cheeks and thick blond hair that stuck up in a cowlick on the back of his head. Henry, who sat in the back of the classroom and never spoke. A farmer's son who disappeared for a week or two in April to help with the planting. Indistinguishable from all the rest of them—or so Lydia thought.

"Henry? What makes you say that?" she asked Melanie.

"The way I've seen him stare at you," Melanie said. "He looks at you more than any other girl."

"Did he say something?"

"No. But you know how boys are," Melanie said with a wise nod. Lydia wondered about her friend's qualifications as an expert in male behavior. As far as she could tell, Melanie's interactions with boys consisted of fluttering her eyelashes, giggling and not much else. Still, this news about Henry was intriguing. Not that she cared about him, particularly; she hardly knew him. But the idea that anyone might be paying attention to her was encouraging.

Despite Melanie's promising news, the social itself went as badly as Lydia imagined it would. The boys lined up against one wall, the girls against another, and a good half hour passed before anyone dared cross to the middle of the room. Eventually, a few awkward pairings stomped across the floor, under the watchful eyes of parental chaperones. Melanie even danced with Lyle Shea, rolling her eyes behind his back for Lydia's benefit. Lydia remained with her back pressed against the wall, despite Melanie's whispered attempts to find her a partner when she thought Lydia wasn't listening.

Henry Armstrong wasn't there.

Unable to bear the humiliation any longer, Lydia finally strode outside, wincing at the sun hovering over the horizon. She saw Mrs. Glover, the woman who ran the general store and acted as local postmistress, sweeping up the store's front porch before closing. Lydia dashed across the street.

"Mrs. Glover," she called out. "I don't suppose you received a package for me, did you?"

Mrs. Glover leaned against the broom with a weary expression that signaled her lack of enthusiasm at being the local representative of the U.S. Postal Service.

"Well, now, I might have."

Even Mrs. Glover's sourness couldn't dispel Lydia's excitement. "May I come in and get it, please?"

The woman sighed heavily. "I was about to close up, but I suppose if you're quick about it…"

Lydia raced inside and ran behind the counter where Mrs. Glover piled oversize mail. The box was toward the bottom—how long had it been sitting there? Her name was clearly marked, along with her address. But the Knox Junction postal service did not include home delivery. It was up to each family to appear up at Mrs. Glover's to claim their boxes and envelopes—when she felt like retrieving them.

"Thank you!" Lydia called as she ran down the steps. She couldn't wait until she got home to open it. Instead, she walked quickly to the porch swings at the Knox Junction Hotel, sat down and tore open the packaging. Nestled inside the box was the latest selection from the Book-of-the-Month Club. The subscription had been a gift from Father on her last birthday. Since Knox Junction had no public library, it was her one connection to the outside world. Each new delivery felt like Christmas.

She was about to pull the book out of the box when she noticed a shadow hovering over her. She glanced up and locked eyes with Henry Armstrong.

For a moment, they stared at each other in

silence. His hair had been flattened with pomade, and he was wearing a stiffly pressed white shirt. His fingers twitched as they moved in and out of his pockets.

"Uh, is the, uh, social over, then?"

"I'm not sure," Lydia said. "I left early."

Henry looked down at his shoes, while Lydia smoothed the paper wrapped around her book. Those two sentences were more words than they'd exchanged during the entire school year. And that could've been the end of it—Henry might have said thank you, and turned toward the school, and Lydia might have walked home and delved into her book and never given Henry another thought.

But something about the package in Lydia's lap caught Henry's attention.

"Book-of-the-Month Club?" he asked.

"Yes," said Lydia, surprised.

"My mother used to get those."

"Oh?"

"Well, she hasn't for a while now. But she kept all her old ones. I read them when I get the chance."

Somehow, in that moment, with hardly anything being said, everything was said. Henry read books, and his mother used to read books, but something had happened and there was no money for indulgences such as Book-of-the-Month Club, so Henry had to work as hard as everyone else, but sometimes, at night when he wasn't too exhausted, he would read and escape into other worlds. Just like Lydia.

"What's your favorite?" Lydia asked.

Henry shrugged and shifted his weight from side to side. "I dunno," he said. "There was one I read not too long ago—*Lost Horizon*. That was good."

Lydia smiled. "I read that one, too. Shangri-La. I love books that make you feel you've gone somewhere else."

"Away from Knox Junction?"

"I don't mean— It's not that I don't like it here…" She watched as Henry's face was transformed by a smile, his clear blue eyes twinkling at her. He looked like a little boy, delighted by a new discovery. Lydia couldn't help smiling back.

"I don't blame you," he said. "Nothing interesting ever happens around here."

"Well, there's the social." Lydia glanced up at him. "I don't want to keep you, if you were going over there."

Henry shook his head. "I'm not much of a dancer," he said. "How 'bout you?"

Lydia laughed. "I'm terrible."

And then Lydia was no longer conscious of talking to a boy—a boy who might actually have some kind of interest in her, no less. She just knew that she wanted the conversation to continue, because there was something about him that made her comfortable. When Lydia offered to show Henry her new book, she knew he'd sit down next to her.

"You know, if you like to read, we've got heaps of books," Lydia said as Henry settled on the swing. "I'd be happy to lend you some."

"Thank you." His obvious delight at her offer was enough to start a warm rush in Lydia's stomach. Years later, she realized it was the first hint of the feeling that would one day turn to love.

The war affected Knox Junction only gradually at first. A few local boys joined up, including Henry's older brother, Timothy. Lydia's mother had to bring a ration book whenever she wanted to buy sugar or coffee. For Lydia's family, however, the war brought redemption. A few doctors from neighboring towns signed up with the medical corps, leaving her father as the sole physician for miles around. Now, rather than struggling to build a practice, he found that demand for his services had soared. Before the family's abrupt departure from Chicago, Lydia had overheard snippets of her parents' conversations, the contemptuous accusations her mother had flung at him regarding "that poor Miller woman." Lydia knew that one of Father's patients had died, and that death had something to do with their disgrace. She'd wondered if Father would ever practice medicine again.

Now that the war had tripled his business, Lydia watched her father revert to the confident physician he had once been. The more patients he treated, the more his shoulders straightened, and the more Lydia heard the sound of whistling in the morning. He made fewer trips to the liquor cabinet after dinner. No longer was Lydia awakened by the sound of harsh voices from her parents' room.

After school let out for the summer, Mother took Lydia and Nell north to Wisconsin, to Grandmother's vacation house on Lake Geneva. Mother claimed it would be good for the girls' health—"The air here is oppressive.

I can't bear it"—but Father's health seemed less of a concern, as he stayed behind.

To one of Grandmother's elderly neighbors, Mother explained the move to Knox Junction as a patriotic duty. "We all must make our sacrifices," she said. "They don't have nearly enough doctors there, and with the war on, David is needed more than ever.

"It's a simpler life," Mother told one of her childhood friends, who lived in a three-story mansion on Chicago's Gold Coast neighborhood. "So much better for the children."

Whether these polite society ladies believed Mother's explanations or merely pitied her, the result was the same. She was welcomed back into the world where she'd grown up, a world of garden parties and croquet matches and leisurely rides on family sailboats. A world Lydia had once believed she was part of. But now she saw it as a brief, idyllic escape. Come September, she'd be back in Knox Junction. That had become her real life.

Lydia had given Henry the address in Lake Geneva on their last day of school, not expecting anything to come of it. But to her great surprise, he did write. And although his letters were short, to the point and distinctly lacking in poetry, she ripped each one open eagerly.

Dear Lydia,
How are things up there? Have you gone swimming in the lake? The only place I've ever gone swimming was the water hole behind our barn. It's all dried up now. It's scorching hot here. How's the weather?

Her letters back were chattier, but similarly superficial:

The women here go to great lengths to track down nylons. They all whisper about who can get them as if they're planning a bank robbery. But I don't imagine you're too interested in ladies' fashions. Sorry I don't have anything more interesting to write about—it's a rather dull routine here. A morning walk, lunch out, afternoon swim, tea with friends of my grandmother's, followed by dinner with someone even more boring. There doesn't seem to be anyone here younger than forty. It actually makes me look forward to high school. Although, I still can't quite believe it—high school! What do you think it will be like?

Knox Junction was too small to support a high school, so students took a half-hour bus ride to nearby Fentonville. During the first few weeks of school, the bus seating settled into a pattern that remained for the rest of the school year. Lydia and Melanie would board the bus first, in town. Later along the route, Henry would get on and sit in the row in front of them. He'd stretch his long legs out along the seat and turn sideways toward the girls, nodding his head once. Sometimes he'd lean back against the window and drift off to sleep. Other days he would halfheartedly respond as Melanie attempted to drag him into conversation.

"What do you think of those Fentonville girls, Henry?" Melanie asked one morning toward the beginning of their freshman year. She flashed Lydia a meaningful glance.

"I dunno," he said.

"Some of them act like big-city girls, don't you think?"

Henry shrugged. "Maybe."

Melanie shook her head, annoyed. She told Lydia later, "Doesn't Henry look like a big scarecrow?" A growth spurt had left Henry awkwardly tall and skinny; he walked as if he was still learning to work his new arms and legs.

"Did you see him this morning, with his hair all pointed up?" Melanie giggled. "It's just like straw!"

To the girls at Fentonville, his lanky body, uneasy posture and obviously handed-down, too-short trousers marked him as a poor prospect. Melanie had stopped teasing Lydia about him. High school offered all sorts of new potential beaus—Henry Armstrong was old news.

"He's not that bad," protested Lydia. But when he wore overalls to school—which he did far too often—he did look like a country bumpkin. Exactly the sort of person the ladies at Lake Geneva would disapprove of.

Without ever discussing it, Lydia and Henry kept their interaction at school to a minimum. But somehow they found moments to talk away from school, Sunday afternoons when they'd stroll along the wide road out of town, searching for a perfect vista for Lydia to sketch. They talked about books, about his brother's letters from overseas, about Chicago, which Henry had never visited. There were no nervous attempts to grab Lydia's hand or stuttering declarations of feelings. They were simply friends. And Lydia never felt she needed anything more.

By their sophomore year, Lydia and Henry had expanded their friendship to help navigate the perils of high school. He asked her to the homecoming dance, saving her from the embarrassment of not being asked by anyone else. They began doing homework together at her house. Lydia's father would sometimes give Henry a ride home in his car, one of the few in town that received ample gas rations.

They might have continued that way for years, neither of them breaking the rhythm of companionship. But the war shattered their comfortable routine.

It was the spring of 1944. Henry didn't board the bus one morning, and he wasn't in math class at the start of the day. Mr. Andrews called roll and noticed that Henry was absent.

"Has anyone seen Henry Armstrong?" he asked.

"He wasn't on the bus," Melanie offered.

"That's an unexcused absence," Mr. Andrews said, marking it down in his book.

Even one unexcused absence was unusual for someone as conscientious as Henry, and when he wasn't at school the next day, Lydia began to worry. She wondered whether she'd be brave enough to telephone his house later. She'd only met his parents once, when they came to the school's annual concert. They were even more soft-spoken than Henry, nodding silently when Henry introduced them. Lydia wondered if they'd remember who she was.

"Um, Mr. Andrews?" George Foster, known as one of the loudest boys in the school, raised his hand.

"Yes, George?"

"My mother heard something about the Armstrongs. I don't know if I..." George seemed unsure, a rarity for him.

"Please come up," said Mr. Andrews. George whispered in his ear. Lydia, from the front row, heard the name of Reverend McDeal, the minister at Knox Junction's only church.

Mr. Andrews was quiet for a moment, gazing down at the floor. "Thank you, George," he said finally. "Take your seat."

Lydia waited for an announcement, but Mr. Andrews continued with roll call and then began reviewing the previous night's homework. Lydia felt her stomach tense with worry. If Reverend McDeal had been called, someone in the house must be very sick. Was it Henry's mother or father? Could it be Henry himself?

By lunchtime, Lydia couldn't stand the suspense anymore. She lingered beside the table where George and his fellow baseball team members sat, drumming up the courage to speak.

"What are you doing here?" asked one of the older boys, a junior or senior.

"I, uh… George?" Lydia's voice was trembling. "Do you have a minute?"

George was obviously shocked at being approached by his class's designated bookworm. He grinned at the other boys as he stood up, enjoying his moment in the spotlight. Lydia motioned him to follow, and she led him to a far corner of the lunchroom, where they wouldn't be overheard.

"Today, in Mr. Andrews's class, you said something about the Armstrongs."

George's self-satisfied expression gave way to wariness.

"Yeah."

"Is something wrong with Henry?"

George looked at her, his face uncharacteristically blank.

"Please," Lydia begged.

"Well, I guess everyone's going to hear about it anyway. It's not Henry, it's his brother. Killed in action."

A heavy chill settled over Lydia's body, making her feel as if she were encased in ice. Timothy. Henry's only sibling, the older brother he idolized. The person Henry's father was training to take over the farm. His mother's pride and joy.

Lydia moved through the rest of the day in a haze, sick whenever she thought of Henry and what he must be going through. She was desperate to talk to him, but terrified at the idea of reaching out. She couldn't possibly call the house. What if his mother answered the phone, hysterical? What would she say? Stopping by for a visit was out of the question.

Seeing the Armstrongs in person, devastated by the news, would be unbearable.

Shortly after returning home from school, Lydia told her mother she was going out to draw. She'd lose herself in something to take her mind away from what had happened. Spring in northern Illinois could shift from freezing to broiling within twenty-four hours, but that afternoon there was still a chill in the air. She tossed a scarf around her neck and pulled on her gloves, tucking her sketch pad under one arm and putting a small box of pastels in her pocket.

She set off down the main road out of town, which led past Henry's farm. She wasn't planning on going to the house, not exactly. But she needed to be closer to him, even if he didn't see her or know she was there. If the connection between them was so strong that his grief affected her physically, maybe he'd sense her nearness and draw some small comfort from it.

The farmhouse where Henry lived lay at the end of a dirt track off the main road. Lydia stopped at the turnoff and looked toward the house. The only vehicle parked in front was Henry's father's truck. No visitors.

She was just trying to decide whether to turn back or keep walking, when she noticed a movement in some trees to her right. She clutched her sketch pad, struggling to come up with an excuse for why she might have chosen this particular spot to draw. Then she saw a glimpse of light hair through the branches. It was Henry.

Lydia's fear about what to say instantly vanished. She dropped her paper and raced over the grass, calling his name. His body stiffened when he heard her voice. As she approached, and saw his face drawn with despair, his eyes rimmed with red, she knew that words wouldn't be enough. She flung herself against him and hugged tight, murmuring, "I'm so sorry, I'm so sorry."

His thin frame felt surprisingly solid to her—what little substance he had was all wiry muscle and bone. One hand rested gently on her shoulder, the other tentatively patted her back.

"You heard," he said quietly, the words muffled by their embrace.

"Yes," Lydia said. "All day, I've been so worried. I can't imagine what it's been like."

She felt him shudder as he tried to speak.

She kept her eyes pressed shut, afraid to see him in such pain.

"It's been awful," he whispered. "My Ma…I don't know what's going to happen to her. It's like she's dead, too. Pop's doing his best, but…"

Lydia rubbed her hands against his back, as if the pressure could push out the hurt.

"Tim was their favorite," Henry said. "Everybody loved him. He was going to take over here someday. He was the one who tended to this apple orchard—did I ever tell you that? He had a knack for growing things. He said I wouldn't have to worry about Ma and Pop, he'd take care of them while I went off and saw the world." Henry's body began shaking with sobs.

"It's going to be all right," Lydia murmured, although she knew it wouldn't. She repeated the words softly, in the tone Mother had used when she was a child, frightened awake by a bad dream.

Henry's fears tumbled out of him—his terror that his parents would never recover, the way he could barely face his own mother, the emptiness that stretched before him without end. Lydia kept her arms pressed around him.

Not looking at him, knowing that he'd stop talking if he met her eyes.

Eventually, Henry's heaving breaths slowed down, and his voice drifted off into silence. His face was red from crying. Lydia pulled a handkerchief from her coat pocket and handed it to him.

"Sorry about that," Henry said, his voice returning to its usual flat tone.

"Don't worry," Lydia whispered. "I'm glad you told me."

"There's no one else I can tell," he said. "No one to talk to. Except you."

They looked at each other, and between them flashed an acknowledgment that everything had changed. A moment before it happened, Lydia knew it was coming, knew Henry would put his hands against her cheeks and guide her face toward his, knew their lips would meet in a soft kiss. Lydia tasted a trace of salty tears on Henry's lips, and she closed her eyes tightly to stop herself from crying.

They might have stood there for a minute, or it could have been hours. Time stopped in that moment, underneath Timothy's apple trees. Henry's strong arms enveloped Lydia's narrow shoulders, as if he was comforting her now, reassuring her that together, they could get through anything.

"Lydia," he whispered, his lips pulling away from hers and brushing against her cheek. "I'm sorry...."

She reached up and moved his mouth back toward hers. "I'm not," she said.

Henry's mouth twisted slightly to one side, as if he was unsure whether to move it toward a smile or a sob. "I love you so much," he said.

"I love you, too." She said the words because it seemed right, but as soon as she'd spoken, she knew they were true.

Then their lips were together again, and his tongue found hers, and they were locked together in a desperate embrace, their mouths hungry for each other in a way that left them gasping for breath. His fingers were tangled in her hair, while her hands pressed against his lower back, pulling him tighter against her. Finally, they drew apart, both shaken. Henry dropped his head and rested his face against Lydia's shoulder.

"Promise you'll never leave me," Henry said.

"I won't," she said. "I won't." And in that moment, she meant it.

Chapter 3

Cassie

For someone who made a living asking tough questions, Cassie was terrified to come out and ask her aunt Nell the big one: Was my grandmother ever in love with someone else?

Aunt Nell was the family eccentric, a role she seemed to embrace and played up at every opportunity. Married three times, she'd re-invented herself with each husband. Starting off as a demure young housewife in the 1950s, she scandalized the family by getting divorced, moving to California and throwing herself into the women's movement in the

1960s (a period Lydia dismissively referred to as "Nell's preachy phase"). That was followed by her earth mother period, when she spent most of the mid-to late '70s living off the land in a series of communes, eventually retiring to a rural village in northern Wisconsin, where she'd spent the past twenty years running a part-time bed-and-breakfast, animal shelter and artists' cooperative.

Cassie saw Nell every few years on major family occasions—distant cousins' weddings, Lydia and Henry's fiftieth anniversary party, Cassie's graduation from law school. But while Cassie loved her great-aunt, they didn't have much of a personal bond. Cassie and Nell had never spent enough time together to have heart-to-heart conversations. In any case, Nell didn't seem the most promising person to turn to for advice.

Still, Cassie's curiosity was stronger than her embarrassment about digging around for family secrets. During a break between meetings at work, she called her aunt. After four rings, she heard the somber voice of Nell's husband, Fedorov.

"Yes?"

Nell had met Fedorov through a group that

raised money for Russian immigrants. He claimed to be a potter, although Lydia noted tartly that he spent far more time sitting on Nell's front porch than in front of a kiln.

"I've never seen a man with a greater talent for doing nothing," Lydia had said after meeting him for the first time. "He's only marrying Nell for the green card—I don't know why she can't see that."

Green card or not, Fedorov had lasted longer than any of Nell's previous husbands—almost ten years—and despite his talent for doing nothing, he apparently knew how to make Nell happy. Whatever his charms, they were well hidden; Cassie had rarely seen him deviate from a state of low-level depression.

"Hi, it's Cassie. Is Aunt Nell around?"

"No. She is with the animal rescue for today."

"Well, could you tell her I called?" Cassie asked.

"Yes. Of course."

Cassie tried to think of something else to say, but came up blank. Fedorov would probably be just as happy if she didn't prolong their encounter.

She thanked him and hung up. Did he possess enough energy to write down the message? Cassie wasn't sure. Even if Nell did get the message, she could be flighty. When she came to Cassie's law school commencement ceremony, she seemed to think it was Cassie's college graduation. Her memory of Lydia's past might be similarly flawed.

Cassie's computer pinged to indicate the arrival of a new e-mail message. Just what she needed. She hadn't even had time to respond to the thirty-four messages waiting in her in-box that morning. She glanced at the screen and saw that the sender was Jeffrey Gannon, one of the firm's senior partners and head of the health-care group she worked for. Her boss.

C-Need summary of major projects you've completed since starting with us. Top priority.
-JG

The terse tone wasn't alarming in itself; Jeffrey always corresponded using the fewest words possible. But the request was odd. Why, when the health-care group was swamped with work, was she being asked to put together a glorified résumé?

Cassie picked up the phone and dialed the number for Jeffrey's assistant, Marie, the one person guaranteed to know everything going on at the firm.

"Hey, Cassie."

"Hi," Cassie said. "Listen, I just got this weird request from Jeffrey to put together some kind of summary of all the work I've done in the last three years. Do you know anything about that?"

"Not really," said Marie. "He didn't mention it to me, anyway."

"Okay."

"Well—but I'm sure it's got nothing to do with you…" Marie's voice trailed off.

"What?" Cassie asked.

"First thing this morning, he got a call from Lowell—" the firm's managing partner "—and after that he was putting through a lot of calls to the other senior partners. And here's the weirdest part. Guess who else called? Milton Greiber from Lofton & Treadwell."

Lofton & Treadwell. The firm's biggest competitor in health-care law.

"Something's definitely up," Cassie said.

"Listen, you didn't hear this from me," said Marie.

Cassie nodded. "I just want to protect myself, you know, in case." Marie had once told Cassie she was the only lawyer at the firm who treated her as a friend rather than a servant. Cassie hadn't planned to make an ally of Marie—she genuinely liked her—but she saw now that this personal connection was paying off. She'd just gotten a heads-up on some potentially life-altering news.

Two rival law firms talking could mean only one thing: merger. And mergers meant consolidation, which meant layoffs.

Was her job in jeopardy?

Cassie's computer pinged again—a message from Cooper.

Can you get away tonight? Got us a 7 pm meeting at the Drake Hotel to discuss the reception. Also, got a great story about Jess and Pedro when you need a laugh. I'll be in the office between 2 and 3 if you want to talk.

Cassie shook her head in irritation. She didn't have time to discuss the latest interoffice-romance scandal at Cooper's office, let alone wedding reception venues. Her job—the center of her life, her identity—might be in jeopardy. That had to be her top priority.

She typed a quick response:

No can do tonight. Sorry. Nightmare at work as usual. Can you go it alone?

She pressed Send, then thought about how to respond to Jeffrey. Asking for a summary of her work might be a good sign. Maybe it meant he was trying to protect her job. They had a friendly working relationship, but he was still the boss. Would he tell her the truth if she asked?

Ping. Another e-mail from Jeffrey arrived in her in-box.

Go what alone? If you can't get me the summary by tonight, try for tomorrow a.m.
p.s. Nightmares at work are no excuse. Part of the job.

Cassie frantically clicked on her sent mail folder. Sure enough, the response she'd in-

tended for Cooper had gone to Jeffrey instead.
Great. Just when she was supposed to be bur-
nishing her professional reputation, she'd sent
a personal message to her boss.

Quickly, she responded to Jeffrey, double-
checking the return address carefully.

My mistake. Meant to send that message
to Cooper explaining why I'd be spending my evening at work yet again. As you
said, nightmares are business as usual.
Will be happy to get you that work summary by the end of the day. No problem.

It was, in fact, a huge problem. How was
she supposed to work on this self-promoting
document when she had back-to-back meetings scheduled well past five? She'd hoped to
take a half-hour lunch break to visit a nearby
bridal salon, but that plan was shot now. All
so she could justify keeping a job she already
had.

Cassie dialed Cooper's cell phone. It went
immediately to voice mail.

"Hey there," Cassie said. "Got your e-mail.
I'm so sorry, but I can't make it to the Drake
today. Horrible day at work, and something

big is up—I'll tell you later, but I don't think it's good. Anyway, I've got to stay late and prove myself. Can you go to the meeting anyway? You can tell me all about it tonight. Thanks."

She hung up, then considered calling back and saying something nice. Didn't most women end conversations with their fiancés by saying, "I love you" or, "Can't wait to see you"? But Cassie was in business mode and it simply hadn't occurred to her.

She typed a quick message.

Just left you a voice mail. Forgot to say I love you. See you later.

Cassie hit Send and watched the words *I love you* disappear from her screen. She tried to remember the last time she'd said them out loud.

Arriving home that night around ten, Cassie kept running certain images through her mind—the way two of the firm's partners had stopped talking when she'd walked by the front desk to pick up a package. Jeffrey's over-casual thanks when she'd delivered a ten-page summary of her professional accomplishments. The sight of Lowell, the firm's managing partner, at the photocopy machines, doing work that was usually delegated to the lowliest paralegals.

Still, as Cassie strolled through the sleek, unfurnished lobby of her condo building, she was determined to leave work at the office for once. Talk to Cooper, try to work up some enthusiasm for the wedding planning that he'd taken on alone. They hadn't even picked a date yet, but the big venues filled up a year or more in advance, so they'd decided to start looking. But so far Cooper had been the only one to do anything.

Cassie opened the door to the apartment and was greeted by darkness. Walking down the hall, she came to the living room, lit by a small table lamp. Had Cooper gone back to the office after his meeting at the Drake? It wouldn't be the first time. But no—she'd spotted his briefcase sitting by the front door, where he usually kept it. His wallet was on the front hall table.

Cassie glanced toward the bedroom and saw that the door was closed. A note was taped to the front.

Sorry I missed you. Have to get up at 5 a.m. for flight to London, so I went to bed early. Leave a note if you want me to wake you up before I go. Otherwise, see you Saturday.

The London trip. She'd forgotten all about it. It was the reason he'd scheduled the Drake tour for tonight, because it was the only time he'd have available until the following week. And she'd completely forgotten.

Leave a note if you want me to wake you up.

It seemed fitting, given that was how they seemed to communicate these days.

Cassie walked back down the hall to the living room, took off her shoes and tossed them on the floor. Another piece of paper was sitting in front of the answering machine.

Aunt Nell called. Said you can call her late.

Was ten o'clock too late for a seventysomething woman? Cassie wasn't sure. But she knew she couldn't sleep, so it was worth a try.

Aunt Nell picked up the phone on the second ring, her voice as cheery as if it were midafternoon.

"Hello?"

"Aunt Nell, it's Cassie. Am I calling too late?"

"'Course not. I make a point of not going to bed before midnight. Don't want to become a boring old lady."

"I don't think anyone will ever say that about you," Cassie said.

Nell's hearty laugh echoed through the receiver. Lydia might see her sister as flighty and unpredictable, but Nell clearly enjoyed life. Cassie found herself wishing she'd taken more time to get to know her. What must it be like to go through life with happiness as your default setting?

"I guess congratulations are in order," Nell said. "When's the big day?"

"We're still working on that," Cassie said. "You know how it is—work schedules. It's really hard to find a time that's good for both of us."

"I don't believe I've ever had a real work schedule in my life!" Nell said. "I do admire you, though. Lydia's always bursting with pride when she talks about you."

"Listen, I was actually calling about Grandma," Cassie said, anxious to get to the point before she lost her nerve. "A weird thing happened yesterday. I was at her house for lunch, and I went to the basement to look at some fabric—well, the background isn't really important, but I found this letter. A love letter."

"Hmm."

"The thing is, I don't think my grandfather wrote it."

"Then who was it from?" Nell asked.

"I don't know. Someone with the initials F.B."

Cassie waited in silence for a moment.

"Doesn't mean anything to me," Nell said. "Do you know when it was written?"

"No, there's no date. Could it be someone in Knox Junction, someone she knew when she was younger?"

"As far as I know, she didn't date anyone else before marrying Henry," Nell said. "And I don't see…" Her voice trailed off.

"What?"

"Well, from everything I've seen and heard, Henry is the love of my sister's life. I don't use that term lightly. Believe me, I thought I was in love many, many times, and most every time it ended in disaster. I'm sure Lydia's taken great pleasure in telling you about all my mistakes!" Nell laughed, but Cassie heard the hurt lurking behind it, the dig at an older sister who would never stop judging her.

"But Lydia and Henry—they were the golden couple," Nell continued. "The ones you knew would get married and live happily ever after. I never suspected there was anyone else."

"I know," Cassie said. "That's why I'm so confused. I'm not sure why—this letter really shook me up."

"Have you asked Lydia about it?"

"Well, I tried to. Sort of. I think she guessed I found it, and then she acted all distant and changed the subject. You know how she gets."

"Not much for sharing her feelings?" said Nell. "I remember dragging her to a consciousness-raising retreat sometime in '71, '72. A complete disaster—but I'll tell you about that another time."

"This F.B.," Cassie told her, "whoever he was, said something about Lydia creating a new life for herself and moving on. So I took that to be a reference to her maybe getting married."

"Unless she was a truly gifted actress, I don't see how she could've juggled Henry and someone else," said Nell. "They started dating when she was sixteen or so and as far as I could see, they were made for each other. But I suppose you already know the whole story."

"The basics," Cassie said. The way Lydia told it, it was as if she'd met Henry, connected instantly and decided to get married—case closed. Was the truth more complicated?

"They started dating in high school, right?" Cassie asked.

"I don't know exactly when," Nell said. "I was three years younger, so Lydia never confided in me. From what I understand, they were friends first. Lydia didn't know too many people, you see. She always kept to herself. When we first moved to Knox Junction, I think she was very unhappy. All of us were. But being younger, I suppose I adjusted faster. I made friends far more easily than Lydia."

"Why did your father move there?" Cassie asked. "It seems like a strange transition, to go from an upscale suburb like Winnetka to a small farm town."

"It had to do with my father's job." Nell paused. "Something had gone wrong in Winnetka, although I couldn't tell you what. Mother was furious at Father, that was obvi-

ous, but she'd never discuss it with us. She'd
very set ideas about what was proper. It's no
wonder I rebelled!"

"So," Cassie went on, "you were saying
Grandma kept to herself after the move."

"Yes. She was such a loner, always reading or drawing or painting. She lived in her
head, and there weren't many people like that
in Knox Junction. One was expected to be
hearty and love the land and come from good
farmer stock. The children at school thought
she was strange, the way she'd spend recess
with her nose in a book.

"But for some reason, Henry found Lydia
intriguing. Maybe because she was so different from everyone else. By Lydia's sophomore or junior year he'd started coming
'round the house. Lydia never invited guests
over—her only friend, as far as I can recall,
was a girl named Melanie. Sweet but fairly
stupid, if I may be brutally honest. So for her
to bring a boy over—I can't even explain how
shocking that was. Boys and girls just weren't
friends the way they are now, you see. If a
girl brought a boy home, it meant something."

"Could she have dated someone else, too?"
Cassie asked.

"I can't imagine there was any other boy in that school who would've appreciated her, let alone fallen madly in love with her," Nell said. "And then, with my parents or me always chaperoning, I don't see how she would have found the opportunity."

"You spent a lot of time with them?"

"Oh, yes," said Nell. "It was understood that Lydia and Henry should never be in the house alone. I'd sit with them at the dining table after school, and we'd all do homework together. Or they'd sit on the front porch while I helped Mother in the front garden. They were often together, but it was never what you'd call romantic. Not in the stereotypical sense."

"No holding hands on the porch swing?"

"Definitely not," Nell said with a laugh. "Although now that you mention it— Hmm, I'm remembering something I haven't thought of in years. There was this one afternoon... must've been spring, because Mother's flowers were all blooming and Lydia was painting them. We spent the summers up in Lake Geneva with Mother's family, so it couldn't have been much later than early June. The weather was lovely, and Lydia had set up her easel on the front porch. She was sitting on a wicker love seat and Henry sat next to her, watching her work. I was sprawled out on the steps, reading Nancy Drew—I remember being obsessed with those books at that age, twelve or thirteen.

"It was peaceful, the three of us there. What struck me was the way Henry sat with Lydia. He didn't talk, or interrupt her work, or try to make conversation to cover up the silence. So many boys in that town—well, they were loud. Loved to draw attention to themselves. But Henry was content to sit and watch Lydia for hours. At the time, I wondered how he could stand doing something so boring. It was only years later that I realized I'd witnessed real love—he was content to share whatever made her happy. I think I've been searching for that most of my life."

Cassie had always told herself the bond she had with Cooper was based on their shared passion for the law and hard work. But now she saw the difference—she and Cooper liked to do the same things but rarely did them together. Their work kept them in separate orbits. She couldn't remember the last time she and Cooper had sat together for hours, sharing silent moments of companionship. Had they ever?

"It was all very small-town America," Nell said. "Henry would pick up Lydia for a school dance. Bring her flowers or a corsage. They always went with friends, of course—Mother would never have let Lydia drive around with Henry alone."

"Sounds like your parents were very strict."

"No more so than any other parents in town," Nell said. "It just wasn't done for a girl to spend time alone with a boy, dating or not. Perhaps *especially* if they were dating. And then, because it was Henry, they were even more careful."

"Why?" Cassie asked. Surely most parents would see a nice boy like Henry as a dream companion for their daughter.

"Oh, they couldn't stand him!"

"Really? Grandma never told me that."

"Maybe she's glossed it over in her mind. But I remember it all well enough. Father— well, he might not have cared so much. But Mother would mutter under her breath in the kitchen, 'I see our *friend* is back.' Lydia would only refer to Henry as her 'friend,' you see, never boyfriend. But Mother knew. She could see the look in his eyes when he was around Lydia. I liked him—he was always kind to me. And then, I always felt rather sorry for him, with what his family went through."

"You mean his brother?" Cassie asked. She knew her grandfather's older brother had died in World War II. His name was carved on a war memorial outside the Knox Junction library, along with those of several other local men who'd been killed in action.

"Yes. When he died, that family fell apart. I know Father checked on Henry's mother a few times, and he said she'd never recover. I don't think her nerves were particularly strong to begin with, and then to have that happen... Timothy was clearly the favorite. So for Henry to be left—I can't imagine what that was like for him."

"But if he'd been through something so tragic, why wasn't your mother nice to him?"

"I asked myself the same question, many times," Nell said. "It was only later, during all the disagreements about Lydia's schooling, that I recognized what was really going on. Mother and Father saw Knox Junction as a temporary interruption in their lives. They hadn't intended to settle there permanently.

It was understood that Lydia and I would leave when it came time for college and go somewhere prestigious. Most of the people in Knox Junction—people like Henry's parents—didn't have a college education. They finished high school, got married soon after and went to work on the farm. That was the pattern."

But Lydia and Henry hadn't gotten married after high school, Cassie knew. They'd both gone to college, in separate parts of the country. Had they wanted to escape Knox Junction? If so, it hadn't lasted long; after their year in Europe, they'd moved right back to town. And now they lived in the house Lydia's parents had planned to move away from but never had. Every day, Henry walked on that front porch where he'd first courted his future wife. Did he ever picture their teenage selves out there, painting and staring at the setting sun? Cassie tried to imagine them as shy young teenagers, but she couldn't quite manage it. She couldn't picture her grandmother, in particular, as a girl, unsure of herself and her future.

"Did your parents send Grandma to

school in New York to keep her away from Grandpa?" Cassie asked.

"Oh, art school wasn't *their* idea!" Nell said. "My parents saw it as a terrible waste. But Lydia got her way eventually, and I'm sure they were happy enough to get her away from Henry."

"But they dated all through college, didn't they?" Cassie asked.

"I assume so, although they didn't see each other often. You have to understand, young people then didn't jet across the country at the drop of a hat like you do. Lydia took the train home once a year, at Christmas. That was the only time we saw her. During the summers, she stayed in New York and worked so she could help with the tuition. I always assumed she and Henry had an understanding."

"You mean they were engaged?"

"Oh, not exactly," said Nell. "She didn't wear a ring or anything like that. It's just— well, I simply knew she'd marry Henry. Not that I wasn't surprised when they came home from Europe as Mr. and Mrs. Armstrong! I suspect they eloped to avoid any family awkwardness. But as much as Mother didn't want to see Lydia married to the local farmer's son,

I know she felt cheated out of the experience of planning a wedding. She meddled far too much in mine a few years later to make up for it!"

"I always thought it was so romantic, getting married in France," Cassie said.

"Well, she was there for that study-abroad program. They had some sort of fight before she left—I'm sure he didn't want her to leave, and Lydia made her grand statement by going off anyway—but it was only a temporary spat. Henry went over there and swept her off her feet and that was that. It was during my freshman year at Northwestern and I was quite resentful that Lydia's drama completely overshadowed my first year of college!"

Something Nell said stuck in Cassie's mind.

"That would have been Grandma's senior year, right?" Cassie asked. "Don't students usually spend their junior year abroad?"

"Well, I don't know," said Nell. "Perhaps art schools do things differently."

Cassie thought back to the letter. The lines about Lydia leaving suddenly, unexpectedly. Creating a new life. Words that might have been written after Lydia sailed off to Europe. Or perhaps the answer lay farther away, dur-

ing those months Lydia lived on her own in
France.

"Are you sure she never dated anyone else
in college?" Cassie asked.

"She never mentioned it," Nell replied. But
now her voice sounded doubtful. "I suppose
she could have. But why keep in contact with
Henry all that time? Surely she would have
broken it off with him?"

"I don't know." Cassie yawned. Almost
eleven o'clock. Only a few more hours until
Cooper left for London. She should get up
to see him off, but right now, sleep was far
more tempting.

"I'm sorry I don't have all the answers,"
Nell said. "But honestly, Cassie, does it really matter? Whoever this letter was from,
it was written a long time ago. We all like to
keep things around for sentimental reasons.
It may not mean anything."

Cassie pictured her grandparents as she'd
seen them so often over the years: sitting
companionably at the dining room table after
breakfast, one glancing up over a section of
newspaper to start a sentence that the other
quickly finished. Whatever had happened
in the past, Lydia and Henry now shared an

unbreakable bond. Any romance might have long since faded from their lives, but Cassie had no doubt they were happy together.

"You're right," she said. "I don't know why I got so obsessed with it."

"We all have our secrets," Nell told her. "If I ever have the courage to write my memoirs, then you'll get some real stories."

"I'd love to read your memoirs," Cassie said. "And thank you—I mean it."

"It's been a joy," Nell said. "Do call more often, won't you?"

"Yes, I will."

After hanging up, Cassie tiptoed into the bedroom, passing Cooper's snoring body on her way to the bathroom. She stopped for a moment, struck by the way his arms were flung haphazardly above his head, the way one knee protruded from the top of the comforter. Awake Cooper always stayed firmly in control, priding himself on remaining cool under pressure. It was one of the qualities she admired most about him. But now, seeing him so unguarded and loose, like a little boy, she was hit by an unexpected wave of tenderness.

As Cassie brushed her teeth, she thought about her grandparents at lunch the day before, comfortable in their shared silences, practically reading each other's minds. What would it be like to have that kind of history with someone? To be with a person who'd known you through all the stages of your life? She'd spent ten years with Cooper, which had once seemed like an eternity. They had grown from teenagers into adults together. But she couldn't shake the feeling that she still didn't know him. Had he really shed the shyness that had been so obvious during their freshman year of college, or had he merely covered it up? Did he ever long to simply be the way he was now, relaxed and unguarded, without worrying about the next step on the corporate ladder? And if he did let his guard slip, would she even recognize him?

Cassie had always considered herself lucky that she'd met her soul mate—thereby avoiding the dating disasters of her friends—but now she wasn't so sure. Perhaps dating other people would have given her more perspective on how a relationship worked. Instead, like her grandmother, she was marrying the first boy she'd ever fallen for. Aunt Nell seemed convinced that Lydia had never dated anyone other than Henry. But the more Cassie thought about it, the more she felt that the secret of the letter lay buried in Lydia's college years. Far from putting Cassie at peace, her conversation with Aunt Nell had only raised more questions.

Chapter 4

Lydia

Senior year of high school was supposed to be fun, but to Lydia it was torture. Everyone seemed to be anticipating the release of graduation—everyone except her. Because rather than heading toward freedom, she faced a future determined by the dreams and expectations of others.

College was nonnegotiable, of course. Mother had a degree from a small but well-regarded women's college in Ohio; Father a medical degree. They expected both their daughters to go on to higher education, even if—as in Mother's case—it was only seen as an opportunity to meet eligible, ambitious young men. College meant a ticket out of Knox Junction. But as the time to submit applications came closer, Lydia became paralyzed with indecision.

Mother took charge, in her usual way, writing to request applications from Wellesley and Smith. Meanwhile, Henry had his own assumption about where Lydia would go, as he casually revealed one day at school.

They were sitting in their regular spot in the high school cafeteria, the same place they always sat and ate their bag lunches, in a corner near the window overlooking the football field. Sometimes classmates would join them, but more often they ate alone, their close connection blocking others out.

"How did your parents take it?" Lydia asked him. Henry had already sent in his paperwork for the agriculture program at the University of Illinois, a huge milestone for him, given that no one else in his family had gone to college.

Henry shook his head. "Not well. You know how Pop is about the farm." Lydia didn't really know, not firsthand. In their years of dating she'd only met Henry's father a few times and had never been invited to the house. Henry's home was no doubt smaller and shabbier than hers, but Lydia suspected that wasn't the reason he kept her away. More likely it was his mother, who had become a recluse in the two years since Timothy's death.

"I told him the classes would teach me how to make the farm more efficient," Henry said, "but he won't listen."

"So what are you going to do?"

"Go anyway. Pay my own tuition. That's why I'm sticking with U of I. It won't cost that much. I can get a job on weekends."

Hovering unspoken between them was the knowledge that Lydia's college choices were not restricted by price. She could go anywhere she wanted.

"If I can save up enough, I want to get a car," Henry said. "That way we could drive back and forth together. That would be great, wouldn't it?"

"What do you mean?" Lydia asked.

"When we leave for school, or during Christmas vacation. We could come home together. No more sitting around waiting for the train."

He assumed she was going to U of I, too. Of course. He had made the decision for both of them.

Lydia tried to find words that wouldn't hurt him. But it wasn't the right time or place— a crowded cafeteria at lunchtime wasn't the ideal spot for a heart-to-heart conversation. Besides, she told herself, she hadn't made up her mind yet. She very well might decide to go to U of I. So she simply reached across the table and put her hand over Henry's. "I wouldn't worry about a car just yet," she said. "The train's fine by me."

Henry blushed, his mouth twisting into a shy smile. They were careful not to show affection in school, always conscious of being watched and gossiped about. To classmates who didn't know they were dating, they could have been mistaken for brother and sister, so casual were their interactions. This clasping of hands was the first time they'd openly expressed any physical affection at school. The fact that the first move had been Lydia's made it all the more surprising.

Away from curious eyes, it was another matter. On those very rare occasions when they found themselves alone—walking down a back road in search of a landscape for Lydia to sketch, or sitting in the deserted school library in the late afternoon—they couldn't keep their hands off each other. Still, they never proceeded further than kissing or holding hands. The ground rules were understood. Lydia was a good girl, Henry was a good boy, and any exploring underneath clothes was strictly off limits.

But lately they'd been bending the rules. It started off with accidents that weren't quite accidents—Lydia pulling her lips away from Henry's and moving them toward the spot where his shirt strained open above his top button. Henry's hand brushing against the tight fabric of Lydia's sweater, fleetingly touching her breasts. If they were to be at college together, living under far less supervision, Lydia wondered if these same unspoken boundaries would hold. Would they be tempted to go further? Because when she was pressed up against Henry, kissing him in a shadowy corner of a high school hallway, she *wanted* to go further. And she was frightened of what would happen if she got the chance.

* * *

"I put the Wellesley information on your bed," Mother said at dinner that night.

"All right." Lydia was less than enthusiastic.

"Have you been reading the brochures? Chosen a favorite?"

Lydia shook her head. "I'm still thinking." Then, looking straight at her parents to gauge their reaction, she added, "It would cost a lot less money if I went to the University of Illinois."

Mother's fingers gripped her fork tightly. "I didn't know you were considering it."

"They say it's a fine school," Father said.

Mother kept her eyes focused on her plate. "Is that where Henry will be going?"

"I think so," Lydia said.

A silence settled over the table. The only sound was of forks and knives gently clinking against the china plates. Mother wouldn't look at Lydia.

"Of course, I'd hate to see you waste your potential," Mother said. "A girl like you, who could go anywhere."

"Shouldn't you go the same place as

Henry?" Nell put in from across the table. "You *are* getting married, right?"

Lydia shot her younger sister a furious glare. That was typical of Nell, drawing attention to herself by making a dramatic pronouncement.

Mother's head snapped around toward Lydia. "What?" she demanded. "Have you and Henry—"

"No, Mother," Lydia interrupted. "Of course not."

"I hope you won't waste your future because of a youthful…*understanding*," Mother said. "No matter how fine a young man Henry may be."

"I do think eighteen is rather young to consider marriage." Father flashed Lydia a sympathetic smile.

Lydia dropped her utensils onto her plate. "I'm not getting married," she said firmly, trying to keep her voice level. "So don't worry." Then, giving Nell one last angry scowl, she rose from the table and strode out the doorway, stamping her feet as she fled upstairs to her room. She blinked hard to keep back the tears. The people she loved most in the world were pushing her in opposite directions, causing her almost physical pain. Her real dream for the future seemed so unlikely and impractical that she was embarrassed to share it with them. Her parents would find it laughable, and Henry would be devastated at the thought of her leaving. If she couldn't count on the support of her family or Henry, she must truly be alone.

It had begun with a story in *Life* magazine, a photo essay about the G.I. bill that showed former soldiers going to colleges across the country. Amid the pictures of grinning young men playing baseball and posing with their fraternity rings, one in particular caught her eye:

> Former lieutenant Roy S. Hartigan saw fierce fighting along the Italian peninsula, but he also gained an appreciation for Renaissance painting. Today, he has put aside his rifle in favor of a paintbrush, pursuing a degree at the New York Institute of Art.

It wasn't Roy S. Hartigan who grabbed her attention; he appeared to be a rather bland, expressionless young man. It was the scene captured in that photograph: young men and women standing seriously in front of easels, brushes in hand, surrounded by walls covered with brightly colored canvases. All those people, together in one room, doing something she loved.

The idea that she could actually study art opened up a world of possibilities she'd never considered. College could be more than a dutiful obligation to her parents. It could be a chance to follow her passion. She wanted to be one of the people in that room. Wanted it more than anything. More, even, than Henry.

At first, the Institute of Art was an elaborate fantasy constructed when she lay in bed at night, trying to sleep. She pictured herself riding the train to New York—how long would it take? Days? Alighting with suitcase in hand at a glamorous, bustling train station; standing in class while a professor with a European accent showed her the proper way to sculpt marble or draw a still life. It was nothing more than a daydream, with no relation to her real life.

But as the college pressure from her parents grew more intense, so did Lydia's urge to escape. She wrote to the most sophisticated person she knew—her distant cousin Eleanor, with whom she had spent time during summers in Lake Geneva—and asked her to find out what she could about the New York Institute of Art, without saying anything to Mother.

Eleanor's reply came a few weeks later, in a large brown envelope.

Having too often made the safe choice rather than the desired one, I am all in favor of you pursuing your dreams. If I can be of any help in bringing your mother 'round to your side, you need simply ask.

Inside the envelope, Eleanor had enclosed a large, glossy booklet about the Institute, along with the school's application packet for next year.

Lydia examined each page until she had it memorized. She read and reread the passages that might bolster her case with Mother: "The Institute strongly upholds the belief that a wide-ranging, liberal arts education is crucial to the development of any future artist…"

"At the Lucille B. Davison women's dormitory, female students live in a safe, companionable setting with the warmth of home, supervised by a live-in matron...

"Among our distinguished alumni are the assistant director of the Metropolitan Museum of Art, the owners of numerous prestigious New York and European art galleries, the noted artist Paul Thewlins..."

All of this was guaranteed to appeal to her mother's snobbery and reassure her protective father. But art school—let alone art school in New York City—seemed like a far-off, unattainable dream. A vast world away from Knox Junction, where three couples in her senior class were already engaged, including her closest friend, Melanie. Henry hadn't yet popped the question—despite Mother's suspicions—but Lydia knew it was coming. College would be a four-year reprieve, at most.

Lydia still wasn't sure she wanted to marry Henry. The disloyalty of that truth filled her with shame, since Henry had been her emotional support for so many years. He even encouraged her artistic leanings, buying her an oil-paint set last Christmas that she'd unwrapped with stunned joy. She'd no doubt she could live happily with Henry for the rest of her life. It was all the other trappings of marriage that left her feeling cold and afraid— moving into a farmhouse at the end of a dirt road; rising with the dawn to feed chickens and milk cows; being expected to produce children at regular two- or three-year intervals. Staying in Knox Junction when there were cities like New York waiting to be explored.

Alone in her room now, Lydia pulled the Institute of Art package from its hiding place under her bed. The application was surprisingly simple: a half page of personal information, a request for a reference from a high school teacher or principal and three samples of artwork. It was nowhere near as demanding as the application from Wellesley, which was sitting neatly on her pillow. For that one, she'd have to write an essay entitled "Why Wellesley?," a seemingly straightforward but fiendishly difficult assignment. The Smith application required something similar. Already, she knew far more about the New York Institute of Art than she knew about either of those more prestigious schools.

She could already picture herself unpacking at the Lucille B. Davison women's dormitory, having late-night discussions with her fellow students about painting versus sculpture. Instead, she'd be filling out applications for schools she didn't want to attend.

Lydia glanced again at the Wellesley application. "Why Wellesley?" Good question. One that, if she was honest, she'd answer: "Because my mother wants me to go."

Lydia smiled, despite her frustration. Just imagine what the Wellesley administrators would say if they read that!

Lydia's hands clutched the paper. She suddenly saw an escape from her dilemma, if she was brave enough to go through with it.

A few months later, when the letters from both Smith and Wellesley arrived, Lydia handed them wordlessly to Mother. Each opened with the phrase "Thank you for your application. Unfortunately…"

"I don't believe it," Mother said dejectedly, scanning the letters repeatedly as though the words would change if she willed them to. "You're at the top of your class."

"I don't think it takes much to be at the

top of Fentonville High School," Lydia responded. "Especially if I'm competing against the smartest young women in the country."

"I knew we should've considered boarding school. Your father wouldn't hear of it, and of course I would have missed you so, but this—"

"Mother, it's all right. There's one more letter I want to show you."

Lydia held out the acceptance letter from the New York Institute of Art. "Look here at the end—" she pointed "—the part about the scholarship."

Mother read the letter in silence, then turned to Lydia with a mystified look. "What is this?"

"I applied, just for fun," Lydia said. "You know how I feel about painting. They seem to like my work, otherwise they wouldn't offer to pay my way, would they?"

Lydia tried to keep her voice level, but her heart was pounding. The gamble had paid off beyond her wildest hopes. She was prepared for the Wellesley and Smith rejections, after the brutally honest application essays she'd written. But still, she was far from assured a place at the New York Institute of Art. Admissions were decided mostly by the quality of an applicant's work, and Lydia had no idea how good she was—or wasn't. That she'd not only been accepted but given a full scholarship made her feel prouder than any A on a test. Perhaps she had talent, after all.

"There's always the University of Illinois," Lydia said softly.

Mother's head jerked up. The choice was clear—allow her daughter to move far away from home to pursue a wildly impractical degree in a large, sinful city or keep her close to home, where she'd settle down with a struggling farmer's son who wasn't nearly good enough for her.

It didn't take Mother long to make her decision.

"Your father will be livid, I'm afraid. But I'll do my best to soften him up. New York is a marvelous place to be young, Lydia—but I trust you're sensible enough not to let it go to your head."

Lydia knew that convincing Father wouldn't be all that difficult. The person she dreaded telling was Henry.

"Huh."

Usually, Lydia found Henry's silences comfortable, especially compared to the nonstop chatter of Mother and Nell. But the day Lydia finally told him about her college plans, she almost wished he'd lash out. Confront her with a reaction she could match with anger of her own. Instead, he looked at her with such quiet dejection that the only possible response was guilt.

Lydia had put off the conversation as long as she could. She'd let Henry assume U of I was her first choice, hinted that the other applications were just to make her mother happy. She'd put off this day of reckoning, hoping to spare his feelings as long as possible. Instead, she'd only raised his hopes, giving him further to fall.

"I didn't think I had a prayer of getting into art school," Lydia said. "I applied as a joke, really. But now, with the scholarship…" Thank God for the scholarship. It let her claim that the decision was out of her hands.

Henry looked at her silently, and she dropped her eyes, acknowledging what they both knew. A scholarship would make all the difference for Henry, who would find it a hardship to pay even the low, in-state tuition of a public university. Lydia had no such restrictions.

"You should do what you want," he said finally. "I know you can't wait to leave Knox Junction. I don't blame you."

They were sitting in one of their favorite spots, by the side of the pond at the edge of his family's property. The trees surrounding the water hid them from the house, but they weren't far from the main road, so they were always aware of being on view. Still, sitting there alone, they would allow themselves a few liberties. They'd sit close enough for their legs to touch, their hands entwined in the grass. Sometimes, after checking that no car was kicking up dirt clouds in the distance, they would kiss, their lips touching softly and slowly, his mouth occasionally gliding down to caress her cheek.

"Henry, this has nothing to do with you…"

"I know."

"I don't want to leave you—oh, I'm so sorry." She stopped as her voice began to shake.

"You shouldn't be sorry for doing what you always dreamed about. I wish I were that brave."

"I'm not brave," Lydia said. She felt, at that moment, the intense weight of her advantages—two loving, healthy parents, a living sister, enough money to do what she wanted, social connections that ensured she would always be taken care of. All things Henry did not have.

"You're brave enough to do what you need to," Henry said. "It's just, before you leave… ah, I don't know how to go about this."

"Go about what?"

"Something I've been meaning to talk to you about for a while, only I keep losing my nerve."

Lydia's shoulders stiffened. Was he planning to propose? Now? She realized with terror that she wasn't sure how she would answer.

But Henry's hands didn't slip into his pockets in search of a ring. They kept plucking at the blades of grass at his sides. He looked at her with the direct stare she found so mesmerizing.

"If you want out, I understand," he said. "Truth is, I don't know how I managed to keep you this long."

"Out? What do you mean?"

"You don't owe me anything."

Alone at night, thinking about the move to New York, Lydia had agonized over Henry and their future. Wondered if she even wanted a future with him. But now, faced with the prospect of leaving him, she wasn't sure if she could go through with it.

"Going to New York doesn't mean it's all over," Lydia said. "We can still be together when I come home." She grabbed his hand and held it to her heart, aware that his fingers were pressed against the top of her breast.

He looked at her for a moment, then leaned in to kiss her.

"You know I love you, city girl," he whispered against her cheek. Usually, their nicknames for each other made her laugh, but at that moment she could barely crack a smile.

"I love you, too, country boy."

"You going to spend the summer in Wisconsin again?"

"Yes. And Chicago. Mother's already planning grand shopping expeditions to put together a suitable school wardrobe."

"Do you think—the night before you leave, would you want to go out?" Henry asked. "Have dinner, maybe?"

"Of course."

"We'll do something nice," he said. "Give you a real send-off."

Lydia smiled. "Surprise me."

Mother didn't make a scene about the dinner with Henry, as Lydia feared, although she would have if she knew the real plans for the evening. Mother assumed Lydia would be out on a double date with Melanie and her fiancé, Bruce Myall. Which she would be, for about ten minutes. The plan was for Bruce to pick up Henry, then Lydia, then Melanie, thus assuring all the parents that the teenagers were heading off together to a movie in Fentonville.

But after waving farewell, Bruce would let Henry and Lydia out for a private dinner, while he and Melanie went off on their own for a few hours to neck in Bruce's car, the main activity on all their dates.

Even though Mother didn't know the evening's true scenario, she was too distracted by travel plans to pay much attention. The whole family would be taking the train to Chicago the following morning, to begin shopping for the next chapter in Lydia's life. The New York Institute of Art might have thrown Mother off balance, but she'd come around with a vengeance, and was now giddy about the prospect of going to New York to help Lydia get settled. It was almost as if she were the one starting a new life.

As she was getting ready to go out, Lydia wondered if Mother might finally be willing to lend her one of her precious pairs of silk stockings. She approached her parents' bedroom, then paused at the sound of her mother's voice. "It's for the best, I see that now."

Father said something, but his voice was muffled.

"Oh, I've no doubt she's fond of the boy," Mother said dismissively. "But she knows as well as I do that she was meant for better. And that family—gracious! Can you picture us sitting down to Sunday dinner with them?"

Lydia heard footsteps approaching in her direction. She pressed her body flat against the wall as Father's voice boomed out from inside the doorway.

"It's the mother than concerns me," he said. "Grief over a child, I can understand. But this moping for years, to me that's a sign of something more serious."

"These things run in a family. You've seen

it yourself," Mother said. "Unstable parents, unstable children. That's the last thing Lydia needs."

Lydia tiptoed back to her room before either of them knew she was there. She thought of Henry's mother, who hadn't left the house in years. Did that sort of melancholy get carried in the blood, from mother to son? Might that explain Henry's lack of passion, his aggravating ability to remain even-keeled at all times?

Henry's love had been, for years, a simple fact of Lydia's life. Much like the flowers blooming in Mother's garden every spring, or the first day of school in the fall. She'd never doubted his feelings. But lately, that love had felt as colorless and predictable as Knox Junction itself. Every day the same, years passing with no change. She dreaded saying goodbye to him, and yet she couldn't deny a certain sense of relief. A feeling that she was escaping before it was too late.

"What are we doing here?" Lydia asked. Bruce had pulled the car over at the turnoff to Henry's house.

"This is your stop," Bruce said with a grin, and Melanie giggled.

Lydia looked at Henry for an explanation. Was their last date, their one chance at a grown-up, romantic dinner, going to be spent at his parents' dining room table?

Henry grabbed Lydia's hand and pulled her from the car.

"Ten o'clock, right?" Bruce asked. Henry nodded, waved, and Bruce and Melanie drove off.

"Come on," Henry tucked Lydia's arm inside his and led her through the grass, onto his parents' property. The full moon partially lit their way, but Lydia felt her feet slipping in the tall, unkempt grass.

"What is going on?" she demanded. "I wore my good shoes…"

"We're almost there," Henry said.

Lydia looked ahead, where a dim light peeked out from amid tree trunks. They were walking toward the apple orchard, a place she hadn't been since the day they first kissed. As they got closer, Lydia saw a blanket spread out on the grass, with a lantern perched in the middle. Carefully arranged on the blanket were two plates, silverware and glasses—a moonlit picnic.

"I know it's not the fancy restaurant I

promised," Henry said, his gaze fixed on the ground. "But I hope you like it."

Lydia stared, unable for a moment to take in what was in front of her. She thought about the preparation this must have taken, the walks he must have made all the way back and forth from the house to gather everything he needed.

"It's beautiful," she said.

Henry let out a sigh of relief. "Oh, good. I thought—well, I wanted to have some time where it's just us."

He took her hand, and held her arm while she sat down on the blanket. The meal itself was plain country food—cold chicken, potato salad, corn, apple pie. Lydia suspected it was leftovers from the family's dinner the previous night, and wondered how Henry would explain its disappearance from the fridge. But she refrained from asking about the specifics and told him it tasted delicious. All the while wondering what would happen once the food was gone, and it was just the two of them out there alone, unchaperoned under the night sky.

"Yum," Lydia said as she scraped her fork over the last of the apple pie on her plate. She popped the crumbled remains of piecrust into her mouth and busied herself with her napkin, trying to cover her sudden awkwardness.

Henry put down his plate and looked her in the eye.

"It's all wrong, isn't it?" he asked.

"Why—what do you mean?"

"This picnic. It's silly. You wanted a nice restaurant, and I brought you here. I'm sorry."

"No, no, don't apologize." Lydia wondered what she'd done to cause this unexpected change of mood. Was her father right? Was his mother's instability lurking beneath the surface?

"It's just—we're hardly ever alone," Henry said. "And now we are, and you're being so careful. You haven't even gone to New York yet, and already you're a different person."

Lydia was taken aback. Their conversation during dinner had been perfectly polite, she thought. Too polite. As if she were royalty pretending to be entertained by the pathetic offerings of a lowly subject.

"You're right," she said. "It's—you see, I'm scared. Of everything changing."

"Me, too."

There was a long pause, and Lydia wondered if this was when he planned to propose.

"Henry, if you were thinking—I mean, if you're looking to the future…I want you to know, I can't…" She didn't know how to finish the sentence.

"Can't what?" Typical Henry. Not letting her get away with being vague. Expecting everyone else to be as direct as he was.

"I can't make any promises," she said. "About the future."

"I'm not asking you to," he said. "The only thing I wanted was to spend tonight with you. That's all."

And in that moment, with Henry's acceptance of her needs, she felt a rush of love that warmed her whole body. She burst into relieved laughter, and after a moment's hesitation, so did Henry. Lydia surrendered to the feeling, tipping over and lying down on the blanket as she was consumed by waves of giggles. Henry smiled down at her, his expression shifting between amusement and concern.

But it felt good. It felt good not to care what she looked like, not to worry about what she should do next, not to notice whether her hair

was mussed or her skirt hitched too high up
her legs. It felt so blissfully right simply to be
there, with Henry, outside in the warm night
air. She gazed up at him with a smile, through
locks of hair that had fallen over her eyes.

Henry reached down to brush the hair off
her face. That gentle touch, the feel of his
hands against her forehead, was enough. She
reached up and grabbed his hand, pulled him
down with her, until his face was next to hers.
She ran her fingers along his cheeks, feeling the rough stubble that dotted his chin.
For a moment, they lay there, frozen, neither willing to make the small overture that
would bring their bodies together. Then Lydia
wrapped her arms around his shoulders and
pulled him to her, and she was lost.

For years, when she and Henry had kissed,
it had been tender. She would tilt her head
up toward his, while he leaned down to meet
her lips. Their hands had explored tentatively,
carefully, afraid of making a mistake. But tonight, they clung to each other desperately,
rubbing their hands over each other's bodies
as if frantic to hold on. Lying there beside
each other, they were equals.

Lydia felt the muscles in Henry's back

tense as their legs intertwined. She moved her hands along his back, pushing his lower body against her. They kissed hard and fast, as if compensating for what their bodies were not yet prepared to do.

"Hold on," Henry muttered. With his feet and one arm, he swept the plates and silverware off the blanket, tossing them haphazardly onto the grass. He pulled the blanket up around their bodies, encasing them in a private cocoon. Without that gesture, the night might have followed the usual pattern of their dates, not progressing further than passionate kissing. Allowing their bare skin in the open, where they could have been discovered, was a line Lydia would not cross. But tucked away inside their cocoon, she felt safe and protected. She didn't have to look at what their bodies were doing. All she had to do was feel.

Lydia's slid the buttons of Henry's shirt through the buttonholes. As she pulled the shirt off his shoulders, she marveled at the tautness of his skin. Years of working on the farm had transformed the skinny, scarecrow of a boy into a man. She rubbed the muscles along his back.

Henry's hands were in her hair, his lips skimming along her cheeks and neck. She arched her back when his mouth approached her shoulders, willing him to move farther down.

"Lydia…" he murmured.

"Yes, yes," she whispered. She undid the delicate, mother-of-pearl buttons on her blouse.

"Do you know how…" she began, shooting a glance down at her brassiere.

He shook his head.

"Here." Awkwardly, Lydia reached one hand around her back to undo the rear closure. Her other hand remained flat against Henry's chest, as if losing contact with his skin would break the spell. She felt Henry's hand fumble around hers, his fingers so wide and rough compared to hers. Then she buried her head in his neck, giving herself over to the sensation of his fingers and lips on her tender skin, feeling her in a way that no one ever had. She pressed into him, begging him wordlessly to rub harder, kiss deeper.

It could have ended there. Henry didn't push for more, never reached any farther than her waist. And if this had been any other night, a night when she would've had to face Henry at school the next day, nothing more would have happened. This sudden descent into full-blown passion would have seemed ridiculous—or worse—by the light of day. But even as she was swept away by the moment, Lydia knew that this night, there'd be no consequences. She would be leaving the next morning. She wouldn't have to face Henry and wonder what this meant for their future. She might never have to see him again.

That knowledge brought a recklessness she would otherwise have lacked.

"Lydia," Henry whispered as she reached for his trousers.

"I want to."

"Are you sure?"

She kept her head buried against his cheek. She couldn't meet his eyes.

"Yes."

The event that had seemed so monumental—the one she'd always assumed would be saved for her wedding night—wasn't nearly as overwhelming as she'd expected. Henry moved gently, as if she were a delicate china doll, and she touched his back lightly, not wanting to break his concentration.

Within a few minutes, it was over. Henry moved off Lydia with a groan, and rolled over onto the grass beside her. Lydia kept her eyes focused on the stars in the sky above her. She heard rustling as Henry adjusted his clothes. When he came back to the blanket he didn't look at her, merely wrapped his arms around her and held her against his chest.

Neither wanted to be the first to speak. They lay there, faces lit only by flickering lantern light, feeling each other breathe in and out.

It was Henry who finally broke the silence. "Lydia, you make me so happy."

"We made each other happy." She wondered if he noticed that she'd used the past tense.

Suddenly, a car horn beeped in the distance.

"Shoot, it's Bruce," Henry said.

Lydia sprang up, clutching the blanket. "Oh, Lord…"

"He won't come over. He'll wait."

But the prospect of being discovered filled Lydia with frantic energy. She fumbled for her bra and blouse, her fingers trembling as she fastened the buttons. She groped blindly in the grass, feeling for the shoes she'd kicked off hours earlier.

"I can't…" she began, approaching panic as she took in the crumpled blanket and scattered dishes.

"Don't worry about that," Henry said. "I'll clean up. I just—you should know—"

"Henry, thank you." Lydia kissed him quickly on the cheek. "Let's not—let's not make this difficult. I'll write you as soon as I get settled in New York." Already, in her mind, she'd left the farm, left Knox Junction, left Henry. Left what had happened between them in the apple orchard.

"Lydia—"

"I have to go." She dashed off through the darkness, toward the distant gleam of headlights. Bruce smirked when he saw her bedraggled figure, although he probably didn't dream how far she'd gone. Melanie climbed into the backseat and fixed Lydia's hair so it would look presentable. Luckily, Mother and Father were absorbed in their magazines when she arrived home, and asked only the vaguest questions about her evening before she dashed upstairs.

It wasn't until the next day, on the train that

carried her far away from the cornfields, that she realized she hadn't said goodbye to Henry. What she didn't know then was that he'd noticed—and drawn his own conclusions.

Chapter 5

Cassie

For the first time in her professional life, Cassie told an outright lie. Not an exaggeration or a half-truth, but a made-up-from-thin-air, all-out falsehood.

"Something's come up—family business," she told Jeffrey soon after arriving at the office on Wednesday morning. "I need tomorrow and Friday off."

He gave her the cool stare he used to intimidate opponents during tough negotiations.

"Everything okay?" he asked.

"Yes, just some things I need to take care

of." Cassie pressed her lips together to keep from babbling. Producing an overcomplicated explanation would only make her look suspicious. Less is more, she told herself.

Jeffrey shuffled a few papers on his desk. "It's not the greatest time, actually."

Cassie waited. While his lack of enthusiasm might have cowed her once, she now felt surprisingly unconcerned. The endless office politics, gossip and mixed signals floating through the firm had taken their toll. If they wanted to fire her for taking a few days off, so be it. Her job wasn't looking too secure in any case. Why jump through hoops to keep it?

"Are you saying I can't go?" Cassie asked.

"No, not if you really need the time."

"I do."

"Then that's your choice," Jeffrey said. "I do expect the Prospect Health Care contract to be ready by Monday, though."

"Of course. It will be." Even if that meant working forty-eight hours straight over the weekend. It wasn't as if she'd anything better to do.

"Okay, then." Jeffrey dismissed her and turned back to his papers. "Anything else?"

Cassie paused, wondering if she should ask what was really going on. If she was in danger of losing her job. But she could tell by Jeffrey's expression that he'd moved on. Taking up any more of his time would only make him more irritated. Jeffrey preferred conversations that were short and to the point, not rambling and speculative. Why annoy him when she'd already gotten what she wanted?

"Thanks."

As soon as she got back to her office, Cassie went online to check airfares to New York. Leaving that night would be ridiculously expensive; if she'd any sense, she'd buy a lower-priced ticket for a trip in a few weeks. Instead, she found herself clicking through the ordering process, then staring at an e-receipt for a flight departing O'Hare that night at seven. If she didn't do this immediately, she might lose her nerve. And other than her job, what did she have waiting for her here?

Cooper would be away for the next few days. She hadn't even kissed him goodbye before he left for London. She'd drifted off to sleep on the couch watching a late-night talk show, and by the time she woke up, wincing at the pain in her twisted neck, Cooper had gone. He must have crept out silently—because he was being considerate or to avoid a conversation? She'd looked around for a note from him on the coffee table or kitchen counter, but there was nothing.

Cassie considered calling Cooper's cell phone to tell him about the trip. But what would be the point? Unromantic, practical Cooper could never understand how much the letter affected her. He had no idea what it was to be raised in a family with secrets. Gatherings at his parents' house were filled with raucous laughter and brutally honest discussions of everyone's personal life. "Why don't you just ask your grandmother?" he would say. But Cassie couldn't. And she sensed that Lydia would never tell her.

Cassie had never been one of those women who dreaded being alone. Cooper's business trips were a chance to lounge around in pajamas, eating ice cream straight from the container and watching weepy movies on cable. But this time around, she wasn't looking forward to the solitude. Something about the way they'd parted—without goodbyes—left a gloomy pall in the apartment. The few friends she could think of calling were all busy: Anne out of town on a big case in Detroit, Katie busy with her kid's birthday party, Julie on a cruise with her boyfriend. All her friends were just as busy as she was, the kind of people you had to schedule outings with weeks in advance. Lately, she hadn't made her friends a priority; now she would pay the price.

After printing out her receipt, Cassie searched for the New York Institute of Art website. She found it quickly, then printed out a map. Cassie had been to New York a few times on business, but those trips had been a flurry of conference rooms and taxi rides and late-night drinks in hotel bars. Her knowledge of the city's layout was sketchy at best.

Cassie flipped through the firm's phone directory, then dialed the extension for Maggie, the travel coordinator.

"Hey, Maggie, it's Cassie. Do you know of any hotels in New York, near Madison Avenue and 67th?"

"Let me check." Cassie heard rapid keyboard clicks. "Sure, there are few nice places within walking distance. Want me to e-mail you some links?"

"Yeah, that would be great."

"Need me to set up a flight, too?"

"No, I've got that taken care of. This is a personal trip, not business."

"Okey dokey. Although if you're going on your own dime, I should tell you that these hotels aren't cheap."

"That's okay," Cassie said. After what she'd paid for her plane ticket, the hotel would look like a bargain. She hoped all the money was worth it. That it would lead her to an answer.

Cassie was used to putting up a confident front; she did it every time she stepped into a courtroom (which was rarely) or a conference-room negotiation (which was far too often). No matter how strong or weak her case, she entered briskly. She would look her opponents in the eye, talk clearly and forcefully. Never give them time to doubt her version of events.

As she walked into the Institute of Art's administration building on Thursday, Cassie strode purposefully in her high-heeled boots, her gray suit and slim-cut red wool coat, a stark contrast to the ripped jeans and flip-flops on the students shuffling around her. After asking a few questions at the front desk, she headed over to the school's library, where she'd been assured they kept copies of past yearbooks.

A few minutes later, she was telling the librarian the story she'd invented, about making a scrapbook as a surprise for her grandmother's birthday.

"Lydia Prescott," Cassie said. "She would've started here in the fall of 1946."

"Those would be in the back room, around the corner there," the librarian said. "You should start with the 1947 book. That would be from your grandmother's first academic year." She was far from the stereotype of a school librarian—bright red hair with oovious black roots, a tie-dyed dress that wrapped around her body like a neck-to-knee bandage. She smiled widely as if to prove that she still had every one of her teeth. "I think it's great, what you're doing."

"Thanks," Cassie said. "I hope she'll like it."

Cassie scanned the bookshelves until she found the rows of yearbooks. Walking backward in time, she strolled past the 1970s, then farther back to the '50s and '40s. With both hands, she pulled out three yearbooks: 1947,

1948 and 1949. Lydia had spent her senior year in France so she probably wasn't even in that yearbook, but Cassie picked up the 1950 volume, too, just in case.

Cassie first turned to the freshman photos at the back of the 1947 book. There she was, Lydia Prescott, looking impossibly young and somewhat frightened. Her dark hair was curled in waves around her face, flipping against her neck just below her jawbone. Her narrow lips were curled upward slightly, hinting at a smile that was never completed.

Cassie pored over the other pages in the book, skimming every caption, but she found no other photos of her grandmother. Same with the 1948 book. The only picture of Lydia was in the sophomore student section—another stiff, nervous headshot. And no photo of any student with the initials F.B.

It wasn't until the 1949 book—Lydia's junior year—that Cassie saw him. A young man with a wide grin, his picture markedly different from all the other carefully posed photos. His swept-back hair gleamed with whatever concoction he'd spread on to tame it down, and his cheeks and nose were sprinkled with freckles. Cassie could see the shoulders of a checkered jacket reaching into the bottom of the frame. He seemed ready to spring off the page, bursting with life and energy.

Frank Blakely.

Cassie looked at the opposite page, where Lydia's photo appeared amid the *P*s. Something about her looked different this time. Her hair, while still carefully curled, hung a little more naturally; her eyes were brighter and less afraid of the camera. Most of all, she was smiling—not a forced grin but an easy, comfortable, happy expression. For the first time, Lydia seemed at ease.

Could that have anything to do with Frank Blakely?

Cassie flipped through the rest of the book eagerly looking for photographic proof of the two of them together. Unlike in the other yearbooks, Lydia actually showed up in a few candid-photo sections, once in a group shot of something called the "Masterpiece Club," and a few pages later in a photo taken inside the school's pottery studio, holding up hands covered with clay. But Frank Blakely was nowhere in those pictures, even though Cassie pressed her face up against the page to peer at the background of every one. The only other picture of him was taken at the school's fall musical, where he appeared to be singing.

Cassie dug in her purse for some scratch paper, then slipped the paper between the pages where Lydia's photo appeared. She put the other yearbooks back on the shelf, then walked back to the librarian clutching the 1949 book.

"Find what you were looking for?" the librarian asked.

"Oh, yes," Cassie said. "Do you know if there are any extra copies of these yearbooks lying around somewhere?"

The librarian shook her head. "Not that far back. Space is at such a premium here, I doubt they'd even be packed away in the basement. We sent a few boxes of yearbooks from the '80s to be recycled a couple of months ago."

"Then can I make copies of a few pages?" Cassie asked.

"Sure. In fact…" The librarian looked around quickly to make sure no one was listening. "Why don't I do it on our office machine? It's got much better paper than the student photocopiers."

"Thanks." Cassie showed her the pages she wanted, then waited as the librarian disappeared through a door behind her desk. Within five minutes, she'd returned, holding the yearbook in one hand and a manila folder in the other.

"Here." She handed over the folder. "Good luck with the album."

"Thanks."

"So, is your mission for today completed?" the librarian asked.

"Not quite. Could you tell me where the alumni office is?"

They didn't want to give her Frank Blakely's address, of course. That was where Cassie's legal training came in handy, because she wouldn't take no for an answer. For every seemingly intractable situation, she'd found, a compromise could eventually be hammered out. If you dealt with the right person.

When she got the standard line about confidentiality from the young woman sitting behind the front desk, Cassie asked to talk to her supervisor. After standing around the waiting room for what felt like forever, she was greeted by the assistant director of alumni relations, a middle-aged woman with a perfunctory smile and weary eyes. The woman recited numerous college regulations against the sharing of personal information. Cassie pushed as far as she could within the bounds of politeness, making repeated references to her sickly grandmother's approaching birthday, but backed off when the woman held firm. No point alienating her. She might even contact Frank Blakely and warn him that someone was snooping around his personal records. To find out the truth from him, Cassie was counting on the element of surprise.

"I understand, of course," Cassie said. "As I explained, I was only trying to put together something special for my grandmother—she's told me all about her friends from school, and I know she's sad she lost touch with some of them. I thought a birthday card from this Frank would make a nice gift."

"As an alumna, your grandmother can certainly write us, and we'd be happy to forward her letter to Mr. Blakely." The woman was clearly not going to be swayed.

"Then I suppose I'll try that," Cassie said. "I just thought I'd take a chance, since I was in town for work anyway...."

The woman gave Cassie her business card.

"If your grandmother would like to make her request directly to me, I'd be happy to take care of it."

"Thank you," Cassie said. "I'll tell her the next time I see her." She shook the woman's hand, then watched her walk away.

Cassie stood in the lobby area a few more moments, pulling on her coat and trying to decide her next move. Shopping? Sightseeing? Suddenly, all she wanted to do was collapse in her hotel room and take off her excruciatingly uncomfortable boots.

"Um, excuse me?"

Cassie turned to the young receptionist sitting at the front desk. Her pierced eyebrow and blue-streaked hair marked her as a student, not a professional secretary.

"Yes?" Cassie asked.

"Look, I checked you out on the database, and I know you're legit." The receptionist tilted her head toward her computer screen. "Cassie Armstrong, right? You're listed as Lydia Prescott's granddaughter."

It shouldn't have taken her aback. Cassie had spent hours tracking personal details about clients and opponents in databases. Still, she was surprised that the school not only kept tabs on alumni, but also their relatives.

"He lives in Palm Beach, Florida," the receptionist whispered. "The guy you're looking for."

Cassie stared at her, waiting for more.

"Someplace called the Coconut Grove Estates. I don't have a phone number."

"I can find that," Cassie said. "Thanks."

"Was this guy, like, her first boyfriend or something?"

"Um, sort of."

The young woman smiled. "I love that kind of stuff."

Cassie strode back to her hotel, trying to block out the honk of taxis and the people speed-walking by her on the sidewalk. Coconut Grove Estates. She pictured a grand, Spanish-style villa inside a gated community, surrounded by palm trees and sparkling blue seas. She knew it would take only a quick Internet search to track down Frank Blakely's phone number. But now that she was so close, she didn't know if she was ready to make the call.

Back at the hotel, mercifully released from her boots and wrapped in a luxuriously soft complimentary bathrobe, Cassie logged on to her e-mail to see if Jeffrey had fired her electronically. Astonishingly, there were only a few messages from work—all of them easy enough to ignore until Monday. The usual assortment of spam, another annoying joke list from Walter, one of the firm's paralegals. And a message from Cooper, in London.

Where are you? Called you at work before going to bed, and your voice mail says you're out for a few days. In case you're interested, I did meet with the woman at the Drake Hotel. She said she can't give us a quote until we give her a total number of guests. Have you thought about it? Do you want to? What's going on?

Cassie frowned at that last accusatory sentence. What was going on?

She quickly calculated the time difference in her head. It was after ten in London, but Cooper probably wouldn't be asleep yet. She could call him, but the thought of trying to explain everything over the phone brought on a wave of exhaustion. Much better to do something constructive, to show Cooper that she did take their marriage seriously and wasn't completely flaking out.

She replied to his e-mail.

Hey!
Things have been weird at work, so I decided to take a break. Thanks for handling the Drake meeting. I'll start work on the guest list right now, and we can go over it when you get back. Good luck. Win big!

As she sent it, she realized it read more like a work memo than a message to someone she loved. But then, they were using their work e-mail addresses. All correspondence was monitored by their firms. Best to keep things all business for now, and maybe it would be easier to explain when she saw Cooper in person.

Cassie turned the television to the Travel Channel, which was showing an escapist documentary about European castles. Perfect. She'd start with the easiest chore: putting together a list of people she wanted to invite to the wedding. Tracking down Frank Blakely could wait.

Cassie flipped open her worn leather address book. Virtually everything in her life ran by computer, but her contacts were still stored in this ragged book, a gift from her grandparents when she graduated from college. Its pages were almost illegible now, with entries crossed out and rewritten and cell phone numbers scribbled in tiny print along the margins. But it was a record of her adult life—tracing friends and relatives through the years as they moved from apartments to houses, from maiden names to married names. The tangled threads that connected her to the rest of the world.

Cassie pulled a sheet of hotel stationery out of a desk drawer and began listing names: college friends, law school friends, Aunt Nell, a few of her grandparents' neighbors in Knox Junction. And then, under *Y,* she saw it— the name that had hovered in the back of her mind, the one she knew she'd have to deal with sooner or later. Eve Young. Her mother's mother. Her grandmother. Cassie's pen hovered above the thick, cream-colored paper. Then she wrote Eve's name—followed by a question mark.

Eve. She'd always insisted Cassie call her

by her first name. "Grandma's for old ladies." She'd laughed dismissively, the cackle rattling in her throat until it brought on a harsh smoker's cough. The last time Cassie had seen Eve, that cough had punctuated almost everything she said. They sat at the tiny table in Eve's cramped trailer, surrounded by the smell of cigarettes and cloying perfume. It was the summer after Cassie's senior year of high school, and she'd stopped by before leaving for college. She'd dreaded the obligatory visit, but it ended up even worse than she'd feared.

"Said in the paper you got some kind of award," Eve said, lighting up another cigarette.

"Yeah," Cassie said. "Valedictorian."

"You must be pretty smart."

Cassie shrugged. "Well, the graduating class wasn't that big. There wasn't a lot of competition."

Eve cackled again. "Lydia must be jumping with joy."

Cassie stared down at the table.

"C'mon, you can tell me. You can't say your grandma isn't thrilled to death that you've done her proud."

"I guess."

Eve slapped Cassie's arm lightly, then her fingers slid off onto the table. "You think if you'd grown up here you would've done so good?"

Cassie kept her eyes focused downward. If she refused to answer, maybe Eve would move on to a different subject.

"Think you would've been dragged down by trailer trash like me? C'mon now, be honest." Eve took a deep drag of her cigarette. "Lydia, I got to give it to her. She's got them all fooled. Loves to come off all meek and mild, but she knows what she wants and she gets it, goddammit. I gotta admire her for that."

There was no point in defending Lydia. It would only encourage Eve.

"Still, I would've liked to see you graduate, you know?" Eve said. "I would've been so proud to cheer for you as you got that award. But I wasn't invited, was I? That bitch made sure I wouldn't see my only grandchild…"

Cassie stood up. "Maybe I'll come back another time," she said.

Eve let out a whoop of laughter. She started

to stand up, then grabbed the table as her body lurched backward.

"Where d'you think you're going?" she demanded.

Cassie heard the slurred letters, saw the dazed look in Eve's eyes. She was drunk.

"I've got to leave now," Cassie said, turning quickly.

"Hey now, you get back here!" Eve barked.

But Cassie kept going, pushing her way past the flimsy metal door, running to her car and trembling as she rammed the key into the lock. She drove away in tears, the smell of Eve's cigarettes in her hair and clothing. She threw everything in the laundry and took a shower as soon as she got home.

Eve's combination of desperate need and harsh scorn hadn't come as a surprise. Lydia had been warning Cassie for years to stay away from her. But Cassie had thought, as she approached adulthood, that Eve would start opening up. Help her understand the parents she'd barely known. Tell her about the family that had been shattered on that blackened highway when Cassie was five years old. Shelly, Cassie's mother, had been Eve's only child. With Shelly gone, Cassie was all the family Eve had left. But if Cassie thought their shared grief would forge a bond between them, she was disappointed again and again. She was mystified by Eve's sarcasm, hurt by her bitterness and frustrated by her unwillingness to revisit the past. Tragedy had made Cassie sensitive to others' pain, but it had only hardened Eve.

At some point, Eve must have been a loving, joyful parent, otherwise she could never have raised a daughter like Shelly. From the little Cassie remembered of her mother, she knew that Shelly had radiated tranquility. Her pale skin, light blond hair and air of calm formed Cassie's first impression of what an angel must look like. She wore her hair long and straight, falling like a shawl around her shoulders. Sometimes she'd let Cassie sit behind her and brush it, or tie it up with ribbons and scarves. If Shelly had lived longer, if she'd made it into her thirties, would she have matured into a more traditional mother figure? Or would she have kept that innocence, that delight in things like butterflies and rainbows?

Cassie idolized her mother, who appeared even more angelic in comparison with her moody, impossible-to-read father. She'd far fewer memories of Paul, most of them vaguely threatening. Him brushing past her when she ran to greet him at the door one night. "Not tonight, kid. Daddy got fired." Staring at him, terrified, because she thought it meant he'd caught on fire. The sound of her father's shouts echoing upstairs as she tried to sleep, her mother's voice calm and soothing. His face flushed as he drained a beer can in one long, drawn-out gulp.

She didn't remember the car accident, although she was in the backseat when it happened. For years, she'd been tormented by that mental gap—if she'd been paying attention, maybe she would have sensed the oncoming disaster. Maybe she could have warned her parents. At the very least, she would have known exactly what happened. Would have known for sure that they died quickly, without pain. As she got older, Cassie realized that her amnesia was a blessing, a way of protecting her from the trauma of seeing her parents' dead bodies.

She did remember the trips to court, during the years Lydia and Eve fought for custody. But the end result seemed preordained, when Lydia and Henry were awarded temporary custody because they were married and Henry had a job, while Eve was single and living on welfare. Cassie was terrified at the thought of leaving the warmth and peace of Lydia's home. Although Cassie had always felt far closer to her mother than her father, she found her mother's mother an overpowering presence, with her platinum-blond bouffant and strident voice. On the few nights Cassie stayed overnight at Eve's, she was bewildered by her grandmother's unpredictable mood swings, the sudden shift from shrill laughter to harsh sobs.

Cassie knew Lydia and Henry were sad about what happened, but their grief didn't keep them from their everyday life. Henry still got up and went to work, Lydia managed to make oatmeal every morning and sweep the kitchen floor every evening. Their house had a rhythm and structure that Cassie found comforting. And so, when the judge finally asked Cassie where she wanted to live, she didn't hesitate before saying, "With Grandma and Grandpa Armstrong, please."

Still, Cassie felt sorry for Eve, and she made dutiful weekly visits to Eve's trailer on

Sunday afternoons. But whatever bond she'd hoped would form never materialized. Cassie wasn't a suitable substitute for Shelly. Eve teased her for being uptight, for doing well in school, for never having any fun.

"Your mother knew how to have a good time," Eve would say, shaking her head. It was a curious critique, thought Cassie; weren't parents supposed to hope their kids didn't have *too* good a time?

Sometime in junior high, Cassie came back from one of her visits to Eve and overheard Lydia talking to Henry.

"Cassie told me Eve offered her a cigarette," Lydia fumed. "Can you believe it?"

Henry mumbled something indistinct.

"I knew she'd be a bad influence. It's not enough that she killed Paul. She's going to ruin Cassie's life, too...."

Lydia's voice had become muffled after that, and Cassie realized her grandmother was crying. She slipped away, shocked as much by the sound of Lydia's sobs as by her mysterious accusation. How could Eve have killed Paul if he'd been driving the car when it crashed?

Cassie was tormented by thoughts of the accident, running what she knew over and over in her mind, trying to understand how Eve could be responsible. After a few almost sleepless nights, she went to the library, determined to track down the truth. She dragged out issues of the local paper from the week her parents died. It wasn't hard to find the story; not much happened in Knox Junction, and the death of an attractive young couple was front-page news.

The relevant paragraphs were toward the end. "Police have determined that the crash was most likely caused by driver intoxication. Blood tests revealed that Paul Armstrong's alcohol level was substantially elevated, and a friend of the couple who did not wish to be identified said they had been drinking most of the evening at the home of Eve Young, Shelly Armstrong's mother, shortly before driving home along I-305."

Her father had been drinking. At Eve's. The woman who liked to show the kids how to have a good time. She'd watched Paul and Shelly stumble off, with her granddaughter in tow, late at night. Maybe she'd laughed as she waved them off to their deaths. Not considering the consequences of all those beers, the way Paul could quickly down one. No wonder Lydia hated her so much.

Cassie's visits to Eve became less frequent after that, slowing to once or twice a year by the time she was in high school. That day of her final visit, as she showered away all traces of Eve's suffocating trailer, Cassie felt nauseous. Alcohol had been responsible for the death of her only child. It had ruined her life—as Eve liked to announce melodramatically—yet there she was, drunk before noon. For Cassie, it was the final straw. She was tired of the trailer, tired of the criticism, tired of Eve. She never visited her again.

Years later, when Cassie was in law school, she received a letter from Eve, who wrote that she'd recently completed an alcohol-addiction recovery program and as part of her recovery was apologizing to all those she'd hurt in the past. The letter had a formal, self-conscious tone that was very unlike Eve's normal speech. Cassie wondered if she'd copied it from some kind of manual.

I am very sorry for talking to you in a rude manner. My alcohol consumption made me insensitive to other people's feelings, and I am sorry if I was hurtful to you in any way....

The return address was an apartment building in the Chicago suburbs; Eve seemed to have left the trailer park behind. Cassie copied the address in her book, then stuffed the letter in her purse, intending to answer it at some point when she wasn't swamped with work. Weeks passed, and then months. The letter fell out somewhere along the way, and Cassie put it out of her mind. One more awkward chore avoided.

But now, in her hotel room in New York, Cassie stared at Eve's address. There was no reason to think she'd still be living there; it was more than five years since Eve had written. Even if Cassie did send her an invitation, it would most likely come back marked Return to Sender.

Deep down, Cassie knew that was no excuse. She could find Eve if she wanted to. Just like she was going to find Frank Blakely. Eventually. Cassie considered herself a decisive person who didn't shy away from tough choices. But now she was paralyzed with fear and uncertainty. Terrified to look for Frank Blakely. Afraid to invite Eve to her wedding.

Outside her window, a car alarm blared into action, making Cassie wince. Living in

Chicago, she thought of herself as a city girl, but New York was on a whole other level. Walking down the crowded sidewalks, surrounded by people in every direction going faster than her, had been exhausting. Even her overpriced, supposedly luxurious hotel room couldn't offer an escape from the never-ending noise.

Cassie tried to imagine Lydia arriving here, straight from the fields of Knox Junction. Maybe the city's energy had been invigorating. But from the nervous look of Lydia's yearbook pictures, Cassie suspected she'd had second thoughts.

Chapter 6

Lydia

As Lydia walked into her first class, she knew she'd made a terrible mistake. Introduction to Drawing had sounded harmless enough, the kind of basic overview course that all art students were subjected to. She clutched her set of charcoal pencils in one hand, part of the required supplies detailed in an extensive three-page list sent to every incoming student. She wore a crisp white artist's smock over her carefully pressed blouse and tweed skirt, her hair pulled back in a sleek ponytail. Assessing herself in the mirror that morning, she was pleased by the reflection staring back at her. She looked like a serious-minded college student at last.

But as soon as she entered the studio, she was paralyzed with shock. Students were already arrayed in a semicircle in front of her, standing at easels with pencils in hand. A few looked quickly at her, then turned back to their drawings. Directly in front of Lydia, in the center of the semicircle, stood the artists' model, her arms draped in a silky fabric that flowed along the floor behind her. Other than that, she was naked.

"Miss Prescott, may we presume?" a voice purred into Lydia's ear. Her shoulders jerked with surprise and she turned to see a tall man peering down at her from behind thick glasses. His long, angular nose seemed ready to poke her accusingly.

"Uh, yes. Lydia Prescott." Her voice wavered.

"In the future, I trust you will not be joining us an hour late?"

"But I thought I was early..." Lydia held up her watch, then felt her stomach sink with embarrassment. She didn't usually need to keep track of time; the entire summer, she'd been at the mercy of her mother's schedule. She'd pulled out the watch—a graduation gift from Father—for the first day of classes. But now she saw it was still set for Illinois time, an hour behind New York.

"I'm very sorry," Lydia said in a rush. "I just realized my watch is wrong…."

The professor waved his hand dismissively. "Consider this your first warning. You may as well do what you can with the remaining time. Over there." He pointed to an easel at the far side of the room. Lydia walked quickly toward it, keeping her eyes focused on the floor to avoid looking at the model.

Her obvious discomfort—when all the other students appeared utterly unfazed by the sight of a naked woman—only made Lydia more self-conscious. She told herself she was a fool for not expecting this; surely, nude models were a fact of life in art classes. Still, Lydia was so flustered by her late entrance, and the sense that she was now somehow marked— the girl who couldn't tell time, the country rube shocked by big-city ways—that she couldn't recover her poise. She dropped her charcoal case as she tried to open it, bringing stares not only from the professor and her fellow students, but the model, as well.

Lydia tried to lose herself in her drawing, focusing on the curves of the woman's skin and the folds of the draped fabric, but her fingers trembled. She couldn't escape the feeling of being watched. As lines and shadows gradually filled her paper, Lydia saw that her drawing was woefully inadequate, especially compared to the glimpses she'd had of the other students' work.

But the worst was yet to come. After about an hour, the professor excused the model and began to critique his students' work. Not content to offer his opinions in discreet, one-on-one consultations, he held up each drawing at the front of the room, pointing out their strengths and—mostly—weaknesses. With a looming sense of dread, Lydia realized that her picture was the worst of all, and that due to her position at the farthest end of the room, she would be the last to get a critique.

"And now, the very tardy Miss Prescott." He ripped Lydia's paper from the easel. He looked at it, frowning for a few moments, then brandished it for the class.

"Any comments?" he asked. The students stared silently.

"I suppose there's really not much to say, is there?" the professor went on. "It's difficult to surmise what this represents. A woman? A whale?" A titter of laughter echoed through the room. "The face is completely out of scale with the body, the legs are curved in a way that is anatomically impossible, and as for the breasts…" The professor took a step toward Lydia. "Have you, in fact, *seen* breasts, Miss Prescott?"

Lydia blushed as the other students laughed. She looked at the professor's chin to avoid meeting his eyes.

"Yes, sir," she whispered.

"Really? How astonishing. Because I would never guess from this." He waved the page in front of her. "Is this representative of your best work, Miss Prescott?"

"No," Lydia protested. "This is the first time I've drawn a model. I've mostly done still lifes and landscapes."

"Ah, a nature enthusiast." He made it sound like an insult. "A pity, then, that you weren't born a hundred years ago. You could have made a good living capturing scenic farmhouses on canvas. However, this is the twentieth century. We hope to train students to aim a little higher. I don't think you'll find much demand for landscapes these days."

Lydia held her arms clenched against her body, stiffened her legs to stop herself from running out of the room. All the way to Pennsylvania Station so she could hop on the first train out of town.

The professor crumpled Lydia's drawing and tossed the ball of paper at her feet. "The purpose of today's exercise was to assess the level of each student," he announced. "Those of you with adequate drawing skills will be rewarded with more challenging assignments. Others, unfortunately, will require remedial training. Starting from scratch, as it were."

Lydia had no doubt which category she fell into. Her first class at art school, and she'd already been humiliated. Lydia had always excelled at school. Being the object of any criticism was painful enough, but to be singled out as a failure so early in the school year was almost unbearable.

She raced out of the studio as soon as the professor dismissed them. She heard other students talk about going to the cafeteria, but she pushed her way out the double doors at the front of the building, desperate to escape to the relative safety of her dorm room. And she might have kept running if it hadn't been for an unlikely savior.

"Hey, there!"

Lydia paused in the lobby of the Lucille B. Davison women's dormitory, where the faded red silk couches and gilt-trimmed end tables hinted at the building's past glory as a luxury hotel. Lydia's mother had smiled delightedly when they first walked in the day before, trailed by a porter carrying Lydia's bags. Her enthusiasm had been dampened somewhat by the sight of Lydia's room, a closet-size space with a narrow single bed, scratched desk and one window that looked out on a brick wall.

"You! In the brown skirt!"

Lydia turned to see a curvy girl with a flushed face, surrounded by a mass of tangled auburn curls. She wore a stained artist's smock that threatened to slide off one shoulder.

"That was some drubbing you got from Casey," she said cheerfully. Lydia felt her cheeks burn. She recognized the girl now; she'd been standing on the opposite side of the drawing studio. On the edge of tears, Lydia turned away before the girl could taunt her any more.

"Say, I didn't mean anything," the girl said, reaching out to grab Lydia's arm. "That is, I wanted to say—gosh, I'm bad at this. Don't take it personally, all right?"

"How could I not?" Lydia asked. "It was a terrible picture."

The girl laughed. "So was mine! But I, unlike you, happen to be filthy rich and Casey wants to keep Daddy's money coming in to pay his salary. Whereas you...you're not from New York, are you?"

Lydia shook her head. "Illinois."

"Chicago?"

"Not exactly."

The girl laughed again, a loud, booming chuckle that shook her entire body. "Country girl, huh? Then you're ripe for Casey's torment. That's his gimmick. Being tough as nails, but only to students who can't defend themselves."

"So what can I do?" Lydia asked.

"Stick with me, kid. I'll watch out for you. Oh, and work like heck on your drawing. It did kind of look like a whale."

The way she said it was so endearing—
a joking tone one friend would use to tease
another—that Lydia felt herself smiling.
Something about the girl's directness was
enormously appealing, especially for someone accustomed to concealing her emotions.

"I'm Lydia Prescott."

"Dutch O'Halloran. Short for Duchess, if
you can believe it. Just one of many things
I'll never forgive my parents for."

"Are you a freshman, too?" Lydia asked.

"Sophomore. Extremely old and wise in the
ways of this crazy school. I was supposed to
take this drawing class last year, with all the
other freshmen, but I made a fuss and insisted
on sculpture instead. I'm horribly spoiled and
demanding, you see. But it turns out sculpture
isn't my cup of tea, so now I'm back to plain
old drawing." The torrent of words stopped
for a moment as she took a breath. "You're
on the third floor, right?"

"Yes."

"I thought I spotted you wandering around
the halls like a lost kitten yesterday. Third
floor's not bad, overall—I haven't sorted out
all the freshmen yet, but we've got a good
group of sophomores and few decent juniors.

The seniors get the suites on six and seven—real swanky. Don't worry, I'll introduce you around."

"Thanks. That's very nice of you."

"Nice has nothing to do with it!" Dutch said, laughing. "I'm thrilled to meet a real small-town girl! This place is crawling with boring debs who think they'll paint a few outrageous canvases to show how shocking they are before settling down with a doctor or lawyer in a Park Avenue apartment. I came here because I wanted to meet people who were different."

Dutch smiled happily, and Lydia knew she'd found a friend. And having a friend was enough to give Lydia hope that she might survive school after all. Her classes turned out to be far more difficult than she'd expected, and she was often embarrassed by her dowdy clothing and total unfamiliarity with New York. But living in a girls' dormitory, surrounded by other young women with similar interests, was a never-ending adventure. Someone was always suffering through a crisis: an unfaithful boyfriend, a sudden attack of pimples, lack of artistic inspiration and a host of other excuses for dramatic collapses and hurried, gossipy conversations. For Lydia, who'd grown up with people who considered it a badge of honor to suppress their feelings, it was like living in a particularly dramatic play. That she was a spectator—never a participant—did nothing to lessen her enjoyment.

Much of the talk—predictably, in an all-girls' dormitory—was about boys. Dutch was forever hatching plans to match up couples, plotting flirtations and dance invitations with the expertise of a chess champion. Lydia took herself out of the running early on by telling everyone she had a boyfriend back home, even though it wasn't technically true. Lydia had sent Henry a quick note, in care of his parents, with her address. She wasn't prepared to cut off all contact with him, but she assumed time and distance would take their toll, and they would inevitably drift apart. The end of their romance would be mutual, and understandable, and they could remain friends. But until she was more sure of herself at school, dating was out of the question. A hometown boyfriend was the perfect excuse to escape Dutch's matchmaking.

Still, she wondered if Henry thought of her. If he found himself reliving that evening in the apple orchard, late at night, as she did, before drifting off to sleep. The day a letter from him finally appeared in her mailbox, Lydia ripped open the envelope immediately. Then, with her hand on the paper, she paused, watching the swarms of girls passing through the lobby. Better to savor it privately. She ran up the stairs, feeling unexpectedly giddy, only to find that a group of girls was gathered in the hallway, blocking the route to her room. They widened their circle when they saw Lydia.

"Hello," trilled Vera, a freshman who had the room next to Lydia's. Vera's most distinguishing characteristic was that she'd gone to boarding school, a fact she made a point of mentioning as often as possible. Superficially friendly, she was already laying the groundwork to be the class gossip, collecting tidbits of news and conjecture about everyone. When she'd heard Lydia was from Illinois, she'd tried to forge a connection, saying some of her best boarding school friends were from the Chicago area.

"Well, I lived in the suburbs for a while," Lydia said. "Winnetka."

"Oh, my gosh, do you know Evelyn Murphy?" Vera had squealed. "She's from Winnetka, too!"

"No, I don't think so. We moved when I was in middle school. I spent the last few years in a town called Knox Junction."

"Oh." Clearly, Knox Junction wasn't included on Vera's mental list of prestigious communities across the country. Since then, she'd shown very little interest in Lydia's activities.

"Hi," she said brightly as Lydia approached. "Did you hear about Peggy and Warren?"

"No," Lydia said. "I'll be back in a minute, all right?" Before Vera could launch into the full story, Lydia smiled and attempted to push past her to her room. But Vera's instincts were well honed. She glanced down at the letter while keeping her shoulder propped against Lydia's door.

"What's that?" she asked.

"Nothing," Lydia said. But her abrupt tone betrayed her. Vera snatched the envelope out of Lydia's hand and peered at it.

"This looks like a boy's handwriting!" she announced. "Is it from your boyfriend?"

Lydia nodded, hoping that would be enough to satisfy Vera's curiosity.

"Ooh, how exciting." Vera giggled. "What's his name again?"

"Henry."

"Is it a love letter?"

"I don't know," said Lydia. "I haven't read it yet."

"Of course you have—the envelope's open. Read it to us, Lydia! We poor girls who don't have boyfriends could use a good love letter."

"I'm sorry…" Lydia began, but Vera had already opened the envelope.

"Stop!" she protested, but Vera laughed and unfolded the page inside. "I hope it's really romantic," she said to the girls gathered around her. "Don't you love a good love story?"

Lydia stood frozen, petrified of what the letter might reveal. She hadn't spoken to or heard from Henry since the night before she left town, when she'd done something she both regretted and couldn't stop thinking about. Would he mention what they'd done? She felt her face flushing.

"'Dear Lydia,'" Vera read in a melodramatic voice. "'How's school? My classes so far are pretty hard. I'm taking Intro to Chemistry, Intro to Botany and Geology of Illinois, all required classes for agriculture majors.

Also an English literature course as my elective. It's nice to have an excuse to read something other than science books. I'm staying in a boardinghouse with three other students since it's cheaper than the dormitories. All four of us share one bathroom with the family, but other than that it's all right. The campus is really pretty. I wish you could see it sometime. How is New York? Is it very loud? I don't know if I could take all that traffic. Remember all those farmer nicknames you gave me? Guess they're true after all.'"

"And it's signed," Vera announced, "'Yours sincerely, Henry Armstrong.'"

Lydia felt her heart settle into a steadier rhythm. He hadn't revealed anything. Then why did she feel so disappointed?

"Lydia's got a boyfriend who's a farmer—how sweet!" Vera was practically gushing now. "He must be really shy, is that it, Lydia? Is that why he couldn't even sign it, 'Love, Henry'?"

Lydia shrugged, grabbing the page from Vera's outstretched hand.

"I think it's absolutely adorable that he signed his last name, too," Vera said. "As if you wouldn't be sure which Henry wrote it!"

Lydia tried to join in the other girls' laughter, but the sound that came out was more of a cough. No matter how much Vera said the letter was sweet, Lydia knew she was being teased. Vera would be using Henry's stilted phrases to poke fun at Lydia behind her back, making the other girls laugh. Vera would be at the center of attention, her preferred position.

Lydia took comfort in the fact that Henry's letter was too boring to provide entertainment for long. Soon enough, the girls would find better gossip elsewhere. Lydia and her country bumpkin boyfriend would be forgotten.

But she was wrong. Vera had even worse humiliation in store.

The blow fell shortly before Christmas vacation. Lydia had become more comfortable at school; she now thought of herself as a student rather than an imposter. Drawing class with Professor Casey had gone from mortifying to tolerable, as she experimented with new methods, taking artistic risks for the first time in her life. She started to find inspiration in the city around her, gawking during field trips to the Metropolitan Museum of Art, listening intently to working artists who visited her classes, staring in disbelief at the paintings in Dutch's family's penthouse apartment.

And then Vera pounced. Like a hunter taking her time stalking prey, she moved in the shadows, setting the trap well out of Lydia's earshot. To Lydia's face, Vera was her usual cheery, chatty self. But Lydia could tell something was going on. She noticed the way Vera and another girl exchanged glances when she passed them in the hallway one night. She sensed the mood shift when she sat down at a table for dinner, only to see Vera, who'd been chattering animatedly, suddenly stop talking.

As she had before, Dutch came to Lydia's rescue. She took Lydia's arm one morning after drawing class and insisted on taking her to lunch at a greasy spoon around the corner.

"But I don't have any money," Lydia said anxiously. Meals out were a rare extravagance, to be saved for special occasions.

"Are you kidding?" Dutch said, laughing. "I wouldn't dream of letting you pay."

"Oh, I couldn't," Lydia said.

"If I have one more of those stale cafeteria sandwiches, I think I'll be sick. And I don't want to eat alone. C'mon—you'll be doing me a favor."

After they'd ordered milkshakes and hot dogs, Dutch got right to the point.

"Your father's a doctor, right?" she asked.

Lydia nodded.

"Well, I'm sure this is all some kind of misunderstanding, but Vera's been saying some things I thought you should know about. You know me—I hate passing on rumors, but this is different."

"What did she tell you?" Lydia asked. What could Vera possibly have to do with her father?

"Oh, she didn't tell me," Dutch said. "She told Sally, and Sally told half the school—as Vera knew she would—and eventually Laura Gilson said something to me. Anyway, all that's not important. Vera's been saying she has a friend who lives in the same town you used to."

"Yes," Lydia said. "Evelyn somebody or other. She asked me if I knew her, but I'd never heard the name. I'm sure I never met her."

"Apparently, Vera wrote to this friend and mentioned your name. Digging for gossip as usual. The friend said she didn't know you personally, but she'd heard of your father, because of something that happened. Some-thing…scandalous." Dutch took a long sip of her milkshake, her eyes focused on the glass.

"My father?" asked Lydia. She felt a chill start to spread through her body.

"That's why I'm sure this is some kind of mistake," said Dutch. "According to this girl, there was a doctor named Prescott in town, and one of his patients died under mysterious circumstances, and his family had to leave suddenly because his reputation was ruined, and the whole situation was very hush-hush. But my point is, the name Prescott isn't that unusual. There've got to be other Dr. Prescotts around, and unless Vera knows this for a fact, she has no business…"

Dutch's voice trailed off as she saw the color drain from Lydia's face. Lydia flashed back to the house in Winnetka, the day she'd been playing with Nell on the sunporch and Mother rushed in, telling them to start pack-ing. Offering no explanation for why they were leaving, brushing off all Lydia's ques-tions. Informing her that there was no time to say goodbye to her friends, because they'd be leaving first thing in the morning for their new home. Her mother's silent fury in that train compartment, her father's glum stare out the window as they rolled away from Chicago. The nights in Knox Junction, when she crept from bed and peered down the stairway, watching her father bent over sobbing, the cut-glass liquor decanter on the table next to him.

Aware of Dutch's silence, Lydia looked directly at her friend. "It must be a mistake," she said.

"Good. I'll be happy to sort things out for you, if you want."

Lydia nodded.

"Vera doesn't mean badly, you know," said Dutch. "She likes people to pay attention to her, that's all. If she can do that by spreading made-up gossip, she will. But I don't think she was purposely trying to hurt you."

Dutch—whom life had treated so kindly— saw the best in everyone. Lydia didn't. She now understood that people like Vera drew strength from others' weaknesses; Lydia's shyness and obvious lack of confidence had made her a magnet for Vera's meddling.

"Thanks for telling me. I really appreciate it."

"Aw, it's nothing," Dutch said. "Now let's

toast to Christmas break! Bet you can't wait to see that boyfriend of yours!"

The idea of seeing Henry again actually made Lydia feel nauseous, from a mixture of nervous anticipation and dread. But Henry was a dim concern in the back of her mind as she rode the train to Knox Junction. The cars seemed to inch across the country. Ever since hearing Dutch's revelations, Lydia had missed her family intensely. She needed to see them again, to prove to herself that the story must be wrong, that her father could never hurt anyone, that whatever happened must have been a terrible mistake. She was determined to find out the truth. When she did, she was sure it would bring her family closer together.

But in the end, nothing went as expected. Mother had organized a nonstop schedule of holiday open houses, caroling and dinners, as if she was anxious to fill every moment with activity. Lydia, of course, was required to accompany her to every event, so Mother could present her like a prize-winning entry at the county fair: "Here's Lydia, just back from *New York!*" Although Lydia called Henry as soon as she got home, she found the busy schedule gave her an easy excuse to avoid seeing him during her first few days of vacation. It was a relief, actually. Lydia still wasn't sure how to talk to him—as a friend or something more? What would he expect from her when they finally saw each other again?

Lydia felt almost as ill at ease with her parents and sister as she did with Henry. While she'd been off at school, her family seemed to have degenerated into four distinct, separate personalities instead of one cohesive unit. Nell had transformed from an easy-to-please tomboy into an overly sensitive, unpredictable teenager who accused Lydia of becoming "snooty" since she left for college. Lydia's father seemed lost in a fog of distraction, disappearing frequently into his office to "work," even though patients rarely visited. Mother constantly talked about fund-raising drives and her new role on the board of directors raising money for the local library, barely letting Lydia get a word in edgewise. Her family, which she'd thought of as her refuge, no longer had a place for her.

It was a few days before Lydia worked up the nerve to confront Mother with the story Dutch had told her.

"Complete nonsense!" Mother protested. "Honestly, why some people find it amusing to distort the truth, I will never understand."

"Then why did we leave Winnetka?" It was a question she'd never had the courage to ask before. But now, after moving across the country and fending for herself in a school full of students ready to look down on her, she was filled with a new strength.

Mother wouldn't meet her eyes. She busied herself rearranging doilies on a side table. "It's true that a patient of your father's died in childbirth. Which, as you know, is far from uncommon, unfortunately. That's why any sane woman gives birth in a hospital, not at home like some sort of peasant. But the weather was terrible that night, and the ambulance didn't arrive in time. Your father did the best he could. It was a bad delivery right from the start."

"Didn't people realize that?" Lydia asked. "Why did we have to leave?"

"People love to talk, Lydia. I'd have thought you'd know that by now."

"Isn't Father a good doctor? Wouldn't they have taken his word about what happened?"

"People can be vicious," Mother said.

"Now, if I wanted to indulge in idle gossip, I'd have remained in Winnetka. That's enough from you, thank you very much."

It was Nell—Lydia's immature, oblivious younger sister—who inadvertently revealed the truth.

"Back to work, I see," Nell muttered on Christmas Eve, after Father left the living room with a quick mention of letters he needed to review. Mother had disappeared upstairs to do some last-minute present wrapping.

"What could possibly be so urgent tonight?" Lydia wondered.

"A bottle, I suppose." Nell gave her sister a sly look. "You do know he drinks in there?"

Lydia shrugged. "Father's always had a cocktail or two after dinner."

"Exactly. And since you left, Mother's been encouraging him to stop, in her usual quiet but overpowering way. Now that she's become some sort of town leader, I suppose she's terrified the mayor will arrive at the house to find Father slurring his words."

"Nell!" Lydia was shocked at her sister's lack of respect.

"He goes in there to hide it from Mother,"

Nell said, undeterred. "Late at night, he sneaks the empty bottles out and puts them in the trunk of his car. I saw him a few weeks ago when he thought I was in bed asleep. It's the same thing he used to do in Winnetka."

Lydia stared at her sister. "What?"

"He had all sorts of bottles stashed in his office there. Didn't you know? Remember when I went through that stage where I kept hiding from Mother and driving her crazy? I snuck into Father's office a few times and snooped around. He would have five or six liquor bottles tucked in the bottom drawer of his desk. At the time, I thought it was medicine, but now I understand what it was. I can't say I blame him, wanting a break from Mother's nagging...."

But Lydia had stopped paying attention. She imagined Father sitting in his home office in Winnetka with a cut-glass tumbler in his hand, the call for an unexpected delivery late at night, after he'd already drained the glass several times. She pictured him weaving up the front steps of a house, staggering as he tried to grasp what was happening. At first, the family would've assumed he was just tired. How long before they realized he was drunk? Mother had said it was a difficult delivery. Maybe the woman would've died anyway. But what if Father's hands shook at a crucial moment? If his mind was so hazy that he lost control of the situation as it took a tragic turn?

"It's gotten worse since you left." Nell was still speaking. "Ever since Dr. Crowley opened a practice in Fentonville, lots of patients have switched. It's no wonder Father gets depressed. He's probably doing half the business he did during the war. You had no idea, did you? Off there in New York having a grand time. Mother's using up all her savings to keep you there. She told me I can't have even one new dress for the school year. Let alone spending money so I can go out for ice cream after school with my friends."

Lydia felt stung by the anger in her sister's voice. "I didn't know."

"Well, it doesn't concern you anymore, does it? You'd better land yourself a rich husband while you're in New York. That is, if you've given up on Henry."

Henry. Their brief phone conversations since she arrived home had the impersonal, superficial friendliness of acquaintances.

Henry's voice, with its flat tones, sounded impossibly slow compared to the quick-talking students who surrounded her at school. He talked about agriculture courses she'd no interest in, his world and future limited to northern Illinois, a place she'd escaped.

She finally made plans to see him on New Year's Day, knowing her parents would be out at a luncheon and Nell had plans with a friend from school. Henry drove up to the house in the same pickup truck he'd driven all through high school. It was as if she'd been transported a few years back in time. Watching him walk up the front steps, feeling his strong arms around her, she could pretend for a moment that nothing had changed. But, deep down, Lydia knew she had already left Knox Junction behind her. This family was no longer her safe haven. This house was no longer her home. And Henry was now part of her past.

"So…" Henry began. They sat in the front parlor, the room Mother reserved for formal entertaining. She and Henry had never been there alone; most of their time at this house, they'd done homework together at the dining room table, or sat in the kitchen as Lydia helped with dinner or made lemonade. They'd swung together at sunset on the front porch. The unfamiliar setting put them both on edge.

After catching each other up on school—the kind of chitchat casual friends would have exchanged—Henry addressed the subject Lydia had been dreading.

"So…how do things stand?" he asked. "I mean, with us."

"Fine," she said.

"Oh, shucks, Lydia, this is like pulling teeth. After what happened with us, you know, at the orchard, I kinda thought…well, we were…"

Lydia felt her face flush. She couldn't meet his eyes. Her glance fell on his hands, clasped tightly in his lap. Looking at those hands, she could still feel the trace of them along her skin. The way they'd fumbled at her brassiere, fueling her desperate need for his touch.

It would be so easy now. They were alone, with no one expected back for hours. She could invite him up to her bedroom, feel that tingle through her body once again. Pull up his shirt and rub her palms along his chest, feeling his heart beat with need for her…

But Lydia held strong. Giving in to Henry

now would only send her spiraling backward. Give him false hope. No matter how much she might be tempted, she couldn't do that to him. Or herself.

"Henry, I don't know," she said finally. "Things are very difficult right now. I need to concentrate on school. I'm sorry."

Henry nodded slowly. He didn't look particularly hurt, or disappointed, or surprised. As if he'd expected this all along.

"The last thing I want to do is make things harder for you," he said. "You figure out whatever you need to figure out, okay?" He stood to leave.

Lydia jumped up, taken aback by his sudden exit. "But, I mean, we can still write to each other," she said. "That is, if you still want to." Henry's letters might be dull and unimaginative, but Lydia couldn't deny she looked forward to opening each one. She kept them in her desk, carefully tied with a silk hair ribbon.

Henry grinned shyly. "Of course I want to keep writing."

They stood together at the front door. Simultaneously, they reached for the doorknob, and as their hands met, a warmth traveled up

Lydia's arm. She felt herself being drawn toward Henry, her hand intertwining with his, their arms touching as he pulled her body against him. Their lips met in a soft, slow caress, his breath heating her cheeks and making her muscles relax in a haze of pleasure. If Henry had pushed for more, she might have lost control.

But he drew back, and the spell was broken.

"No point getting us all wound up, right?" he asked softly.

"Right." She straightened, feeling self-conscious once again. "Thank you for understanding."

"This isn't goodbye, is it? I'll see you over the summer?"

"Of course."

But he didn't.

After a long talk with Mother about family finances, and another long talk with Dutch once she was back at school, Lydia formulated a plan. Her scholarship covered only tuition; her living expenses, books and art supplies had been paid for from Mother's rapidly dwindling savings. If Lydia wanted to stay in school, she'd have to earn some money, hopefully with enough extra to send to Nell for new clothes. Dutch said her father would be happy to help her find a job. "He knows half the shop-owners in New York," she'd exclaimed, "and the other half wishes they knew him!" And so, in the spring, she wrote letters to her parents and to Henry, telling them about the wonderful opportunity she'd been offered in a framing shop, how she'd be a fool to turn it down. The prospect of staying in New York as her schoolmates packed up and headed home was not as difficult as she'd expected. The more time she spent away from Knox Junction, the more distant it felt—a small town of narrow minds and limited opportunities, a place where she no longer fit.

If she was going to make a success of school—and a success of her life—she would have to stay focused. Not be distracted by painful family secrets or the temptation of Henry's kisses. She and Henry still exchanged letters, but Lydia was careful to write in the tone of a sister rather than a girlfriend. The memory of Henry's hands on her body faded, only occasionally resurrected late at night when she lay in bed, unable to sleep. And so she continued for the next two years, dutiful in her classes, spending every school holiday working in the shop owned by a friend of Dutch's father, completely in control of her life.

Until she met the man who changed everything.

Chapter 7

Cassie

The call came as Cassie was half dozing in the bathtub, with barely enough energy to pick up the handset on the wall beside her. She'd treated herself to a ridiculously over-priced room-service dinner, which she ate while zoned out in front of a *Full House* rerun. A bubble bath seemed like the perfect way to complete her transformation from hard-charging lawyer to slack-jawed couch potato. She'd just slid into the water and laid her head back on a rolled-up towel when the phone rang. For about half a second, she considered ignoring it. But years of being on call twenty-four hours a day had taken their toll.

"Cassie Armstrong," she said tentatively.

"Thank God!" Cassie immediately recognized the caller's voice. It was Marie, her boss's assistant. Talking at her usual mile-a-minute pace, rushing to avert yet another crisis.

"Why aren't you answering your cell?" Marie demanded.

"Um…well, it's in the other room. I guess I didn't hear it ring."

"Listen. Jeffrey wanted me to put through a call to you, even though he knows you're out of town. So I figured I'd check in with you first and give you a heads-up. Thank God you told me what hotel you were staying in— anyway, are you ready for me to connect you with Jeffrey?"

"Uh, could I have a minute? I just…" She didn't have the heart to tell Marie that she was lying in a bubble bath while everyone at the office was still at their desks at 10:00 p.m.

"I'll put him through in thirty seconds, okay?" Cassie heard a click, then the violin music that indicated she was on hold.

Thirty seconds. Jeffrey would never be calling on a Thursday night unless this was something major. E-mail was his preferred mode of communication for work-related conversations. This could mean only one thing: Cassie had half a minute to prepare to be fired. She climbed out of the bathtub and wrapped her body in the plush bathrobe hanging on the back of the bathroom door. If she was getting the ax anyway, it wouldn't really matter if Jeffrey heard the sound of water splashing in the background, but Cassie couldn't quite shed her need to appear professional. Not yet.

She sat cross-legged on the floor of the bathroom, clutching the phone in her hand. Now that it was coming, the call she'd dreaded, she had to fight back tears. Mentally, she practiced sounding gracious: "Of course, I completely understand.... It's been a pleasure working with you.... If you should hear of any other opportunities..."

"Cassie?" Jeffrey's voice broke through her self-pitying reverie.

"Yes. Hi." She didn't bother with small talk. Now that the moment had arrived, she wanted to get it over with as quickly as possible.

"Listen, Cass, I'll get right to the point. The

firm's going to be making a few changes. This is still hush-hush, but we've just grabbed Milton Greiber from Lofton & Treadwell."

"Grabbed?" Cassie pictured Greiber being pounced on by security as he tried to break into the firm's offices.

"Poached. Stolen." Jeffrey laughed. "He's going to be our newest partner, which, as you can imagine, is a huge coup. We're putting out a press release on Monday, but for now this is beyond confidential, okay?"

"Sure," Cassie said, still waiting for the blow to come.

"I'm not sure how much you know about the firm's long-term strategic planning, but we've been looking to expand to the West Coast for a while now. Greiber started at Howell, Sheffield & Huntington in San Francisco, so the plan is to have him open a new office for us out there. He wants some strong backup players with him, and the senior partners have been discussing who'd be most appropriate. Cassie, I'm pleased to tell you that your name came up as a top choice."

Cassie's head was spinning. She'd braced herself to be fired, but instead she was being offered a transfer. To San Francisco. A city she'd never even visited.

"You're one of our stars, Cass. I'd love to keep you here in Chicago, but I can't deny you this opportunity. If you pull your weight like I know you can, you'll be on the fast track. I could see you making partner within a year, if you really wowed Greiber."

A partnership had been dangled in front of her as the ultimate goal, but it had seemed so far off that it was almost unreal. This offer was concrete. She could be a partner within a year. This wasn't just a transfer, it was a promotion.

"Jeffrey, I don't know what to say...."

"Well, that's a first."

"I mean—God, yes. It sounds like a great opportunity. I'm honored that you thought of me."

"You've more than proven yourself around here, Cassie. You work harder than any associate, and that's compared to a bunch of workaholics! Listen, are you going to be back here tomorrow?"

"Um." Cassie stalled, her mind racing. "I wasn't planning on flying back until Sunday, but I'm sure I could get standby if I went to the airport tomorrow morning…."

"No need to rush back here on a Friday—especially since this won't be announced officially until Monday. We can go over all the details then. Have you been able to take care of everything? The family business?"

"Uh, sort of," Cassie said. "Mostly."

"Well, do what you need to do and enjoy your last few days of freedom. You'll be working like a dog when you get back here, but I promise it'll all be worth it."

"I know it will."

After hanging up, Cassie remained on the bathroom floor, trying to take it all in. She trailed her fingertips in the bathwater, which now felt lukewarm and unwelcoming. San Francisco. A new office. A fresh start. Her heart pounded at the possibilities.

She stared at herself in the mirror that spanned one wall of the bathroom. Her dark blond hair hung in bedraggled clumps around her cheeks and her skin was splotchy. The oversize bathrobe made her look like she'd gained thirty pounds. But her lips were curled up in a smile and she let out a yelp of relief.

This was the reflection of a law-firm super-star. Cassie Armstrong, partner.

Cassie spent the rest of the night pacing nervously around the hotel room, more than once picking up the phone, then hanging up before dialing. Her first reaction was to call her grandparents, the two people who valued her happiness even more than their own. But San Francisco—how would they take that? Lydia didn't hide her disappointment on those rare occasions when Cassie couldn't make it to Sunday lunch—how would she react to the news that her only granddaughter would be a four-hour plane ride away?

Cooper would understand exactly how big a deal this was. When they'd both started their jobs, they'd jokingly bet on who would reach partner first. However, given the late hour in London, Cooper would be asleep. Was it worth waking him? It occurred to Cassie that she hadn't even thought of Cooper when Jeffrey made her the offer. She'd pictured herself moving to San Francisco, setting up the new office, finally having a say in how the business was run rather than being at the beck and call of others. Cooper—the man she was planning to spend the rest of her life with—hadn't figured into her fantasy at all.

He'd move with her, of course. He had great experience; he could get a job anywhere. But Cassie knew it wouldn't be that simple. He loved his job in Chicago. His entire family was there. He lived his life according to well-established routines, from monthly poker games with his brothers to yearly outings with his father to Chicago Bears football games. Cooper may have been the academic star of his family, but he had told Cassie that his parents and siblings kept him connected to the world outside the law firm. Cassie pictured Cooper without that bond, in a new city where he had no job and no friends. He would be completely dependent on her. Could their relationship survive that kind of strain?

Uncomfortable with these thoughts and where they were leading her, Cassie decided to do what she always did when faced with a difficult decision—pretend it didn't exist. She would focus on the here and now, then deal with work after she got home. There was no reason to announce the news to anyone until it was for sure, anyway. Who knew—by Monday the whole deal could've fallen through and if she'd told everyone, she'd look like a fool. Better to keep quiet until she saw it on paper and knew what the terms were. She hadn't spent years poring over dense corporate contracts for nothing.

Still, she tossed and turned for hours that night, before giving up on sleep and switching on the lights around two a.m. After flicking through seventy-five channels of infomercials and made-for-TV movies featuring D-list actors, she turned to the one guaranteed distraction she could think of. She powered up her laptop and took a piece of scratch paper out of her purse. Frank Blakely. Coconut Grove Estates.

After a few seconds on Google, Cassie discovered that Coconut Grove Estates wasn't the exclusive gated community she had imagined. According to its website, it was "South Florida's premier retreat for show-business seniors," a retirement home for impoverished former actors and other performers. The photo showed a garish pink high-rise surrounded by palm trees, with people in various stages of decrepitude sitting on park benches out front. "Call today!" the website cheerfully announced, with the not-so-cheery reality obscured in small print at the bottom of the page ("Income maximums apply; prospective residents must show proof of financial need.").

Cassie wrote down the number. Friday and Saturday, her next two days in New York, stretched out open and unplanned—a rarity in her scheduled-to-the-minute life. Sometime in the next forty-eight hours, she would call Frank Blakely and finally get the real story behind the letter. Then she could move on to the next chapter of her life.

"Coconut Grove Estates!" a female voice trilled when Cassie called the next morning.

"I was trying to reach one of your residents, Frank Blakely," Cassie said uncertainly.

"Please hold, and I'll connect you." Cassie waited in silence, then heard a metallic chirp as the phone rang.

"Frankie here!" a male voice boomed. Cassie held the phone receiver away from her ear.

"Um, Mr. Blakely?"

"That's me, doll. How can I help you?"

Cassie had been prepared for suspicion; she'd never expected Frank Blakely to greet a stranger so cheerfully. It made what she was trying to do seem unfair, somehow.

"Um, my name is Cassie Armstrong," she began. "My grandmother went to the New York Institute of Art in the 1940s, and I believe she was in your class. Lydia Prescott?"

As she spoke, Cassie recognized that talking on the phone was a huge disadvantage. In negotiations, she was always able to tease out what her opponents didn't want to tell her by watching their eyes and hand gestures. Did Frank flinch at the sound of Lydia's name? Was he blushing at a long-buried memory?

"Lydia..." Frank drew out the sound. "Huh. It's been a long time."

"Yes, I know...." Cassie stumbled through the explanation she'd practiced in the shower that morning. "You see, my grandmother's birthday is coming up, and she's often told me how happy she was at art school—how she made so many wonderful friends, but now she's lost track of most of them. I thought, for her birthday, I could give her some cards and letters from people she hasn't talked to in so long."

"And she mentioned *my* name?" Frank asked.

Cassie felt guilty lying to such an obviously good-natured old man. "Well, this is supposed to be a surprise, so I was looking through her old yearbooks for some ideas, and it seemed I remembered hearing your name somewhere...."

"I was only there for two years," Frank said. "Transferred from the University of South Carolina after my sophomore year— figured if I dreamed of making some grand artistic statement, I'd better get myself to New York, right? Not to mention the sheer misery of living in South Carolina for someone like me. The Institute of Art was sheer heaven after Hillbilly Land, I'll tell you that."

"So you were happy there?"

"Oh yes, sweetheart, I positively blossomed. I arrived without a clue, I had visions of myself as an avant-garde artist, but had no idea how to go about it. I still give the school money, even though my Social Security checks don't stretch as far as I'd like. They gave me a chance, and I'd like to help them rescue other poor souls from backwater towns."

"So, my grandmother, Lydia?" Cassie urged.

"Was she interested in theater?" Frank asked. "They do a wonderful spring show every year—at least they used to, and the sets were phenomenal, as you can imagine, with all those artist types to work on them."

"I don't think so," Cassie said. "I did find a picture of her in something called the Masterpiece Club."

Frank laughed. "Oh, Art for the Smart! That's what we used to call it, those of us who weren't glamorous enough to belong. It was a club for the really *serious* students— visits to snooty galleries and private art collections. I was too busy painting sets. That's about all I used my art degree for, I'm afraid."

He seemed genuine. Which didn't mean he wasn't lying. Cassie had been through enough lawsuits to know that truly gifted liars never gave themselves away. But the way he was talking—without a trace of defensiveness or suspicion—made Cassie doubt her hunch. Maybe this man hadn't written the letter after all. Maybe F.B. was someone else altogether.

"Well, I'm sorry if I've bothered you," Cassie said, preparing to end the conversation. "I just thought I'd try, on the off chance..."

"If I saw a picture of her, maybe that would

jog my memory," Frank said. "But darling, to be honest, it wasn't the girls I was obsessing over. Now, if you'd asked me to remember some of the dreamy boys in my class, that would be a different matter!"

Cassie caught her breath.

"I can't tell you what a sanctuary the Institute of Art was for me," he continued. "I didn't even know what gay was then—we didn't have a word for it, just *sissy,* or *ninny,* or a number of other derogatory terms I didn't want to be associated with. I won't bore you with the particulars. Suffice it to say that I met the love of my life there. He and I were together for almost fifty years, can you believe it?"

"Wow."

"Lost him to cancer a few years ago. That's when I moved in here. Wasn't doing too well in that condo, all by myself, with nothing but memories. It's much better here—the characters in this place are a hoot."

"I can only imagine." Cassie laughed. "And—well, you're lucky you found someone. Many people spend their whole lives searching for the right person."

"I hear you, sweetheart," Frank said. "I'm

sorry I couldn't be more help, but good luck with your big surprise. I tell anyone who asks that I don't have any regrets, but there's one thing I would've liked—a granddaughter or grandson to make a fuss over me in my old age."

"I do my best," Cassie said. But she didn't. Not really. This story she'd concocted was a lie. She'd never planned anything special for Lydia or Henry. She fit her grandparents into her life when it was convenient. And soon, when she moved across the country, it wouldn't be convenient at all.

After hanging up, Cassie pulled out the photocopied pages of Lydia's yearbook. She looked at Frank Blakely's picture, his wide grin announcing his contentment to the world. You couldn't tell who was gay from yearbook pictures, but you could see who seemed happy. Which young man had become the love of Frank's life? Cassie scanned the pictures, wishing she'd thought to ask Frank his name. Would asking have brought back the pain of his loss, or would Frank have been happy to talk about the person who'd brought him such joy?

Cassie glanced at Lydia's picture again. Her

grandmother's face revealed little except careful grooming. Still, her eyes had a sparkle that was missing from her previous yearbook photos. Her smile was more natural. She seemed to have come into her own.

Cassie flipped through the other pages she'd copied. There was Lydia, standing in the second row of the Masterpiece Club. The group Frank had referred to as Art for the Smart. The men and women surrounding her certainly appeared well put together. They all wore carefully pressed blouses and shirts, with hair that looked freshly combed. Lydia held her head high, straining slightly to be seen over the hat of a woman in front of her.

Cassie's eyes wandered over the other young faces. They appeared so grown-up in their sophisticated outfits, but these people were in college, probably no older than twenty or twenty-one. Yet they looked a full generation more mature than the students Cassie had passed in the school yesterday, shuffling around in stretched-out sweatpants and faded T-shirts.

Her eyes were repeatedly drawn to the center of the photo, where one particular face seemed to leap from the page. A dark-haired man with a thin moustache and piercing black eyes. It was as if he were staring directly at her, through time. His face looked vaguely familiar. The angle of his gaunt cheekbones, the way his chin thrust out underneath his mouth. The expression that combined arrogance and confidence. A commanding presence that separated him from the bland faces surrounding him.

Cassie checked the caption and saw that he was the Masterpiece Club's advisor—a professor, although he barely seemed older than his students. She studied his face, and suddenly realized where she'd seen it before. Those dark eyes, that direct stare… He looked just like the pictures she'd seen of her father.

Chapter 8

Lydia

His name was Victor DiStefano, and from the minute Lydia met him she was lost.

It was at the first meeting of the Masterpiece Club, to which Dutch dragged her against her wishes.

"I won't fit in," Lydia protested as Dutch pushed her along the hallway toward the student lounge where the meeting was being held.

"Why not?" Dutch demanded.

"Isn't it for—well, students with better connections than me?"

Dutch laughed. "You mean rich kids?"

"Yes."

"Let's see, I'm rich, so I guess you're right." Dutch's eyes sparkled with amusement, but she didn't dispute Lydia's remark. Only the truly wealthy, Lydia had noticed, could discuss money so light-heartedly.

"Oh, come on, Lyd, the field trips sound like fun," Dutch said. "Don't you want to escape this stuffy old place once a week? Besides, I heard the new club advisor is dreamy."

But when Lydia walked into the student lounge, she saw immediately that Dutch was wrong. Victor DiStefano was not dreamy, a word that conjured up an image of soft-focus tenderness. Victor was vibrantly, thrillingly alive. He stood facing the doorway as they entered, arms folded across his chest, his dark eyes staring directly at each student who walked in. Lydia froze when she saw him, overwhelmed by his intensity. His black hair was swept off his forehead and brushed straight back, curling slightly where it met the top of his collar. A slim moustache drew attention to his lips, twisted slightly in amusement.

He met Lydia's panicked expression, then

smiled reassuringly, tilting his head toward a worn green couch to his right. Following his wordless command, Lydia scuttled toward the couch, where Dutch soon joined her. After about five minutes, as other students entered and everyone exchanged questioning looks, Victor clapped his hands. The sound was electric. Everyone instantly sat up straighter, waiting intently for him to speak.

"Welcome to the first meeting of the Masterpiece Club," Victor said, giving the name dramatic emphasis. His rich, deep voice had a musical rhythm, like that of an actor delivering lines of poetry. "To begin, I would like to announce that we'll be doing things differently this year. In the past, from what I've heard, this club was an excuse to skip classes and gawk at the private art collections of rich alumni. No more. This year, the club has a new mission—teaching you about the real lives of real artists. We will visit studios where the major artists of tomorrow are creating future masterpieces. We will go behind the scenes at this city's finest private galleries to find out how the art market actually works. We will browse some of the best art supply shops in the country, places where you will be inspired to try new things."

He paused, looking around the room to confirm he had their full attention.

"I want this club to change your life."

His words cast a spell over Lydia and her fellow students. Not one of them coughed or fidgeted as they waited for Victor to continue. From the corner of her eye, Lydia could see Dutch staring at him slack-jawed.

"I want members who are deeply committed," Victor went on. "People who want to learn and will contribute something to every meeting. To that end, membership will be determined by private interviews with me. My goal is to have no more than fifteen members—which means many of you will not be accepted. But for this club to thrive, and allow for an open exchange of ideas, it is necessary."

Lydia glanced around the room. There were easily thirty students crammed in there. Lydia felt the familiar weight of disappointment. Victor DiStefano had the kind of forceful personality that would easily overlook someone like her. How could she possibly compete with these other students, who had no doubt spent summers sketching in Tuscany and regularly attended Metropolitan Museum galas with their wealthy parents?

"I'll start on this side of the room." He pointed to his left, the opposite direction from where Lydia was sitting. "One by one, each of you will come down the hall to my office for an interview. I apologize to those of you who will be kept waiting—" he nodded quickly to the students on the other side of the room "—but I would like to complete this process today, so our next meeting can be devoted to more important topics."

As soon as he'd walked out with his first interviewee, the lounge buzzed with conversation.

"I was right, wasn't I?" Dutch said. "Can you believe how good-looking he is? Like an Italian Laurence Olivier. And maybe just a bit of Cary Grant. Gosh—I'd listen to him talk about anything!"

"Dutch, I can't do this," Lydia said. "What am I going to tell him?"

"Just be yourself," Dutch said reassuringly. "Compared to all these stuck-up rich kids, you'll be a breath of fresh air."

After more than an hour of fidgeting, Lydia made her way to Victor's office, which turned out to be little more than a supply closet with a desk along one wall and an armchair next to it. Victor sat in a wheeled, leather office chair behind the desk, his legs stretched out. He waved his arm toward the armchair, and Lydia sat down, knees pressed together and her hands folded primly in her lap. Facing him this close, with his gaze focused on her alone, made her light-headed.

There was no small talk. After writing her name on a paper in front of him, Victor asked, "Why do you want to join the Masterpiece Club?"

"I want to become more familiar with the art world," Lydia said, reciting the line she'd prepared during her wait in the lounge.

"You see, that's exactly what I'd hoped to avoid," he said, shaking his head. "A rational, sensible-sounding reason that means nothing."

Lydia flinched at his words.

"Art should be about passion," he continued. "It should come from the heart." He leaned over until his face was only a few feet from hers. Up close, Lydia saw that he was far younger than her other professors, the moustache and steely gaze giving him a more mature appearance than his smooth skin and unlined face merited.

"What is your passion, Lydia?"

His question hung in the space between them. He watched her intently, his stare breaking through her defenses.

"I don't know," Lydia finally admitted. "All I'm sure of is that I'm happiest when I'm painting. I lose track of where I am and what time it is."

"That's how it should be," he said. "Like a love affair."

Lydia felt her face burn. He was trying to shock her, testing her for signs of weakness, and she'd failed already.

His smile was compassionate rather than amused. "You've got potential," he said, sitting back in his chair. "At least you're honest, and that counts with me. It's very refreshing. We'll see what we can do, okay?"

Lydia sat silently for a moment. "Does that mean I can join?"

Victor laughed, a quick burst of sound that was over almost as soon as it started. "Yes, Lydia Prescott. Welcome to the Masterpiece Club. Just between you and me, I tried to have the name changed. Masterpiece Club sounds like it was dreamed up at a debutante ball at the Plaza Hotel, doesn't it?"

Lydia smiled and shrugged.

"You're not from New York, are you?" he asked.

"No, Illinois. Small-town Illinois," she quickly clarified.

"Don't say it like you've got something to be ashamed of," he said. "I'm not exactly blue blood myself, as if my name weren't enough of a tip-off. You can imagine the reaction of the more traditional faculty when they heard their newest colleague had an Italian last name—despite their admiration for Da Vinci and Botticelli." He tossed his head back scornfully, then smiled. "I've always had a soft spot for outsiders."

And that was where it all began, in a moment of compassion inside a tiny, airless office. Victor DiStefano didn't look down on her family or her hometown; in fact, he liked her better because of it. Lydia sensed a bond between them, an acknowledgment that she stood apart from all the other students in the club. No matter how intimidating or demanding Victor was from then on, Lydia was never threatened. For the first time since arriving at the Institute of Art, she felt special.

It had been quite a coup for the school to hire Victor DiStefano, Dutch told Lydia later. He was only a few years out of school himself, but had already made a name for himself as a writer on contemporary art, able to scout out talent in the dingiest, most unassuming studios. Bringing Victor on as a faculty member had given the school instant cachet and a connection to the up-and-coming young artists he championed.

His other, more subtle talent was his ability to adapt to the needs and insecurities of each person he encountered. Lydia watched in wonder as he encouraged all the students in the club to speak their minds and share opinions. He traded flirtatious double entendres with the girls who were forward, then switched to intense, philosophical conversations with the serious ones. He muttered off-color jokes to the boys with the most swagger, even as he drew out the shyest with stories of successful artists who had begun their careers plagued by self-doubt. But he seemed to take a particular interest in Lydia, as Dutch soon noted.

"You ever notice how he makes sure you're listening?" she asked one night, sprawled on the floor of Lydia's room.

"Really?"

"He always seems to be checking on you," Dutch elaborated. "Like he wants to see that you're there, paying attention."

Lydia shrugged, but her stomach fluttered with excitement.

"Just be careful," Dutch warned. "The other girls are starting to get jealous."

"What do you mean?" Lydia had spent almost three years carefully navigating the treacherous school hierarchy, deferring to popular girls like Vera. To hear Dutch—her confidant, her biggest cheerleader—suggest that she was doing something wrong made her feel panicked.

"Teacher's pet isn't all it's cracked up to be," Dutch said solemnly.

"I can't believe—I mean…" Lydia's voice trailed off. What exactly was Dutch hinting at? Victor had never treated her with anything but respect.

Dutch laughed as she got to her feet. "Don't

get so worked up," she said dismissively. "Believe me, I know you'd never do anything wrong. *Everybody* knows it."

That night, even as she fumed at Dutch's insinuations, her friend's words opened up an intriguing possibility. Lydia looked up to Victor DiStefano with the awe of a lowly subject dazzled by a king. He seemed to exist in a different world from her. But the other girls wouldn't be jealous if Lydia had merely made a fool of herself by getting googly-eyed over a professor. They must have seen a spark of interest when Victor looked at her. They must have sensed a connection that went deeper than teacher and student.

Lydia had heard whispered gossip about girls who had affairs with teachers, short-lived escapades that unfolded in darkened classrooms after hours, or over secretive dinners in dimly lit restaurants. Such affairs were hushed up, to be hinted at only after the fact. But Lydia had never imagined herself in their shoes. As Dutch had said so emphatically, she was one of the good girls. But when she closed her eyes that night, she saw Victor's face. He was gazing at her intently. Trying to see into her soul. The dim memories of

Henry that used to haunt her faded, replaced by thoughts of Victor.

In the weeks that followed, Lydia grow more self-conscious around him. Sometimes she could barely look at Victor during club meetings, afraid that she'd reveal too much. She was reluctant to talk about him, embarrassed by her silly schoolgirl crush. And gradually, as the months passed and Lydia withdrew, her friendship with Dutch broke under the strain. From the beginning, their relationship had been based on honesty, but now Lydia couldn't bring herself to admit that the meetings with Victor were often the highlight of her week. Dutch had a way of turning everything into a joke, and Lydia didn't want to be teased.

Preoccupied by her work and her daydreams, Lydia barely noticed that her best friend was growing more distant. Instead, she replayed every conversation she'd had with Victor. He seemed so close to saying something important—or was that wishful thinking? He flirted just enough to keep her wondering. His hand would rest on her shoulder a moment too long; he would start a sentence, then stop abruptly and turn away. Lydia wondered what might happen at the end of the school year, when she was no longer his student. Could he possibly treat her as an equal then? And what would that mean?

Then came a chance to tip the balance. It was a rainy Wednesday afternoon in early spring, and the Masterpiece Club was touring a Greenwich Village artists' cooperative, two decrepit rooms filled with half-finished canvases and sticky paint splattered across the worn wood floors. A group of young artists shared the space—a few even slept there on mattresses they rolled up during the day—and they told the students about their struggles to make a living while pursuing their dreams. Lydia watched her fellow students' faces, most of them registering a combination of curiosity and horror. Clearly, they couldn't picture themselves working in such depressing conditions, sleeping on the floor of a tenement with no hot water and a tiny hotplate instead of a stove.

But Lydia was inspired. Here was a group of young people, not much older than her, following their passion. Just like Victor told her she should.

"What do you think?" Victor sidled up to

her as she stared at a canvas covered with streaks of bright yellow paint.

"Incredible," Lydia said. "When you look at all these pieces together, you can see how each of them is influencing the other's work."

"Good for you." He seemed pleased. "No one else has seen that."

"I'm jealous, actually," Lydia said. "My work has been stagnant for so long. I mean, I've been trying new techniques, but nothing has really captured me."

"Maybe you haven't allowed yourself to be captured," he suggested.

"I suppose that's it." Standing side by side with Victor, staring at the painting rather than each other, Lydia found it easy to talk honestly, without her usual self-censoring. "I don't think I've changed since arriving at school," she continued. "I'm still the same person, so it's no wonder my art hasn't progressed, either."

"Perhaps it's time to challenge yourself," Victor said. "Even if it frightens you."

"I'm sure you're right," Lydia said. "I'd love to be part of a cooperative like this. Be inspired by other artists. But I would never fit in."

"That's where you're wrong," he said. "In fact—no, I shouldn't."

"Shouldn't what?" Lydia turned to face him. Victor glanced around quickly, checking to make sure he wouldn't be overheard.

"Listen—this is strictly against the rules, but they're having a party here on Thursday night to celebrate Lois's new gallery show. You should come."

Lydia's heart began to pound. "Really?"

"You mentioned wanting to work in a gallery someday, right? This would be a great opportunity for you, a chance to meet some of the younger artists."

It wasn't a date, Lydia told herself. Of course not. Then why was she struggling to suppress a delighted grin?

"The gallery opening goes until nine o'clock," Victor explained, "so things wouldn't get started here until later. Would that be a problem?"

He looked at her, his doubtful expression acknowledging the risk she would be taking. The women's dormitory had a strict ten o'clock curfew on weeknights. There were ways around it, of course, but good girls like Lydia didn't do that sort of thing.

"I think I could manage," she said.

"Keep this between us, all right?" he said. "Don't want anyone getting the wrong idea." His hand brushed gently along her back, then he was gone. Lydia felt his touch linger long after he'd gone. She decided she'd think about the party. Carefully consider the pluses and minuses. But deep down, she knew from the moment he touched her that she'd go.

The preferred late-night exit from the women's dormitory was a fire escape off the second-floor lounge. Lydia had heard other students talk about sneaking out, but she'd never had a reason to try—until that night. The lounge was empty when she crept in at a quarter to ten. Perhaps if someone had been there, Lydia would have been too embarrassed to attempt it. As it was, she saw the uninhabited lounge as a sign that luck was on her side. She was meant to go to the party.

The only person she might have confided in, Dutch, had taken to making fun of Victor. Lydia wasn't sure if it was because she genuinely didn't like him or if she was trying to bait Lydia into a confession. Telling Dutch about the party would have brought either scorn or laughter. Lydia didn't know which would be worse. So she left without telling anyone, her great adventure a tightly guarded secret.

Lydia climbed down to the sidewalk and walked down the street to hail a taxi. As the car sped downtown, her heart raced almost as fast as the vehicle's engine. It was her first time out alone in New York at night, her first time in a taxi by herself. Without the distraction of a gaggle of girls surrounding her, the city lights shone with a new intensity. Even as she smiled out the window at the scenes flashing by her, Lydia tried to prepare herself for disappointment. She mustn't expect too much. Victor might ignore her in favor of his artist friends, or he might not even be there. She braced herself for every possibility—except what actually happened.

Lydia had dressed carefully in a tweed skirt and dark-blue wool twinset, a necklace of faux pearls arranged carefully along the sweater's collar. Victor had told her this party would be an investment in her future, a chance to show herself as a poised twenty-year-old woman instead of a naive student.

But the image Lydia created for herself

turned out to be completely wrong. After knocking loudly on the studio door—hoping she'd be heard over the jazz record playing inside—she was greeted by a woman a few years older than her, wearing tight black trousers and what looked like a man's shirt, holding a cigarette in one hand and a cocktail in the other.

"Yes?" she said, eyeing Lydia doubtfully.

"I'm here—um, Mr. DiStefano invited me," Lydia said.

"Mr. DiStefano!" The woman laughed, then took a deep drag of her cigarette. "You mean Victor?" She angled her head to one side and blew smoke past Lydia. "He didn't tell me he was bringing a date."

"Oh, no, it's not…" Lydia stammered. "I mean, I'm one of his students." So much for blending in with the sophisticated crowd.

"How adorable," the woman said, but her expression remained suspicious. "Come right in. Victor's holding court at the bar." She pulled the door wider and waved Lydia inside. The bar appeared to be a pile of wooden packing crates with liquor bottles crowded on top. Victor stood behind the crates, bottle in hand, talking animatedly to a group of women. Lydia paused in the doorway.

"Come on," the woman at the door urged, pushing at Lydia's back. "No one here bites." She leaned toward Lydia's ear and whispered, "Not if you don't want them to." Then she laughed, a harsh sound that made Lydia flinch, before turning back to the door.

Lydia took in the scene around her. Brassy, discordant jazz blared from a record player. To her right, groups of people hovered around the makeshift bar, gulping from cocktail glasses and almost disappearing in a thick haze of cigarette smoke. In the middle of the room, a woman wearing a red silk robe was moving sinuously to the music. Lydia glanced around for the woman's dance partner, but she seemed to be alone. Almost three years at art school had given Lydia ample experience with eccentric people, but she'd never felt quite as lost as she did right then. She was about to turn around and leave when a man appeared at her side. Victor.

"Lydia!" He seemed genuinely pleased to see her. "I wasn't sure you'd come."

"Well…" Lydia began. But she couldn't think what to say. She'd rehearsed sophisticated party chatter as she was getting dressed, but now that she was here, she knew she couldn't fool him. He saw her awkwardness, the way her proper outfit set her apart. And he didn't seem to care.

"Let me introduce you around," he said, taking her by the hand. The introductions passed in a jumble of names that Lydia instantly forgot, because all she could concentrate on was her hand in his, the sensation of his touch.

He poured her a scotch and soda, then insisted she join a discussion about the death and/or resurgence of portraiture. She sipped her drink as Victor and his friends—young men and women with unkempt hair and defiantly wrinkled clothes—argued for the sake of debate, reveling in one-upping each other. Lydia had spent her life avoiding conflict, ignoring the truth if it kept everyone else happy. To see the rules of proper conversation abandoned was disconcerting—but surprisingly thrilling. Especially since Victor looked at her from time to time with a knowing glance, as if the two of them shared a secret no one else could decipher.

And so, after a few more drinks and a few

more glances, when Victor put his arm around her shoulder, it seemed natural to lean her body into his. In later years, she tortured herself by reliving that moment, because it moved them from teacher and student to something far more dangerous. She always took the blame for everything that happened afterward, simply because she relaxed her body into his, sending a signal he couldn't ignore.

As she pressed against him, Victor's hand slid over her skirt, finally resting on her hip. His lips brushed her cheek.

"You want to get out of here?" he murmured.

Lydia said nothing, merely followed him as he steered her toward the front door. She pictured the two of them sitting together at a dimly lit café, talking intently in a way they'd never been able to before. Instead, Victor led Lydia across the hall, opening another door to reveal a cramped studio apartment, with a bed along one wall and a minuscule kitchen along the other. Light from a single overhead bulb illuminated the center of the room, leaving the rest in shadow.

"This is Adrian's place—the sculptor," Victor said, wrapping his arm around her. "Not much to look at, I know, but at least it's private." Lydia heard the door click behind him.

That click—the acknowledgment that she was alone with him, hidden from view—wasn't enough to alert her that she'd made a mistake. For those first few minutes, as Victor rubbed his hands along her back and legs, she felt only butterflies, a giddy thrill that the object of her romantic fantasies was now focused on her alone.

It was as his hands grew more insistent that she began to doubt. They stood in the center of the room, Victor's face buried in the curve of her neck, as Lydia tried to reach his face and kiss him. Then she felt him pushing his fingers under her skirt, tugging at the garters holding up her hose. In the silence of her room late at night, she'd imagined Victor's hands moving along her skin just like this, a thought that had filled her with an excited glow. But those visions had always included Victor escorting her to smoky bars and avant-garde concerts, gazing at her during long, soul-baring conversations. Victor wooing her until she finally gave in. The man who was groping her now in this dingy, unfamiliar room was a stranger.

She tried to wriggle away, but his hands wouldn't release her. They pressed against her bottom, crushing her against the bulge in his trousers. It came as a shock—an attack against her unprepared, unprotected body—and she flinched.

Victor lifted his head and looked at her, amused.

"C'mon, baby," he said. "Don't be scared." Then he froze. "This isn't your first time, is it?"

Lydia couldn't speak. Her hesitation gave Victor his answer.

"That's what I thought," he said with a smile. "Still waters run deep, don't they?"

He began to pull her toward the bed. Lydia struggled to remain upright, to escape his grasp.

"I don't—I don't think…" she stammered.

"Stop thinking," he said with a laugh. "You'll never be an artist if you keep thinking. Start living."

She did say no. But she said it in such a soft, pleading voice that he didn't seem to hear. Before she knew it, Lydia was lying on the bed, Victor's body pinning her down. But she didn't kick or scream. She tormented herself with that later, the idea that she might have fought him off. But in that moment, when it all seemed so unreal that she barely understood what was happening, fighting him was impossible. She couldn't make a scene, draw all those people at the party into this miserable room to witness her disheveled clothes and tangled hair. To see Victor smirk at her hysteria.

It was only decades later, when Lydia first heard the term date rape, that she understood what had happened to her. The rush of relief, the acknowledgment that it wasn't her fault, almost brought her to tears, even though she was a middle-aged woman by then. She wept for her younger self, the self who'd shouldered the blame for years. Because even as she blinked back tears while Victor ripped off her underwear, her entire body rigid as he pounded against her, making her cringe with pain and bite her lips to keep from screaming out, she hated herself, not him. She'd led him on by coming to the party. She'd lost track of how many cocktails she'd gulped down. She'd pressed herself against him. She'd given him permission by admitting she wasn't a virgin. As his moustache rubbed her cheeks raw, she cried silently, worried even then what he'd think if he saw her tears.

When it was all over, Victor got off her quickly and stood up. Lydia kept her eyes closed so she wouldn't have to see his triumphant expression. She let the tears roll slowly down her cheeks, forming narrow streams along her jawbone.

"Lighten up, sweetheart," she heard him say. "You can't have it both ways, you know."

She had no idea how long she lay there motionless on the wrinkled sheets. Eventually, she sat up and took in the wreckage of her carefully selected outfit: sweater crumpled on the floor, skirt jammed up above her hips, ripped underpants and hose at the foot of the bed. Wincing, she walked over to the sink and wet her underwear, then wiped her legs before tossing it with her ruined hose in a trash can. She smoothed her skirt and ran her fingers through her hair, but without a mirror it was impossible to see how disheveled she looked.

There was another problem. She'd left her purse in the studio across the hall, where Victor was probably entertaining the crowd as if nothing had happened. The thought of entering that room, of seeing him again, made her nauseous. But she needed money for the taxi home. She had to get away. Slowly, she opened the apartment door and peeked out into the hallway. The music sounded louder than ever, and a group of women stood in the doorway of the studio facing her, laughing and smoking. Lydia recognized the woman who'd let her in earlier in the evening.

The woman met her eye, her expression amused.

"Still here, I see," she said.

Lydia started to speak, but the words seemed likely to come out as a sob. The woman left her companions and strode over.

"You okay?" she asked.

Lydia shook her head. "I—I have to go home," she finally said, her voice wavering. "But my purse, it's over there." She nodded toward the studio.

"And there's someone you'd rather not see. I get it. What does your purse look like?"

Within a minute, the woman had located Lydia's purse and handed it to her. "Get out of here," she said, but her tone was kindly.

Almost protective. "Try to forget whatever happened."

Lydia stumbled down the stairs and collapsed in the taxi she flagged down outside. During the ride back, all she could focus on was her last hurdle: getting back inside the dorm without being detected. She staggered up the fire escape and through the study-lounge window unseen, tiptoeing up the stairs and down the hall to her room without encountering anyone. She might as well have been a ghost.

She grabbed a towel and robe from her room and walked to the bathroom at the end of the hall. She turned on the water in the shower as hot as she could and washed and rewashed her skin in the scalding stream, unable to consider sleep until she'd cleansed off every trace of the evening. The memory of Victor's fingers made her shiver despite the steam. Once, long ago, after her night in the apple orchard, she'd reveled in the memory of Henry's touch; in bed, alone, she would remember the sensation of his hands, his lips. Thinking about Henry brought on sobs of regret and self-loathing so wrenching they threatened to break her to pieces.

Henry loved her, and this was how she repaid him. The only way she could wake up tomorrow and still want to keep living was to forget every second of tonight. Lock it away in a part of her brain where it would never escape. Confide in no one, never acknowledge what had happened. Erase it from her life story.

Lydia stayed in her room for the next two days, pretending she had the flu. When she finally emerged, she appeared to be her usual self: the good girl, the one who never broke the rules or caused a stir. For a little while, she thought it might work. She would drop out of the Masterpiece Club, of course, but otherwise return to her usual routine. Continue as normal.

But it wasn't long before she realized her evening with Victor would have repercussions she'd never considered.

Chapter 9

Cassie

Locating Victor DiStefano wasn't hard. One phone call to the alumni office, and Cassie found out he was still in New York, living less than a mile from her hotel.

Cassie was tempted to call right away, while she was still buzzing with adrenaline. But years of legal training had taught her the importance of research. Victor DiStefano might be her grandfather. Or had she imagined the echoes of her father's features in that mysterious yearbook photograph? If she wanted to find out the truth, she'd have to find out more about him. She'd seen the strategy work many times at the negotiating table. Lull your opponents into a false sense of security by starting out with easy questions. Then catch them off guard with information they didn't know you had. That was when they got ready to make a deal.

Cassie typed Victor's name into Google and skimmed through the results. Amazon. com listed him as the author of a few books of art criticism, most of them out of print. The site for a New York neighborhood newsletter posted minutes from a community meeting, where Victor was listed as one of the speakers protesting the demolition of a historic building. The *New York Times* website had a 1996 obituary for someone named Flora Highwood DiStefano, "noted contemporary art collector and board member of the Museum of Modern Art... She is survived by her loving husband of thirty-five years, writer Victor DiStefano." There were no children.

As the links became less relevant—mentioning Victor DiStefanos who clearly weren't the one she was looking for—Cassie acknowledged that there was nothing more to learn from this source. She dialed the phone number.

A gruff voice answered after the first ring. "DiStefano."

Cassie decided to be honest. He would either talk to her or not. Best to discover right away which it would be.

"Victor DiStefano?" she asked. "You used to teach at the New York Institute of Art?"

"Yes," he said, drawing out each letter slowly.

"My name is Cassie Armstrong. My grandmother was a student of yours, I think. Lydia Prescott."

Cassie listened for any kind of reaction. All she heard was silence.

"Did Lydia tell you to call me?" he eventually asked. He had a rich, resonant voice, and he spoke as if he was used to his words making an impact.

"Not exactly, no. I'm in New York doing some research on her life—"

"And you want to meet me," he interrupted.

This was it. Her chance.

"Yes," Cassie said.

"There's a coffeehouse on 61st, just off

Madison. Café Au Lait. Could you be there in half an hour? Eleven o'clock?"

"Sure. See you there."

Too jittery to sit in her hotel room, Cassie arrived at the café ten minutes early. After peering in the window and seeing no one over the age of forty, she decided to wait outside. Pacing nervously on the corner, she scanned the people walking along the sidewalk. Spotting him first would give her an advantage, she knew, an opportunity to observe him unawares.

If Victor had been teaching when Lydia was a student, he'd have to be well into his eighties by now. Cassie prepared herself accordingly, watching for a slow-moving figure, possibly hunched over or clutching a cane. So when Victor finally appeared, she didn't notice him until a few seconds before he reached her. He moved gracefully along the sidewalk, a slim figure with perfectly straight spine and shoulders. Thick white hair swooped back off his forehead, and his white moustache and beard were neatly trimmed. He wore a dark-green velvet jacket over a black shirt, with a paisley silk ascot around his neck. On anyone else, such an outfit might have looked like a costume, but it gave Victor an eye-catching elegance. If he was this compelling as an old man, Cassie could imagine how magnetic he must have been fifty years ago.

"Cassie Armstrong?" he asked.

"Yes." She started to extend her hand, then retracted it when he didn't offer his. "Thank you for meeting me."

He held the door of the café open for her and waved her through. After they'd settled in armchairs facing the front window and ordered drinks, Cassie got down to business.

"So, my grandmother," she began. "You do remember her?"

"Yes," Victor said. "She was in a group we called the Masterpiece Club. Students visited artists' studios and were given behind-the-scenes museum tours—that sort of thing."

The words flowed without hesitation. Had he rehearsed what he wanted to tell her?

But Cassie was used to smooth talkers. And she knew that silence threw them off. So she looked at him expectantly, waiting for him to continue, and he took the bait. "Lydia was a promising student. But I think she found the pressure of school too much. I believe she dropped out."

"She studied abroad her senior year," Cassie explained.

Victor nodded once. "Ah."

He picked up his cappuccino and began sipping the foamy top layer. That couldn't be the whole story. There had to be more. Cassie decided to switch tactics. Leaning back in her chair with a friendly smile, she changed the subject.

"Did you like teaching?" she asked.

Victor shrugged. "Well enough, I suppose," he said.

"How long did you teach at the Institute?"

"About ten years. I left in 1960, the year I got married."

"So—you moved on to another job?" Cassie asked.

"It was suggested that I find something else." Victor smiled wryly. "My wife, Flora, was one of my students, you see. The powers that be didn't take very kindly to our marriage."

Flora Highwood DiStefano. Known for her charitable work and her role on the board of the Museum of Modern Art. You didn't get those lines in your obituary without a substantial bank balance. Cassie could guess what the scenario had been. A wealthy, attractive student; a young teacher looking for a comfortable life. A whirlwind romance followed by years of luxurious living, with no need for Victor to hold a steady job ever again. Still, they'd stayed married for thirty-five years. There had to be some kind of love there. Or was it just a mutually beneficial business relationship?

"So, this project of yours," Victor said. "What exactly are you researching?"

Cassie met his steely gaze with a stare that was equally intent. Time for her trump card.

"Family history," she said.

"And you think your family history has something to do with me?"

Cassie didn't respond, just watched him for a sign of acknowledgment. But his eyes revealed nothing.

"So," he said eventually. "Whatever happened to Lydia?"

Cassie gave Victor the basic facts: Lydia had married her high school sweetheart, had a child and moved back to Illinois, where she still lived.

"Only one child?" Victor asked.

"Yes, my father," Cassie said. *Who looked*

like you, she thought, straining not to blurt out the words. *Who might have been your son.*

"And your father lives in Chicago, as well?" Victor asked.

"He died when I was little," Cassie told him. "My grandmother raised me."

Victor nodded slowly. "Lydia always struck me as resourceful."

"You seem to recall her quite well." Cassie pounced on his words.

Victor shrugged. "I remember many of the students in her class. It was my first year of teaching. I wasn't much older than them, and nervous as hell."

"I find that hard to believe," Cassie said with a flirtatious grin.

"Why?" he asked. "What did Lydia tell you?"

For a fleeting moment, Cassie caught a hint of worry in Victor's voice. She considered lying, telling him she knew everything. But that would only feed his ego. It suddenly seemed crucial that Victor think Lydia was living a happy life, undisturbed by thoughts of him.

"She didn't tell me anything," Cassie said.

"I saw your picture in one of her yearbooks, and your face looked…"

She waited, watching Victor for a sign of regret, or longing. An admission that Lydia had meant something to him. That what Cassie suspected was true.

Victor sipped his cappuccino, looking down at the cup to avoid meeting her eyes. "If you're hoping to make some sort of financial claim," he murmured casually, as if they were discussing the weather, "I should warn you that the money's all tied up in binding trusts. You won't get far."

Cassie caught her breath, aghast at the implication.

"I'm not interested in your money," she said coldly. "Besides, what claim could I possibly make?"

The truth hovered between them. She saw it in his eyes as he looked her over. Assessing her as a threat rather than as part of himself. She knew then that she didn't want to hear the real story. Not from him.

"I'm sorry I can't be more help," Victor said smoothly. "But good luck with your work. I hope you find it…fulfilling."

Cassie's tea still felt too hot to drink, but

she couldn't face sitting there even five more minutes, making small talk with a man she now despised. He hadn't suggested meeting because he planned to tell her what had really happened with Lydia. He was only worried about what Cassie wanted from him. He would be no more forthcoming than her grandmother. Victor and Lydia hadn't been raised in a tabloid, talk-show culture, where the road to validation was paved with personal revelations. Their generation knew how to keep secrets.

"I have to get going." Cassie stood abruptly. "I'm just in town for a few days, and I've got a very busy schedule."

Victor stood up next to her. "It was a pleasure meeting you," he said, inclining his head. Then he looked at her intently. "Does Lydia know you're here?"

Cassie shook her head. "No," she said quickly. "No."

"Ah." Victor nodded slowly. "Then perhaps it's best if we keep this meeting between us. Our little secret."

Cassie almost stumbled in her hurry to get away from him, tugging her bag over her shoulder and bumping her arm against the door as she opened it.

Despite his evasions and feigned indifference to Lydia, Cassie no longer had any doubts. When Victor stared at her with his dark, inscrutable eyes, she'd been transported back to the apartment she'd lived in with her parents, the place that filled her mind with vague memories of brown shag carpeting and wood-paneled walls. It was the same look her father used to give her.

Victor DiStefano was her grandfather. And he knew it.

Cassie caught a flight out of LaGuardia later that day. She wasn't supposed to leave until Saturday afternoon, less than twenty-four hours later, and it cost a fortune to change her ticket at the last minute. But she couldn't stay in New York any longer, now that her quest had been revealed for what it was. Pointless.

Yes, she'd gotten an answer. She knew that her grandmother had had another lover once, an affair serious enough that she got pregnant and chose to keep the baby. But the discovery hadn't given Cassie the relief she'd expected. The letter itself, the message that had started her journey, was still a mystery. The only person who could possibly have sent it was Victor, although Cassie still had no idea why he'd signed it F.B. Had it been some sort of code between them? Cassie tried to imagine her grandmother in France, pregnant and alone, reading the emotional letter from the father of her unborn child. But the unbearable passion contained in the letter had obviously died over time. When Cassie talked about Lydia, there was no trace of longing in Victor's eyes. No hint of the feelings he must've had for her once.

If Lydia had kept the letter all these years, it must still have meaning for her. But it obviously meant nothing to Victor. The enduring love the letter promised was only a fantasy. Perhaps being left for Henry had embittered him forever. How would it feel to know another man was raising your child?

Cassie thought about Victor, living off his rich wife for thirty-five years, so used to attention that even the passage of time hadn't tempered his arrogance. But what had she expected? A tearful, loving reunion? An invitation to the next DiStefano family reunion?

Given who Victor was, she felt relieved that she'd never have to see him again. But still, the change in his feeling mystified her. How could he have gone from loving Lydia passionately to complete disinterest?

By the time Cassie got off the plane, waited at baggage claim for half an hour, waited another half hour for a taxi and finally made the long ride back to her condo she was utterly exhausted. She opened the front door and walked into silence and darkness. She'd expected Cooper to be there and to unburden herself by telling him the whole story. Cooper had always been, first and foremost, a friend. Confiding in him would be a relief, and maybe he could offer some much-needed perspective. He never let himself be swayed by emotions, and she longed for his common sense. Longed for the days in college when she could talk with him about anything, without being judged.

But Cooper must still be in London. She was embarrassed to admit she didn't remember when he was coming back. She turned on the lights in the living room and checked the desk calendar sitting on the side table. Cooper's neat, angular handwriting stretched across the page for Saturday: "Cooper back from London, British Airways #314, 3:15 p.m."

She would see him tomorrow. They could work it all out then. She saw the answering machine light flashing and pressed the button.

"Hey, Cassie, it's Ella!" One of the other associates at the firm. "I know it's supposed to be *super* confidential, but I got a heads-up about your big promotion. Oh, my God, you must be thrilled! Just wanted to tell you how excited I am for you! Call if you want this weekend—I'll be at the office, of course."

San Francisco. Her meeting with Victor had completely overshadowed the new job. The job that had seemed so thrilling yesterday had somehow faded from her consciousness.

The next two messages were also friends from work, buzzing about the news. For people who swore by attorney-client privilege, the lawyers Cassie knew were terrible at keeping inter-office confidences.

The final message was from her grandmother.

"Dear, it's me," Lydia said, enunciating carefully as if she didn't think the machine would register her voice otherwise. "I called your office, but your message said you were out. I wanted to check that you're still coming for Sunday lunch."

Her grandparents. They didn't know about the job offer, either. How was she going to tell them she was moving across the country?

She'd have to go to lunch and explain it in person. Show them that she was excited, so they could be happy for her. She picked up the phone and called.

"Cassie!" Henry said happily when he answered up. "Your grandmother said you weren't in the office today."

Why did they both need to comment on her absence? As if being away from work for one day was so revolutionary. Come to think of it, Cassie realized, it was.

"I had, uh, a business trip," she said quickly. "Last-minute."

"Where'd you go?"

"New York."

"Ah, the Big Apple," Henry murmured. "Following your grandmother's footsteps, eh?"

"What?" Cassie asked in a panic. Did he know she'd been snooping around the Institute of Art?

"Although I don't suppose you saw much of the city, with work and all," Henry said. Cassie breathed a sigh of relief. He had no idea what she was really up to.

"I was only there once, years ago," he continued. "Wasn't for me. Too crowded and too dirty."

"Well, it's still pretty crowded and dirty," Cassie said. "Anyway, I'm back now, and I wanted to tell Grandma I'll be by on Sunday."

"Great. Glad to hear it."

His contented cheerfulness made her want to go on. Give her grandparents a warning.

"The thing is, Grandpa, it looks like there are going to be some changes at work."

"Oh?"

"They're offering me a promotion. A big one. But it would mean moving to San Francisco."

"Ah." Cassie waited for more, but true to form, her grandfather kept his feelings well hidden.

"So, it's a pretty big decision," she said.

"Sounds like you haven't made up your mind yet," Henry said.

"Well, I have…" Cassie began. Then she realized she hadn't, not really. Mentally, she'd accepted the offer, the same way she'd always accepted whatever project the firm's partners handed her. You didn't turn anything down if you wanted to get ahead. So she'd simply assumed she'd go, without working through the reality of packing up her stuff, saying goodbye to the people she loved most in the world, possibly even Cooper.

"You know," Cassie started over, "I guess I'm not sure. Not one hundred percent."

"You've got a tough decision," Henry said.

Most of the time she was growing up, Cassie had been grateful for her grandfather's reticence. When he'd run his own landscaping business, he'd treated his employees with the same respect he showed his wife and granddaughter. Lydia, who did the bookkeeping and often helped Henry by drawing garden plans for clients, was the one in charge of family discipline. Theirs was clearly an equal, loving partnership, but their temperaments often struck Cassie as wildly divergent. Her grandmother was easily aggravated—whether by rude drivers or Cassie's refusal to eat anything other than orange food throughout second grade—while Henry strode through life calm and unruffled. He had the magical ability to soothe Lydia with no more than a light touch to her back or a slow smile. As if a silent message was being passed between them. Usually, Cassie was awed by her grandfather's gentleness. But at times she wished for more of an authority figure. Someone who'd tell her the right thing to do when life felt overwhelming.

"This would be a whole lot easier if you'd just tell me what to do," Cassie said with a laugh.

"I may be old, but I'm not necessarily wise," he said. "Your job, your life, your choice. Except…" His voice trailed off.

"Except what?"

"I've never bossed you around, Cassie," Henry said, "and I don't aim to start now. I'll wish you the best if you go. But only if you do it for the right reasons."

"And what are the right reasons?"

"Heading toward a goal rather than away from something. Go if you want to be in San Francisco, and it's a job you'll like. But don't go if you're looking to escape whatever's here."

"Escape? Why would you say that?"

Henry let out a sigh. "I don't pretend to

know a lot about women," he said. "All I was thinking is…for a girl getting married, you don't seem too excited."

Cassie was stunned. She and Henry never talked about her personal life; those conversations were reserved for Lydia. And even with her, Cassie talked about Cooper only in the most positive terms.

"I've been busy, that's all," Cassie said lightly. "Distracted."

"All right, then," Henry said. "Forget I said anything. I usually know better than to meddle in this sort of stuff. I want the best for you, you know that. I don't want to see you make the same mistakes I did years ago…"

There was silence as Cassie waited for him to continue. Henry rarely talked about the past, and when he did, it was always about happy times. Stunts he and his fraternity brothers had concocted while he was at college, or how he'd failed miserably the first time he'd tried to braid Cassie's hair. But now Cassie could sense that he was referring to something far more serious.

"When I was younger," Henry finally said, "I'd walk away from problems. Wait for things to sort themselves out. Took me a long time to learn that wasn't the right way to go about it. If there's a problem, you have to face it head-on. Otherwise—well, otherwise you're never free of it."

Cassie held her breath in anticipation. Henry and Lydia had lived together happily for fifty years. They were the envy of their friends, a neighbor had once told Cassie. In all the years she'd lived with them, Cassie had never heard her grandparents raise their voices to each other. Now, she wondered if such tranquility was a way to escape problems without solving them. Had her grandparents' marriage been more precarious than she imagined?

"Is anything wrong?" Cassie asked cautiously. "With Grandma?"

Henry laughed. "Oh, no. I was thinking of something that happened a long time ago, when I was a foolish young man. About your grandmother, though—she's upstairs, but I don't think she's asleep yet. You want me to get her?"

"No, just tell her I'll see her Sunday."

"Will do," Henry said. "Is Cooper coming, too?"

"I'm not sure." She couldn't admit that she

hadn't spoken to her fiancé in almost a week. "I'll ask him." Which she would, if she ever saw him again.

Chapter 10

Lydia

It took Lydia nearly two months to realize she was pregnant. She prided herself on being a doctor's daughter, wise about the workings of the body in a way other girls weren't. But when weeks passed without a period, she didn't jump to the obvious conclusion. Her cycles had always been irregular, and her parents' vague explanations of where babies came from hadn't included a checklist of symptoms. Deep down, Lydia had assumed that a baby could only be conceived if both parents wanted it, if the act that produced it was one of love. The thought of a baby being created against her will—by force—seemed so unjust as to be impossible.

Lydia hadn't felt right for weeks, but she put her lethargy down to the trauma she'd been through, plus a cold that she picked up along the way. She'd spent a few days recovering in her room, telling any girls who knocked to check on her that she wasn't feeling well. When she emerged, it was only for short excursions: required classes, a visit to the library to research a paper, dinner in the cafeteria. Her greatest fear was running into Victor in a hallway or lobby. She kept her forays outside the dorm as brief as possible, moving through the campus like a fugitive, with her head down and her eyes on the ground.

Dutch was the one who inadvertently steered Lydia toward the truth. Lydia had rushed to the bathroom one morning shortly after waking up, her stomach twisting with nausea. Bending over the toilet, she produced no more than dry heaves and a lingering bitter taste in her mouth. *Not fair*, she thought to herself. On top of everything else, now she had stomach flu.

Emerging from the bathroom, she almost

bumped into Dutch, who was coming down the hall in her bathrobe. Dutch looked her over and frowned.

"What's wrong?" she asked.

"I might have the flu," Lydia said. "I don't feel good."

While Dutch was still perfectly civil—as she was to everyone—she was no longer Lydia's protector and booster. It had been months since they'd had a conversation that was anything more than an exchange of pleasantries.

But that morning, Dutch stopped and put a hand gently on Lydia's forehead, her face wrinkling with concern.

"You do feel a little warm," Dutch said. "Do you want me to bring you breakfast?"

Lydia shook her head forcefully. "No, I don't think I could keep it down."

"Okay," Dutch said. "Should I tell Matron?" The women's dormitory supervisor, Mrs. Edith St. Clair, was a fussy, proper Englishwoman who'd originally come to New York as a nanny for a wealthy family. Now, she was den mother to two hundred female students, whom she ruled with a combination of firmness and maternal warmth. Her insistence on treating the women in her care as overgrown toddlers made her somewhat resented, but she was the first person anyone turned to in a crisis.

"No, not yet," Lydia said. "I'll see how I feel later."

"Try to rest, then," Dutch suggested. "I'll pick up some ginger tea for you at lunchtime. It's very good for an upset stomach— my mother started drinking it when she was pregnant, and she always gave it to us when we felt sick."

The word practically shouted out at her: *pregnant*. Suddenly, all the pieces of the puzzle slammed into place in Lydia's mind. The nausea, the missed period. She thanked Dutch, then hurried back to her room, her head spinning.

Pregnant. The idea of a baby growing inside her made Lydia feel sick all over again. She collapsed on the side of the bed, clutching her wastepaper basket in her hands, but the nausea eventually passed.

She couldn't possibly have a baby. Not now. She was due to graduate next year. The future stretched out before her, full of possibilities. She made a quick calculation: the party had been in March, so nine months from then would be December. Halfway through her senior year. She'd have to drop out, leave school, go back to Knox Junction…

The thought of home was what finally brought tears. A letter from Henry sat on her desk, one she'd read countless times, as she did all his letters, trying to tease out some hidden meaning. Even when she felt increasingly frustrated with his straightforward, all-too-predictable prose, there was something comforting about his writing. His letters always began with an update on his classes, followed by the latest news from Knox Junction. He'd ask a perfunctory question about how school was going for her, then end with the sort of sentiment high school students scrawled in friends' yearbooks: "I wish you the very best with everything," or "I hope college is everything you hoped it would be." He would add one line about missing her, as if that filled his quota.

For Henry, it seemed, nothing had changed between them. He even occasionally made offhand references to their plans together:

I finally told my father that I wasn't going to come back to the farm. You can imagine how that went over. We always agreed farming wasn't what we saw in our future, right?

Or, in this latest letter:

Are you planning to work at that store again this summer? Sounds like good money. New York must be awful expensive, but I'd still like to see it someday.

Was he asking if he could visit? He'd never so much as hinted at it before. It was understood that money was tight, and whatever they earned must go toward tuition, books and other necessities. Cross-country travel was a luxury. Lydia remembered the last time she'd been home, over Christmas, when she'd managed to stay busy to avoid seeing Henry more than a few times. They'd fallen into their usual rhythm of conversation, but Lydia no longer felt drawn to him physically. She'd been distracted by the idea of Victor DiStefano then, and Henry's laconic ease had been no match for Victor's commanding presence. Even as she talked to Henry and held hands with him in the front seat of his truck, she wondered how he could ever have had such a hold on her. He felt like a brother rather than a lover, whereas Victor made her long for more....

Lydia grew hot with shame. She realized that there was only one person she could confide in, one person worldly enough to take this news in stride and sophisticated enough to know what to do. One person who would want to keep this secret as much as she did.

Victor.

It was Wednesday, the day the Masterpiece Club met, and Lydia knew he'd be in his office before the meeting. Her nausea had subsided by the afternoon, and she took time to apply lipstick and powder before leaving her room. Despite her determination to be confident and self-sufficient, her legs were trembling as she reached his office door. She tapped lightly on the glass, then heard him bark, "Who is it?"

Instead of answering, she pulled open the door. Victor was leaning back in his chair, his feet propped on his desk. At the sight of Lydia, he put his feet down and sat up straight, waiting for her to make the first move.

"Are you free?" she asked.

He glanced quickly around her to see if there was anyone nearby. Then he nodded and gestured toward the worn-out armchair across from his desk. Lydia stepped into the room, but remained standing. Even in this classroom building, with students passing through the hallway, she was afraid to be alone with him. She half closed the office door behind her, but left an opening wide enough for a quick exit.

Victor watched her, his expression doubtful. Small talk didn't seem to be an option. Lydia wanted to get the conversation over with as fast as possible.

"I'm pregnant," she said.

Victor's jaw dropped open, and he sighed.

"And what do you want me to do about it?" he asked. His eyes flashed with irritation.

Lydia had no answer.

"You're sure it's mine?"

Lydia took a deep breath to stifle the scream that threatened to erupt. "Yes," she said coldly. "Positive."

"I hope your father's not insisting we get married," he said.

Lydia shook her head. Although a hastily arranged wedding was the way most unintended pregnancies were handled, she decided she'd weather any public humiliation rather than be married to this man.

"Good," Victor said. "Then you'll take care of it."

She knew what he was implying. She'd heard her parents whispering about patients who had tried to end unwanted pregnancies. One of them had died. She remembered her father referring to the doctor who had done it as a butcher. She didn't have any details, but she'd been left with the understanding that reputable doctors didn't perform this sort of operation.

"I—I don't know where to go," Lydia said.

Victor shrugged. "That's women's business, isn't it? I have no idea."

Lydia stood rooted in place. She wanted to leave, but she hadn't gotten what she needed. She still felt as lost as she had when she first walked in.

"Look—all I know is, you can't wait forever," Victor said. "The further along you are, the tougher it gets." He suddenly seemed worried. "You haven't told anyone, have you? About me?"

"No."

"Thank God for that, at least. I need this job, Lydia. Listen—I could probably scrounge up fifty dollars or so. That should help cover it. Provided you keep quiet."

"Don't worry," she said. "I don't want anyone to know."

He opened a desk drawer and began fumbling among the papers inside. He pulled out a few crumpled dollar bills, tossed them on the top of the desk, then checked another drawer. Lydia looked at the money, creased and worn. She turned and walked out without a word.

All the way back to the dormitory, she admonished herself for not waiting. She desperately needed the money, and he certainly owed her some assistance. But the reality of standing there, waiting for him to dole out the money dollar by dollar, was too humiliating to bear. Being in the same cramped space with him had made her feel ill.

It had been naive to think he would help, in any case. She was on her own. No one to confide in, no one to share the burden. She walked through the lobby of the dormitory, choking back tears. Around her, girls were giggling and gossiping, anticipating the imminent end of the school year, while Lydia's whole future was darkening before her eyes. She would have to quit her summer job, leave school, find a place to live where no one knew her. And what would happen to the baby?

The lobby began to blur as the tears filled her eyes. Then a distinctive voice, with a clipped British accent, caught her attention.

"Everything ship-shape, my dear?" Mrs. St. Clair's face appeared in front of her, her eyes narrow with concern behind thick glasses.

"It's nothing." Lydia tried to remain calm, but her voice quavered with stifled sobs.

"Nonsense," Mrs. St. Clair retorted. "Come to my office."

She steered Lydia to the room off the lobby from where she observed the dormitory's everyday ebb and flow. Mrs. St. Clair walked over and lowered the shades so they could talk privately. Lydia had never been called in for a personal meeting before. The sight of Mrs. St. Clair's pulled shade usually meant a girl was in trouble for sneaking out after curfew or—the very worst offense—being discovered with a male student in her room.

"Now then," Mrs. St. Clair said. "What's the trouble?"

Faced with such no-nonsense sympathy, Lydia's tears broke free. This prim, dignified woman was the last person she'd thought she would ever confide in, but at that moment she seemed like the only person who cared. Someone who'd greet even the most shocking scandal with nothing more than a click of the tongue and a cup of tea.

With barely a pause for breath, Lydia outlined the basic story. The only detail she refused to share was the name of the baby's father, and Mrs. St. Clair didn't push. Instead, she listened to Lydia's confession with an impassive expression, nodding every now and then to encourage her to continue.

"I'm two months along," Lydia finally concluded.

Mrs. St. Clair nodded and started writing on a piece of paper.

"We have a few decisions to make, then," she began. She smiled kindly at Lydia's miserable face. "My dear, do you think you're the only girl to come in with a story like this? I've been here almost twenty years—you're far from the first. In the early days, I tried to encourage the young men to take responsibility, but it rarely worked out. Now, you said you did talk to him—the father?"

Lydia nodded.

"And he made no offer of marriage?"

"No. Just money. But—I couldn't take it."

Mrs. St. Clair tapped her pen on the desk. "Very well. We have two choices. There are medical solutions to this kind of problem, as you may have heard. Do you need further information?"

"My father's a doctor," Lydia said. "I've heard about the, uh…the medical option. But I couldn't go through with it."

"The other possibility is that you have the baby and give it up for adoption. I find it the very best thing to do—a way to help a deserving couple who're unable to have children of their own. Now, I'm not familiar with facilities in Chicago—that's where you're from, am I correct?—but I'm sure if we speak with your mother…"

Lydia shook her head quickly. "I can't tell my parents."

"I know the prospect is daunting, but I often find that parents rise to the occasion…."

Lydia tried to imagine the scene—Mother on the verge of hysteria, Father pouring yet another drink. The look on Mother's face when she realized that her eldest daughter, the one on whom she pinned all her hopes, had shamed them. Her family was precarious enough as it was. She couldn't disappoint them like this.

"I can't go to Chicago," Lydia said. "Is there somewhere else?"

"Of course. I have personally escorted a few young women to a charming home in up-state New York. Very peaceful and tranquil. They do a lovely job with the girls. Extremely discreet. There are a number of other places, as well—a few here in New York City. I've even had a few girls go as far as Europe."

Lydia's head was spinning. What would she tell her parents if she went off to upstate New York? Could she somehow convince them she was still in school? Could her mail be forwarded without their knowing?

"Where in Europe?" she asked.

"I have a dear friend in Paris," Mrs. St. Clair said. "Mrs. Weatherly. A former nanny, like myself. Ran off with a French tutor— quite a scandal, and of course it didn't end well. She runs a pension, a very respectable place, but she's been known to help a girl in trouble from time to time. We tell the parents it's a study-abroad program, if the girl wishes."

Paris. Lydia had had the stereotypical

dreams of any aspiring artist—fantasies of herself sketching Notre Dame Cathedral by sunset. Wandering the halls of the Louvre for inspiration. This wasn't the way she'd pictured her first visit, but it might be more bearable than months by herself in upstate New York. And a study-abroad program would be the perfect cover story. There was only one problem.

"I think that's what I'd like to do," Lydia said. "But, you see, the money…um, how much might it cost?"

"That can be taken care of," Mrs. St. Clair said. "The school does offer scholarships for deserving students to study abroad, you know. A word to the right person, and I'm sure we can work something out."

Lydia managed to summon a weak smile. For the first time in days, the low-level nausea that had accompanied her almost constantly faded.

"I don't know what to say. I'm so grateful…"

"My dear, your face is all the thanks I need," said Mrs. St. Clair. "I'm truly sorry this had to happen to you. You haven't had the easiest time here. Let me get things under way, make some inquiries. If you're already a couple of months along, I assume you'll want to get started rather quickly, before it becomes more obvious." She looked pointedly at Lydia's stomach.

"Yes," Lydia agreed. "As quickly as possible."

"I'll see what I can do," Mrs. St. Clair promised. "In the meantime, I would suggest writing to your parents and telling them you're being considered as a last-minute addition to our study-abroad program. Perhaps you can tell them another student has had to cancel unexpectedly, and you've been offered her place. I will write to them, as well."

"Thank you." Mrs. St. Clair stood up, and Lydia did, too. They looked at each other for a moment, then Lydia reached toward Mrs. St. Clair and hugged her. The matron stiffened at the unexpected contact, then relaxed. She gently patted Lydia on the back.

"Rest up, my dear," she said. "It will all be fine in the end."

Lydia walked up the stairs to her room, giddy with relief. She would escape for a few months, and her parents would never know. No one would. She'd have the baby, then she could return for her final semester of school as if nothing had ever happened.

When she got to her room, she found a telegram slipped underneath her door. She grabbed the paper and ripped it open hurriedly; telegrams could only mean bad news. She scanned the words in shock:

Coming to New York. Long story. Arrive Empire Express, Penn Station, May 20, 5pm. Will you show me the Big Apple? Henry.

May twentieth. Henry would be there in three days.

Lydia sat in Pennsylvania Station's waiting room, her hands curled around a copy of *Life* magazine. The Empire Express was supposed to pull in an hour ago, but periodic announcements told her that the train was "temporarily" delayed. Her nerves were about to shatter.

"Empire Express! Now arriving on Track Ten!"

Lydia shot up from the wooden bench and craned her neck to see around the grand hall. A sign behind her read Tracks 10-15. She froze with indecision, unsure whether to walk out to the track or remain where she was. As she was trying to make up her mind, a stream of people began filing out through the doorway. The figures passed in a faceless mass, until suddenly there he was. Henry, his broad shoulders crammed into a too-tight jacket, his head turning back and forth to take in the massive scale of the station, hands clutching a battered suitcase that seemed to be held together with tape. Looking every inch the dumbstruck out-of-towner.

"Henry!"

His face lit up when he saw her, and his pace quickened. Then they were together, his arms enveloping her. Lost in his firm grip, she rested her head on his chest for a moment. She'd forgotten how comfortably she fit there.

"Hello!"

Lydia jerked her head upward to see a face peering at her from behind Henry. Embarrassed, she pulled herself away and put a hand up to fix her hair.

"Lydia, this is my friend Lou," Henry said. "Louis Rutherford. I told you about him, I think."

Lydia nodded, although she couldn't remember ever hearing the name; Henry's various fraternity brothers blended together in her mind. Lou gave her a wide grin. He had large white teeth that threatened to burst out of his mouth. The kind of face her mother would describe as homely, but with a cheerfulness that made him appear more handsome than he was.

"My brother works here," Lou said, reaching out to shake Lydia's hand. "My mother and I had a trip all planned to visit him as soon as school finished, and then my father came down with shingles, which is awfully painful, and she thought she'd better stay with him, but we'd already paid for the train berth, and then I remembered Henry had a girl out in New York, so I asked him if he'd like to come along." Lou took a deep breath and smiled again, apparently proud of his skill in summarizing the story.

"Though it's only a loan," Henry said. "I'm going to pay you back for the train fare."

Lou slapped Henry on the shoulder. "No hurry." He turned to Lydia. "My brother's expecting us at his apartment, if you want to join us for dinner."

Henry glanced at Lydia. "Gee, thanks, but I think we'll…"

"I get it," Lou said. "You two go catch up. You want me to take your suitcase, Henry, since I'm catching a cab?"

"Thanks." Henry said, handing it over. "I'll see you at your brother's later." After confirming that Henry knew the address, Lou waved and headed out.

"I hope that's all right," Henry said. "Lou is a great guy, but kinda talkative."

Lydia smiled. "I can only imagine what it was like riding across the country with him. Are you hungry?"

"Uh-huh. But dinner's on me."

"Oh, you don't have to…"

"I want to," he insisted. Lydia wondered if Henry had any idea what New York restaurants cost. She refused to humiliate him by chipping in for dinner, so she'd have to choose the place carefully to prevent him from spending all his money his first night in town.

"Have you ever been to an Automat?" she asked. "There's one in Times Square that's very popular. We could walk—it's not far."

Henry seemed happy to follow her lead.

They walked out of the station, almost shoulder-to-shoulder in order to stay together in the swarm of early-evening commuters. It was jarring to watch Henry in this setting—a man who seemed most at home in an open field, seen against a background of blue sky and endless grassy vistas. Here, he looked smaller, lost among all the people, his face gazing up toward the skyscrapers in wonder. Lydia had never felt protective of him before.

At the Automat, she showed him how to drop coins in a slot and then open the glass door to pull out each dish. She told him she wasn't very hungry, and it was true—her appetite was still unpredictable—so she chose only soup and tea. Henry got pot roast, green beans, mashed potatoes and a roll.

Small talk filled the time as they ate. Henry told Lydia about Lou and the characters they'd encountered on the train. Lydia talked about her classes and a few of the paintings she'd been working on. Always hovering in the back of her mind was the knowledge that she'd have to tell him she was leaving. Mrs. St. Clair had stopped by Lydia's room in the morning to tell her she'd arranged scholarship money to cover her travel expenses. She would be sailing for Europe even sooner than expected. But she didn't know how to bring up the subject. Not yet.

"Do you think you'll be coming home for the dedication?" Henry asked.

Lydia snapped back to attention. "What? Sorry?"

"The dedication. The war memorial. It's going to be the Fourth of July weekend. Since your mother had such a big hand in it...."

Lydia vaguely remembered a mention in one of Mother's letters about a statue commemorating local men who'd died in the war. She'd assumed it was another of her projects that generated grandiose talk but minimal results.

"I didn't know it was so close to being finished," Lydia said.

"Oh, yeah. No surprise, really, seeing how hard your mother's been working. Ma said she's so dedicated, you'd think she lost someone herself. Then your mother told her something really nice—about how Tim was everyone's son in a way."

"Wait." Lydia was mystified. "My mother talked to your mother?" Through all their years of dating, Lydia's parents and Henry's had never officially met. Henry's mother was notorious in town for never leaving the house.

"Didn't you hear?" Henry asked. "When your mother started raising money for the memorial, she wanted to get all the families involved. Everyone in the county who'd lost someone. From what Pop told me, your mother marched right up to the house and insisted on seeing Ma. She wouldn't take no for an answer. They ended up talking for hours. Your mother even got Ma to come with her to look at plans for the statue." Henry glanced down at his plate, embarrassed. "You know how my mother is. We could hardly get her to leave her room after Tim died. But your mother's very convincing."

"I know." Lydia still couldn't picture the two women together. Bonding over heartbreak.

"The memorial isn't even the biggest news," Henry went on. "These days, all people are talking about is the hospital."

"Hospital?"

Henry laughed. "Don't your parents tell you anything? They're building a new Veteran's Hospital in Fentonville. We're all excited. It was either there or Peoria, and it turns out Dixworth—you know, the senator?—his nephew was killed at Normandy, and his name's going on the memorial in town. His family met your parents, and I guess your father convinced Senator Dixworth that Fentonville would be the best place for the hospital. The senator pulled some strings in Washington, and now everyone's saying your father's sure to be appointed chairman or head doctor or whatever the top guy is called."

Henry peered at Lydia, amused. "You didn't hear about any of this?"

Lydia shrugged. "I guess Mother wrote about the memorial a bit, but the hospital—no, I didn't know about that." Henry, it seemed, knew far more about her family than she did. When had that happened?

Henry scraped up the last of his mashed potatoes and pushed the plate aside. Lydia tried to stifle a yawn, but he noticed. She'd been so tired lately—yet another unwanted consequence of pregnancy.

"I'm sorry if I'm keeping you up," Henry told her. "I know you've got final exams and that kind of thing."

"No, no," Lydia said. "I just got up too early today." They sat there, surrounded by the hum of voices and the clatter of dishes. Lydia was too exhausted to move, let alone take the conversation to its next, unbearable stage.

Henry slid one hand across the table until his fingers brushed hers. "I…I don't know how to say this exactly, but I did save up some money. I was thinking…well, if you want, I could get a room in a hotel one night." He avoided looking at her, keeping his eyes focused at the table.

Lydia stiffened, and Henry pulled his hand back.

"I'm sorry," he apologized. "Bad idea. I didn't mean to make you think, you know, that I meant anything by it." He still wouldn't meet her gaze.

"Henry." Lydia waited until he looked up. His pained expression, his obvious embarrassment, made her long to shatter the awkwardness. Break through all the insinuations and evasions and talk honestly with each other, the way they used to.

"Do you love me?" she asked. If he loved her, maybe that would be enough to make up for what she'd done. Enough to forgive her anything.

Henry laughed. "What a silly question! Of course."

He smiled at her, his face settling into a fond smile. This, then, was all he would ever be capable of—thinking of love as something simple and easy. Never understanding that it could have a dark side, too. She knew then that she couldn't tell him. Henry was too good, his view of the world too uncomplicated, ever to understand. How would she be able to come back from Europe, after everything she'd endured and pick up where they'd left off? Even if Henry never found out, she'd always hate herself. And if she told him the truth, her betrayal would destroy him, and he would hate her, too. If she really loved him, she would cut all ties now. He would be hurt, but his recovery would be relatively swift. If she told him what she'd done, he might never get over it.

"Henry, I won't be coming home for the Fourth of July," she said. "The thing is…I'm going abroad. To Paris."

Henry looked at her, puzzled.

She began the speech she'd rehearsed in her room earlier that day. "It's a study-abroad program for art students. There was a last-minute cancellation, and this spot opened up—with a full scholarship. So, you see, I couldn't pass it up. It's the chance of a lifetime."

"Sounds like it." Henry didn't seem convinced.

"It looks like I'll be leaving rather soon, in a few weeks, probably. And then I'll be there for the school year, taking classes…"

"You'll be gone a whole year?" Henry asked.

"Um, maybe," Lydia said. "Possibly." How could she tell him that she didn't know, that it all depended on when the baby arrived and how she felt afterward? That her entire future was a hazy blur?

"Huh." Henry tapped his fork on the table. He didn't appear angry, or disappointed. Just surprised.

"So, this chance that suddenly came up," he said. "Does it have anything to do with me?"

She could have lied. Could have soothed him with comforting words. But Lydia was tired of lying. There was so much she couldn't tell Henry that she was desperate to finally tell him part of the truth.

"Be honest, Henry," she said. "It's not

the same between us anymore, is it? We've changed."

Henry said nothing.

"We love each other," Lydia continued, "but it's all routine. Like brother and sister. You know what I mean, don't you?"

Henry sighed. "Yeah. That's why I thought of the hotel."

How could she tell him that she was terrified of doing anything physical—even if she'd had the energy—because it might hurt the baby? And she was afraid to hug him, in case he felt a bump in her belly.

"I guess I don't understand what you want me to say," Henry stated.

Exhaustion washed over Lydia. She felt like dropping her head on the table and drifting off to sleep, escaping this conversation that twisted and turned with no answer in sight.

"You're tired." Henry stood up. "Let me take you home."

They rode in a taxi in silence to Lydia's dorm, staring out the windows on opposite sides of the car. Lydia's mind raced, trying to find words that would wrap up the situation the way she wanted, with no hurt feelings and a clear resolution. But there was nothing to say.

She fumbled in her purse for money when they arrived, but Henry brushed her off and paid the fare, no doubt using some of the money he'd saved for the hotel.

She waited for him in the doorway. Male visitors were strictly off-limits in the lobby in the evenings.

"So, how long are you in town?" Lydia asked.

"Five days," Henry replied.

An awkward pause dragged on. "You said something about me showing you around," Lydia said.

"Oh, don't worry about that," Henry said. "I know you're busy, getting ready for your trip."

Lydia felt a rising panic. This couldn't be it. She'd thought she would have a few more days to think over what to say, another chance to make him understand.

"Good luck with your trip," Henry said. "Do you want me to write?"

"I'm not sure," she said. "I mean, I don't even have my address yet."

"Right."

"But I could see you again, before you leave," she offered. "Maybe Friday, we could have dinner, see a movie...."

Henry shook his head. "We can't keep doing this, Lydia," he said sadly. "I don't know what you want from me."

I want you to ask what's wrong, she pleaded with her eyes, *because if you ask me directly, I won't be able to lie to you. I want you to say it doesn't matter, that you love me no matter what I've done.*

She swallowed the lump in her throat. "I don't know, either."

"I hope you find whatever it is you're looking for," he said. He started to lean over as if to kiss her, but stopped, one hand clumsily hitting her arm. Then he walked quickly down the block, away from her, without turning back.

Lydia's ship sailed two weeks later, at the beginning of June. She stood on deck as the ship prepared to leave, watching groups of people on shore waving and calling out to passengers around her. The New York skyline sparkled in the morning sunlight, but Lydia kept her attention on the crowd, checking every face for one she recognized. She'd not seen Henry since the night they'd said goodbye, and he had long since left town. He didn't even know which day she was leaving or on which boat.

But somehow, she couldn't help scanning the dozens of people standing there, hoping she'd see him. She could picture it as though it were a film. She'd be leaning over the deck rail, wiping away a tear. The final boarding announcement would blare over the loudspeakers, and then, suddenly, Henry would be pushing his way through the crowd, clutching a bouquet of roses or a bottle of champagne. Their eyes would meet across the open space. They would call out to each other, and Henry would dash up the gangplank, hopping on board moments before the boat pulled away. They would rush toward each other, all fights forgiven and forgotten as they kissed passionately.

That was how it would work in the movies. But this was real life. And in real life, Lydia was setting off for Europe alone and terrified.

Chapter 11

Cassie

The e-mail from Cooper was stunningly direct.
Hear you've got an offer in San Francisco.
Am I the last to know? Is the wedding still
on? Please advise.

Cassie checked when it had been sent. Friday morning. Twenty-four hours ago. She couldn't remember the last time she'd waited more than a few hours to check her e-mail. Cooper would see her failure to respond as an indication of a serious problem. And by now he was unreachable, on his way to the airport or already on the plane back home.

He'd never addressed her so coldly before, in person or in writing. One thing she could count on with Cooper was that he'd wait to hear the whole story before drawing a conclusion. He didn't let feelings get in the way of logic. It was what made him such a good lawyer, if not the most romantic boyfriend.

Cassie had no doubt that he was furious. But explaining to Cooper what had happened would mean making sense of things she didn't understand herself. How could she tell him that she still didn't know what to do? A night's sleep hadn't given her the perspective she'd hoped for. Her grandfather's words echoed through her mind: *Don't make the same mistake I did.*

Cassie considered meeting Cooper at the airport. She could make everything up to him by being there in person, showing him she still cared. But would he be excited—or embarrassed? Most likely the latter. Cooper was traveling with other lawyers from the firm and he'd probably be mortified if she showed up. He'd never been one for public displays of affection. Cassie wondered if they would continue to find their way home from the airport after they were married. Wasn't that what husbands and wives did, picked each other up at the airport, despite horrendous traffic and overpriced parking?

Cassie read the e-mail again. She'd been ambivalent about the wedding for months, using any excuse to put off the items on her to do list. But her panicked reaction to Cooper's message brought her feelings into sharp focus. He was giving her an out. She could call the whole thing off and walk away. But she didn't want to.

Losing Cooper would mean more than losing a fiancé. It would mean losing her best friend, the person who'd helped her transform herself from a self-conscious, studious girl to a confident, professional woman by always believing in her. The one person—besides her grandparents—who wanted the best for her. The person who was planning their wedding because he was committed to their future together, while she treated their relationship more as a business partnership than a bond of love. She'd blamed Cooper's unromantic nature for her own inability to show emotion. But she'd never told him she wanted more.

Hadn't even known she longed for more, until she read her grandmother's letter.

Scared into action, Cassie decided to make things up to Cooper by being productive before he got back. She needed to show him she was happy about getting married. She reached for the folder she'd designated for the wedding, which was pathetically short of information. She scanned through her to-do list, which Cooper had printed months ago. Invitations were at the top of the page.

Fine. She turned on her computer and began checking out stationery websites, periodically requesting samples. As she made notes, she realized she couldn't list approximate prices because she'd no idea how many invitations they needed. She and Cooper had agreed they didn't want a big wedding, but that could mean anywhere from twenty to a hundred and fifty people.

She searched her tote bag and came up with the invitation list she'd written on hotel stationery in New York. She mentally tallied up the names, until she arrived at the last one. Eve. She remembered the awkward apology Eve had sent after rehab. Wondered if Eve had really been capable of turning her life around.

Cassie pulled out her address book and stared at the address she'd written down years before. Could Eve possibly still be living there?

She picked up the phone and called the operator.

"I'd like to get a number for Arlington Heights, Illinois," she said. "Eve Young."

After a moment, the operator said, "Sorry, no listing for that name. Would you like me to extend the search to surrounding suburbs?"

"Yes, please."

"Okay, then… Well, there are a few E. Youngs around…ah, here's an Eve Young in Northbrook at 1254 Ash Lane."

Cassie copied down the address.

"Would you like me to connect you?" the operator asked.

"Yes—no, give me the number…" Cassie added, but it was too late. The phone was already ringing. Cassie's first impulse was to hang up. But if she could handle calling Victor DiStefano out of the blue, she should be able to deal with her own grandmother.

"Hello?" an unfamiliar voice asked cheerily. Cassie wondered if she had the wrong number.

"Um, this is Cassie. Is this—Eve?"

A sharp intake of breath, then the woman exclaimed, "Cassie!" Cassie heard a trace of the woman she'd known, a hint of the roughness that used to degenerate into harsh coughs.

"I know this is unexpected..." Cassie began.

"I'm so happy you called," Eve said. "I can't even tell you. Wow. Whatcha been up to, sweetie?"

Cassie gave her highlights—law school, the high-powered job, the upcoming wedding.

"I hope he deserves you," Eve said.

"Oh, yes," Cassie said. She'd started to ask herself if the problem might be the other way round. What if she didn't deserve Cooper?

"Listen," Eve said. "I don't suppose you're free, this being Saturday night and all, but would you like to come out for dinner?"

Cassie's mind raced. Cooper would be coming home tonight. She'd been planning to make dinner for him, creating the illusion of a happy home. But the lure of finding out more about Eve, who sounded so happy, so different, was too strong to resist.

"Sure," Cassie said. "I'd love to."

Cassie spent the rest of the day in a frenzy of activity, printing out pages from the invitation sites she'd liked best, typing up a list of guests, and wiping away the layer of dust that had settled on every surface of the apartment. Shortly before she left for Eve's, she rushed to a gourmet market around the corner and bought a roast chicken dinner for Cooper, then wrote a quick note and left it on the kitchen counter:

I got a last-minute dinner offer from my grandma Eve, the one I haven't talked to in years. Couldn't resist. Sorry I'm not here to welcome you back, but I won't be late. Dinner's in the fridge. Can't pretend it's home-cooked, but it smells fantastic. Please try to stay awake until I get back. We have so much to talk about.

Cassie paused, then wrote one final line.

I love you.

But she wondered if it would make any difference.

Eve lived in a compact town house in one of the suburb's newer developments. The paint on all the window trim was pristine, as yet undamaged by Chicago's harsh winds and unpredictable temperature shifts. Neat rows of miniature rosebushes lined the front walkway. A painted tile hanging above the doorbell announced, Good Company Always Welcome.

Cassie and her grandmother stared at each other after Eve opened the door. In some ways, Eve still looked the same—overprocessed white-blond hair swept up in a bouffant, deep creases around her eyes and mouth highlighted by a thick layer of beige face cream, garish gold earrings and necklace, an oversize sweater with gold appliqué leaves worn over tight leggings. The one noticeable change—and it was striking—was Eve's face. She no longer conveyed the sour suspicion with which she used to greet visitors. Instead, she looked at Cassie with a clarity she'd never shown before. As though she was seeing the world straight on, rather than through a haze of alcohol and resentment.

Clearly, she was waiting for Cassie to make the first move. Cassie stepped into the foyer and stretched out her arms. The two women came together in a hug, and Cassie could feel Eve's shoulders trembling as she began to cry.

"Oh, Eve, please," Cassie said, trying to comfort her.

Eve stepped away with a quick laugh, wiping her face with her sleeve.

"Pathetic, huh? I'm weepier now than when I was a drunk. Come in, come in. I'll give you the tour."

As they walked through the town house, Cassie marveled at the changes in Eve's lifestyle. She still smoked—"I couldn't quit everything!" she joked—but otherwise this tidy home was worlds apart from the trailer Cassie remembered with such disgust. One of the two bedrooms had been made into an office, and Cassie saw textbooks piled on the desk, next to an orange iMac computer.

"Wondering how I can afford all this, huh?" Eve asked. Cassie had to smile. Eve had never bothered with politeness; she'd always been refreshingly direct. That hadn't changed.

"The lottery!" Eve announced.

"You're kidding."

"Nope. It was a few months after I got cleaned up. I'd been out of the rehab place for a while, and it was getting awful tempting to take a drink now and then. No job, living in a crappy apartment away from everyone

I knew.... So, anyway, I bought this ticket. Been buying them for years, and I never got more than a few bucks out of it. But this time, I hit the jackpot. Not the ten-million-dollar kind—but good enough. Somewhere 'round eight hundred grand. And then the government came in and took almost half of it. But I had enough to buy this place and start taking some classes."

"Yeah, I saw the books on your desk upstairs."

"I'm going to volunteer at this counseling center, the place that helped me get sober," Eve said. "Can you believe it? Me, some kind of role model? I figure, if I can clean up my act, anyone can. Thought I might have something to offer. Anyway, the lottery win taught me a big lesson. I never won when I was getting blotto all the time, but I won when I was sober. It was a sign."

She looked at Cassie, her eyes tearing up.

"And now you've come back. Like I said—good things started happening."

It wasn't until the dinner plates had been cleared and they were sitting in the living room with coffee that Cassie mentioned her parents. She noticed a framed photo sitting on a side table that showed her mother and father standing together, hand in hand; Shelly was wearing a white halter-top dress and Paul had on a cream-colored suit, with wide lapels and flared pants. Cassie picked it up and looked at it more closely. Her mother stared slightly to the left of the camera, as if she'd been distracted, her mouth curved in a gentle smile. Her father was smiling, too, his head leaning down against Shelly's. Cassie saw the resemblance to Victor DiStefano that had so stunned her in the yearbook photo. But here, in this unexpectedly happy face, she also recognized a trace of Lydia in the way Paul's smile made his eyes crinkle with delight.

"It's from their wedding," Eve said.

Cassie knew her parents had gotten married in Las Vegas on a whim, during a cross-country driving trip, but she'd never seen a picture from their wedding day.

"Where did you get this?" Cassie asked.

"I found it in the apartment when I was cleaning out your mother's things, after..." Eve's voice drifted off.

"It's funny," Cassie said, setting the picture carefully on the table. "Everyone I know plans these huge weddings, with ten bridesmaids and seating charts and elaborate meals. And yet I had no idea about my own parents' wedding."

"That was Shelly's way," Eve said. "Making all her decisions at the last minute. She loved to be spontaneous. I didn't realize they were thinking about marriage until they came back here and she showed me the ring."

"They should've put a little more thought into it, huh?"

"Why?"

"Oh, come on," Cassie said. "You don't have to worry about hurting my feelings. I know they never should have gotten married."

"Why in the world would you say that?" Eve asked in surprise.

"Just—well, I remember them fighting all the time."

"They were no better or worse than other couples," Eve said. "They fought, then they made up. If you ask me, the fights were part of the attraction from the beginning. Neither of them was perfect."

"My father certainly wasn't," Cassie said.

"Neither was Shelly," Eve insisted. "Always too dreamy. Couldn't decide what to do from one day to the next, let alone keep a job. Couldn't even keep a boyfriend before Paul came along."

Cassie had never considered that her mother might bear some responsibility for the family's problems. In her memories, her father was always the villain.

"Paul was trying to find his way, too," Eve continued. "He had a quick temper, that's for sure, but it faded just as quickly. I never worried about him lifting a finger to hurt Shelly—or you. He'd been through a difficult time with his parents—and who wouldn't, being raised by two people as perfect as Lydia and Henry? How could anyone live up to that example?"

Cassie braced herself for the insults she'd spent her childhood deflecting. But instead, Eve sighed.

"I'm sorry," she said wearily. "I'm trying to stop bad-mouthing people behind their backs. I'm sure Lydia did her best with Paul. That's what was so cruel about what happened—it looked like things were finally working out for him. He was so optimistic about the future that night."

"You mean the night they died?"

Eve nodded. "They came over to my trailer

that evening. You knew that, right? Brought you along for supper. We ate, and then you and Shelly lay down on the floor, playing with a few of her old dolls I kept around. Paul and I sat at the table, having a beer or two, like we always did. And I'll never forget—he was like a new person. Said he'd had it all out with his mother, and he'd made his peace with her."

"How?" Cassie asked.

"I don't know," Eve said. "I guessed he'd stood up to Lydia for once, and she'd figured out she had to treat him like a man from then on, not a little boy she could order around. Paul was smiling, and talking about the new painting business he was going to start up. He'd been doing all sorts of construction jobs, but he'd decided he wanted to be his own boss. And he had a real eye for color— got that from Lydia, I guess. Shelly was so excited about it, even said she wanted to take accounting classes so she could help out with the money. Shelly! Accounting! I can't tell you what a shock that was."

"But…" Cassie paused, unsure how to phrase the next question. "He was drinking a lot, wasn't he?"

Eve nodded. "I never should've let them

leave. It's the greatest regret of my life. I had no idea how many beers I'd drunk, let alone Paul. We were celebrating. We were happy. When they left—oh, Cassie, I felt better than I had in a long time."

Cassie sat in silence for a few seconds, processing this new information. "I guess I always thought they were…I don't know, drowning their sorrows."

"Oh, no," Eve said. "We were celebrating a new beginning. That's the only thing that's kept me halfway sane all these years. Knowing their last night was happy."

As Cassie drove home, she thought over Eve's words. Her parents were no worse off than any other couple. They were happy. She scanned her repertoire of childhood memories. Of all the days and nights she'd spent with her parents, very few moments remained, mostly scenes in which her mother was happy and her father angry. But what if she only recalled those times because they were extraordinary? What if the many normal days that came in between had faded precisely because they *were* routine?

And then she remembered. She'd turned off

the highway at her usual exit, driving along the residential street that led to her condo, when she had to swerve suddenly to avoid a cyclist who was almost invisible on the darkened road. Idiot, she thought. And no helmet, of course. Helmet or sidewalk—didn't he know the rule?

Helmet or sidewalk. It was a phrase ingrained in her memory, but she hadn't thought of it in years. A rule her father had taught her. He'd bought her a rusty pink bicycle at a garage sale and taught her to ride it in the driveway in front of their apartment building. The first time she'd tried it out, he'd fastened a helmet on her head.

"Helmet or sidewalk," he said. "If you're not wearing your helmet, you can only ride on the sidewalk."

She remembered giggling and waving to him when she'd managed to pedal halfway down the block without his help. He'd waved both hands above his head, letting out a proud whoop.

Cassie hadn't ridden a bike in years. Hadn't thought about that day in even longer. She wondered if more memories like this were buried deep in her subconscious. Memories of her father that wouldn't hurt her to revisit. She wondered if, over time, she'd be able to think of her father with love rather than apprehension.

After parking in the basement garage, Cassie pressed the elevator's Up button repeatedly, anxious to get to her apartment. For the first time in months, she was giddy at the prospect of seeing Cooper, eager to share good news. She flung the front door open and raced inside.

Cooper was sprawled on the couch in the living room, the television remote in one hand and a beer in the other, watching basketball on TV. Cassie took in his stretched-out sweatpants, his ragged college T-shirt, his matted-down hair and look of utter exhaustion. And she knew she was in love with him. He was the one person with whom she wanted to share everything, every naked emotion and self-conscious doubt.

She couldn't tell him. His disinterest was too strong. He refused to meet her eyes.

"Howdy, stranger," Cassie said, making an effort to sound casual as she plopped down on the floor next to the couch. "When did you get back?"

"About an hour ago," Cooper said, his eyes moving momentarily from the TV to her face. "Delays at Heathrow, surprise, surprise."

"Did you have dinner?"

"Yeah."

"Did you see the invitations? I left some for you to look at."

"Uh-huh. I'll check them out tomorrow."

His lassitude was unbearable. Cassie grabbed the remote from his hand and pressed his fingers against her cheek.

"Hey, Coop, about San Francisco…"

She had his attention now. He tilted his head down to face her.

"Nothing's been decided," she said. "They're making a big announcement on Monday, but I haven't officially said yes."

"So, they made you this offer with no warning?" Cooper asked.

"Yeah," Cassie said. "They snagged some big-shot partner from Lofton & Treadwell who's going to start a new office out there."

"Oh. I thought…"

"You thought what?" Cassie asked. "That I was secretly interviewing out there behind your back?"

"Yeah. Something like that."

The fact that Cooper considered her capable of such deception was staggering. She lived with him—how could she have been plotting a new life without his knowing? The answer hit her with a force that almost took her breath away. They lived together, yes, but their lives were separate. They'd both been so logical when they first started dating, agreeing never to interfere in each other's work or be consumed by coupledom. It had seemed so important that they remain strong individuals. Despite their engagement, Cassie now saw that she was still living her life as if she were single. As if Cooper's life were not intertwined with hers.

Cassie held Cooper's hand and stroked his fingers lightly. "Look, we can talk about it. It's not my decision alone. I want you to have a say."

"Huh." Cassie watched Cooper distance himself from the conversation, escaping before he could get hurt. When he was younger, he'd once told Cassie, he avoided being drawn into fights between his older brothers by going limp and silent. Now he was retreating from her.

"Cooper," Cassie pleaded.

"Geez, Cass, you talk about this being our decision, but we've barely talked in days."

"Well, we're both so busy…"

"Right," Cooper interrupted. "That's always our excuse, isn't it? Did it ever occur to you that I keep busy to fill all the time you're away?"

"What do you mean?"

"I never wanted to be a workaholic," Cooper said. "Sure, being a lawyer means putting in long hours, but I thought that the two of us—that we'd make time to be together. Just hang out and talk. But we never do."

"I want to, I do," Cassie said.

"But instead, you run off on some mystery trip without bothering to tell me. Were you scoping out places in San Francisco?"

"No, I was in New York."

Cooper sat up on the couch, removing his hand from Cassie's, and stared at her in confusion.

"So, let me get this straight," he said. "You're up for a huge promotion, and you decide to take time off to go to New York. To do what—buy shoes or something?"

"No, nothing like that," Cassie said. "It had to do with my grandmother."

Cooper stared at her in disbelief as she told him about discovering the letter and tracing Lydia's life in New York, talking to Frank Blakely and Victor DiStefano. Her conclusion that Victor was the author of the mysterious letter and her own biological grandfather. When he didn't respond, she continued, explaining how she'd reconnected with Eve and gained a new sense of peace about her parents and her past.

"All this because of a letter?" Cooper asked.

"Yes," Cassie said. "I'd never seen one like this before. It was so passionate. It's like—all this time has passed since it was written, but it still felt vital. It's the most romantic thing I've ever read."

"I didn't think you were the type to get caught up in all that hearts and flowers stuff." Cooper still seemed confused.

"I'm not," Cassie said defensively. "It's not what you're thinking—it's not like a store-bought Valentine's card. It was so honest it felt almost violent."

Cooper's eyes wandered back to the television. "Well, I guess we could learn something from that," he said.

"What do you mean?"

"Being honest with each other." Cooper reached for the remote and switched off the game. The sudden silence made Cassie nervous. As if he was about to make a grand announcement. One she wouldn't want to hear.

"I've always been honest with you," Cassie said.

"Okay, then," said Cooper. "Are you going to take the job in San Francisco?"

"I don't know. That's the truth."

"Are we going to get married?" he asked.

"Yes," Cassie said vehemently. "Yes."

Cooper sighed.

"Do you think we're going to get married?" she asked quietly.

"I don't know," Cooper said. "That's my honest answer."

Cassie's heart sank. "Well, thanks for telling me the truth, at least."

"Look, Cass, I'm exhausted and jet-lagged. I can't get into a whole discussion about this now."

"I understand."

"Mind if I go to bed?"

"No—go ahead."

Cooper stood up from the couch, stepping around Cassie, who was still seated on the floor. Cassie watched him trudge off to the bedroom, heard the sound of water running as he washed his face and brushed his teeth. And that was where the evening would usually have ended—Cooper going to bed, Cassie sitting in front of the TV with a mug of tea. Polite roommates with their own separate routines. Their own separate lives.

It wasn't enough. Most nights, Cassie wouldn't have cared. But not now, not with all the things she'd learned rushing through her head. She listened for Cooper's footsteps in the bedroom, then the groan of the mattress as he got into bed. She slipped through the bedroom door, leaving it ajar so the light from the living room illuminated a sliver of the bed. Shedding her clothes, she slid underneath the sheets, pressing her naked body against Cooper's back. She nuzzled his neck and caught a subtle hint of the cologne she'd bought for his last birthday.

He couldn't be asleep already, no matter how jet-lagged he was. But he didn't respond to her touch, just lay motionless, facing away from her. Cassie put her head down on her pillow and closed her eyes, eventually drifting off to sleep with her arm around his waist, hoping her touch would be enough to show him how much she wanted to hold on. To him. To them.

"Sorry Cooper couldn't make it," Cassie told her grandparents the next day, when she arrived for lunch. "He just got back from London and he's exhausted." Which was the truth. He'd gotten up briefly to use the bathroom early in the morning, then had gone straight back to bed, shaking his head when she'd asked if he wanted to come to her grandparents'. Cassie showered, read the Sunday paper, got dressed and left without talking to him again.

Lydia said, "Too bad," but she clearly wasn't surprised. Cooper hadn't made an appearance at one of their weekend lunches for weeks. Cassie generally blamed work—Cooper's standard excuse—but she wondered if his refusal to come today had a deeper meaning. If it was yet another indication of their separate lives.

"So, let's talk about this big job in San Francisco," Lydia urged, leading Cassie toward the dining room. "Your grandfather told me the news, but as usual, he didn't provide nearly enough details."

"I don't know the specifics," Cassie said. "I won't find out until tomorrow." This opportunity—an offer that had had her practically hyperventilating in New York—was losing its gleam. She tried to change the subject.

"Actually, it's been kind of nice not thinking about work for a few days," she said. "I can't remember the last time I took more than one day off in a row."

"And don't think I haven't been worried about you running yourself ragged," Lydia scolded. "So, Henry told me you went to New York?"

"Yeah," Cassie said, scooping up another mouthful of shepherd's pie. "Uh—I needed a little break."

"Where did you stay?"

"Midtown. Actually—" she turned toward Lydia "—not far from the Institute of Art."

"Oh?" Lydia asked. Her face revealed nothing other than mild curiosity.

"Yeah. I walked by one of the buildings."

"Decrepit as ever, no doubt," Lydia said. "Artists seem to find it a point of pride to live and work in the shabbiest places possible."

Henry and Cassie laughed.

"You didn't seem to mind it at the time," Henry said, giving Lydia a teasing glance.

"I was a lot younger then. Naive enough to think dirty meant authentic."

"Well, the school must have taught you something," Cassie said. "I've always loved those paintings in the front hallway." A few of Lydia's paintings, mounted in simple wood frames, had hung in the hall for as long as Cassie could remember. Her grandmother had told her they'd been painted in Paris, and to Cassie, they represented the strange and exotic. She used to be mesmerized by them as a child. Wild, scraggly trees in bright red and orange. An old farmhouse surrounded by fields, envisioned in unexpected shades of shocking pink and yellow. The fact that her proper grandmother was capable of such intense images had always mystified her.

Lydia nodded. "Well, when I was in France I was able to experiment. Maybe there was inspiration in the air. Once I moved back home, with the baby, I never found much time to paint. And then I started quilting and...well, painting lost its allure."

"She did some wonderful drawings in

France, too," Henry said. "You've still got that portfolio, haven't you, dear? Didn't she ever show you, Cassie?"

Lydia tsked discouragingly. "Don't bore the poor girl, Henry."

It wasn't until they'd finished dessert that Cassie convinced Lydia to pull out the portfolio Henry had mentioned. It was packed inside a flat plastic storage box under Lydia's bed, two large pieces of black cardboard tied closed with a silk ribbon.

"My masterpieces," Lydia said with a laugh, spreading the papers out across the bed.

Cassie looked at the pictures, mostly pencil sketches mixed in with some watercolors. They were all landscapes, undisturbed by human figures. Fields of corn being pelted by a harsh rain. The old train station in the center of Knox Junction, which had long since degenerated into an abandoned ruin. The flower beds in front of Lydia's house.

"You did all these in Paris?" Cassie asked. She refrained from asking what she longed to know: When you were pregnant? When you were reading and rereading that letter from Victor DiStefano, trying to decide what to do with the rest of your life? But she couldn't just blurt that out, not here, with no preparation. Not when the two of them were standing so peacefully together, comfortable in their shared silence.

Cassie ran her hands through the papers, searching for a sketch of Notre Dame Cathedral, a view of bridges over the Seine. But she found none of the vistas one would expect from an art student in Paris. No evidence that she'd even been there. It seemed that no matter how far she ran, Lydia could never escape Knox Junction.

Chapter 12

Lydia

Outside her window, Lydia could see the classic Parisian rooftops, sidewalk cafés, wrought-iron balconies overlooking a grand boulevard. But whenever she took up a paintbrush, all she could create were pictures of home—images of Knox Junction seen through the prism of a nightmare, swept with angry reds and eye-scorching oranges. They were unlike any landscapes she'd produced before, raw and powerful. But while Lydia was struck by their intensity, the paintings disturbed her. They were physical proof of how much a hold home still had over her.

Her current home—at least for the next six months—was on the top floor of what Mrs. Weatherly called the "Pension Anglaise," a crumbling rooming house that attracted a small but apparently loyal contingent of frugal British travelers. The sloping roof forced Lydia to walk hunched around the bed, and the ceiling leaked steady streams of water when it rained. The summer air could be stifling, even when all the windows were open, and the bathroom was at the far end of the hall, where Lydia had to share it with three other guests.

Still, the view was inspiring, and Lydia spent hours sitting on a lumpy cushion in the window seat, observing the rhythms of city life. When she'd first arrived, she'd wandered the streets by herself, taking in the traffic on the avenues and shoppers browsing at tiny flower stalls, signs that Paris was slowly recovering from the war. Twice a week, she joined a small group of fellow Americans for French and art history lessons at a run-down school that catered to foreign students. But as her belly grew stiffer and rounder, it seemed to form a barrier between herself and others, and she became increasingly self-conscious. After class, she kept to herself, avoiding the other students who might otherwise have become friends. As the summer passed, she spent more time alone in her room.

Mrs. Weatherly checked on her often with gentle concern. She was the only person Lydia talked to on a daily basis. She insisted Lydia join her for dinner each night, fussing over her protruding belly and sharing folk remedies for back pain and swollen ankles.

"Do you have children?" Lydia asked one night after they'd finished eating. Mrs. Weatherly seemed familiar with the trials of pregnancy, but Lydia had never heard her talk about her family. Nor had she seen any sign of Mr. Weatherly.

Mrs. Weatherly smiled sadly. "I was in your shoes once," she admitted. "That's why I have a soft spot for girls in trouble."

"What happened to your baby?" Lydia asked.

"We took them to the convent in those days. We were told they were adopted into very good families." Lydia heard a twinge of regret beneath Mrs. Weatherly's British reserve.

"Afterward, I couldn't return to England—everyone knew about my situation, you see. But British nannies were quite in demand here, so I stayed. Worked for the family who owned this building, when it was a private residence. It was in far better repair then, I assure you! When they decided to move to Provence, they were very particular about who bought the house. They wanted it to go to someone who cared about it as they did. I had some money saved up from when my parents passed on, and the family was willing to sell it to me at a very reasonable price."

"And your husband?"

Mrs. Weatherly laughed. "Didn't Edith tell you? There's no Mr. Weatherly. Never was. A widow is able to live much more freely than a spinster, as you can imagine. I concocted a wonderful story about him—an officer, serving his king in India, drowned tragically while sailing back to visit me. I have a photo in the parlor—haven't you seen it? A cousin of mine, in full military regalia, and I've been known to refer to him as Mr. Weatherly and gaze at it tearfully when the situation demands."

Lydia smiled.

"Life does go on after this, my dear," Mrs. Weatherly said. "Your family, your friends—they know nothing about your... situation?"

"No," Lydia said.

"Then you can go back to your old life with no one the wiser. I, on the other hand, was foolish enough to be part of a full-blown scandal. There was no recovering from that. Your prospects are far better than mine were."

"I hope so," Lydia said. But she knew she'd go back a changed person, no matter what Mrs. Weatherly thought. And where exactly would she be returning? Could she face finishing school in New York? Or would she end up back in Knox Junction, a failure?

"I find that girls cope best if they use this time to better themselves in some way." Mrs. Weatherly shifted into nanny mode. "I can't have you brooding in your room day and night. It's not good for you and not good for your baby. Edith tells me you're an artist?"

"Well, I like to paint and sketch. I don't know if that makes me an artist."

"There's a lovely art shop not far from here," Mrs. Weatherly said. "I'll take you tomorrow."

If nothing else, throwing herself back into

her work gave some much-needed structure to Lydia's days. She would spend her mornings walking through the city, sketchbook in hand, stopping to draw whatever buildings or scenes caught her eye. But when she pulled out her paints in the afternoon, those sketches refused to transfer onto canvas. Instead, the images she was driven to produce were of Knox Junction—the sunflowers in the backyard, the twisted drive leading to Henry's house, the lines of trees in the apple orchard. Scenes where the sky extended forever, where the grass grew wild, where she didn't feel shut in and constantly crowded by other people. Landscapes untouched by humans, in colors so vivid they sometimes shocked her.

"My goodness!" Mrs. Weatherly exclaimed when she saw one of the paintings. "You're full of surprises! These are really quite good, you know. Have you thought about selling them?"

But Lydia soon discovered that she could never support herself through art. Her few tentative forays into small galleries all ended with the same advice; the dealers admired her technique and use of color, then told her landscapes simply didn't sell. Perhaps if she created Parisian cityscapes that could be sold to tourists… But her country scenes—no matter how unusual the colors—would have no appeal for collectors. The serious collectors all wanted abstracts.

So Lydia painted for herself alone, hoping to drain herself of the visions that haunted her. Her preoccupation with Knox Junction was all the more mystifying considering that she'd never been so cut off from home. Mail delivery from the United States was unreliable at best, and Lydia received few letters from her family that summer. Mother's next note was full of news about the war memorial and veterans' hospital, achievements that had finally allowed her to make peace with her life in Knox Junction. Father scribbled a quick note at the end of one page:

I imagine you're fluent in French by now. Don't let those Charles Boyer types turn your head.

She had to smile to that. Except for the fact that she was pregnant, she was living the life of a nun.

Nell sent only one letter, but it turned out

to be the most important. Most of the letter was typical of her sister—a chatty, disorganized mix of hometown gossip and random thoughts ("Wouldn't it be swell if I went to Hollywood and became a movie actress?"). It was toward the end that she wrote the words Lydia read and reread for days afterward:

> I saw Henry at the war memorial ceremony, and I asked if he'd heard from you yet. He told me you'd had a fight and he doesn't have your address. I can't imagine what all the fuss was about. Have you broken off with him completely? He's still head over heels about you, you know.

Had Henry told Nell it was over? Because it was—at least Lydia assumed it was—after their awkward parting in New York. But if he'd really considered her escape to Europe the final straw, why would Nell think he was still in love with her? She couldn't picture Henry confiding in her flighty younger sister. He barely confided in Lydia, the person he supposedly felt closest to in the world.

Lydia glanced at the date on the letter. June twenty-fifth. It was now July, and she was four months pregnant. Henry would be back at school before long. Maybe he'd start dating, now that she'd cut him loose. The idea of Henry enjoying himself—perhaps escorting a pretty young sorority girl to a formal dance—while she sat alone in her attic room was too painful to dwell on. Still, as she told herself when she felt especially melancholy, she couldn't have it both ways. Couldn't long for him when he was far away, only to find fault with him whenever they were together.

She answered Nell's letter a few days later, carefully creating the illusion that she was living a full life, rather than spending her days in an attic room. Trying to sound casual, she addressed the topic she'd been dwelling on:

You asked about Henry. I'm not sure if it's going to work out for us. We're so different, after all. If he asks—perhaps you see him in town sometimes?—please tell him that I'm very busy and don't have much time for correspondence, but perhaps I'll see him when I return.

As she scanned the letter, rereading the lines to check for misspellings, Lydia was struck by the coldness of her words. She *had* gone cold, she realized. She wondered if it would be her fate to live the rest of her life without warmth or emotion. Until a surprise visitor brought her back to life.

The sun was beginning to set over the rooftops outside Lydia's window, filling her room with a soft yellow glow. Lydia was washing her face in preparation for dinner with Mrs. Weatherly, trying to wipe away the evidence of a late-afternoon nap. Mrs. Weatherly, who prided herself on being useful at all times, did not approve of sleeping during the daylight.

There was a gentle tap at the door, followed by Mrs. Weatherly's voice. "Dear, are you in there?"

"Yes." Lydia hurriedly dried off her face. "Come in."

Mrs. Weatherly opened the door and strode in, her lips pursed with concern.

"Lydia, you have a visitor."

The announcement was so unexpected that Lydia simply stared.

"A young man. From America, by the sound of him. I thought you might need a minute to compose yourself. Wouldn't hurt to give him some time, as well. He seems quite nervous." She looked pointedly at Lydia's stomach. "I presume he's aware of your situation?"

Victor. He could have tracked her down through school; Mrs. St. Clair had the address. Lydia felt weak.

"Where is he?" she asked.

"In the parlor. I don't approve of young women entertaining men in their rooms unchaperoned. I'm sure you understand."

Considering that entertaining a man unchaperoned had gotten her into this mess, Lydia understood perfectly.

"Tell him I'll be down shortly."

After Mrs. Weatherly left, Lydia examined herself in the small mirror propped up on the dresser. Her hair, which hadn't been cut since she arrived in France, hung past her shoulders, held away from her face on one side by a silver clip. Her dress was a hand-me-down from Mrs. Weatherly, worn by countless unwed mothers before her, a cotton floral shift that pressed snugly against the curve in her stomach. Gray circles lingered under her eyes. She looked tired and beaten down. Not the image she wanted to project to Victor.

She dabbed bright red lipstick on her mouth and wrapped a red knit shawl around her shoulders. The makeup brightened her complexion somewhat and the shawl helped cover the bulge under her dress. She could pass for a sophisticated, confident woman, at least temporarily. Breathing deeply to settle her stomach, she walked carefully down the four flights of stairs, her emotions swinging wildly between anger and curiosity.

Before opening the parlor door, she pulled the shawl tighter in front of her and lifted her chin high. She would not let Victor see her weak. But as soon as Lydia entered the room, her cool facade fell apart and she stood dumbstruck, unable to move. Her visitor wasn't Victor. It was Henry.

"Lyd!" he exclaimed. His hair was cut short. The clumps that used to stick up in the back of his head like straw were now shaved away. He wore a dark suit, crumpled from travel, and battered leather shoes. He looked older. Tired.

He stood when he saw her, smiling hopefully, his arms outstretched. She stiffened, pressing the shawl tightly against her stomach, terrified he'd come closer and discover the secret her body could barely conceal. Seeing her frozen posture, Henry paused, then dropped his arms to his sides.

"I guess I should've given you some notice," he said.

"Henry, your letter…" she said. She wanted to tell him how much his words had shaken her. But faced with Henry in person, she fell silent.

"When you wrote back, I didn't care what happened months or years ago," he continued. "All I needed to hear was that you loved me. You remember, Lydia, how we always knew each other's feelings, like they were our own?"

Lydia flashed back to the day she'd heard Henry's brother had been killed, how her heart had ached as if her own sibling had died. She nodded mutely.

"There were so many things I needed to tell you," Henry said, "and waiting for all those letters to go back and forth would have driven me crazy. I needed to see you in person."

"But the trains, the ship's passage—it must have been so expensive," Lydia fretted. "And what about school?"

"I took a leave of absence," Henry explained. "I can make up my classes later. And the money—well, Pop sold some of our land. He finally accepted that I wasn't coming back to work the farm. And with him getting older, it was getting harder to do it all himself."

The farm was Henry's father's life. Selling even part of it must have been wrenching.

"He gave me some of the money—it was to get started with this business I've been thinking about, but I wasn't going to use it for anything yet. I hopped on a train to Chicago and pretty much came straight here."

"The money," Lydia protested. "It was supposed to be for you...."

Henry shrugged, the casual lifting of his shoulders she'd always found so comforting, as if he was flicking off problems that would have crushed anyone else. "I can always earn more. I kinda thought I had only one shot at this. At us."

Desperate to stall him, to put off the inevitable reckoning, Lydia blurted out, "What's this business you're planning?"

"Landscaping. Gardening for rich folks, I guess you could call it. Things are changing at home, Lydia. They're expanding the highway from Chicago, and new houses are going up all around Fentonville. There's a lot of work to be had laying out plantings and parks, that sort of thing." He tried to sound casual, but Lydia could tell he was excited. He had found his passion, a way to escape the drudgery of the farm but still be outside, working the land he loved.

"That's wonderful," Lydia said.

Henry shook his head quickly, as if to rid his ears of her too-polite words.

"Lydia, I might as well say what I came to say. I've been thinking a lot, and I know I was unfair. Expecting you to come back to Knox Junction and settle down like it was nothing. So, what I wanted to say is—well, if you'll let me have another chance, I could come to New York. If that's where you want to be, I'd give it a try."

Lydia smiled at the thought of Henry in New York. He'd be miserable cooped up in the city. For that matter, so would she.

"I don't want to go back to New York," she said. "Believe it or not, I miss Knox Junction."

Henry laughed. "You're kidding."

"No," Lydia said. "You remember that sketch I sent you?"

Henry nodded. "The orchard."

"Ever since I got here, all I draw is Knox Junction. The dinky little town I thought I hated. But it's home. It's home because you're there. If that's where you want to live and work, you should."

"And you?" he asked.

"I'll come back if you want me to." A sudden wave of shyness forced Lydia to lower her eyes so she wouldn't see his expression.

"Then let's make it official." Henry stepped forward and took her hand gently in his, then dropped to one knee. "Lydia, you would make me the happiest man in the world if you'd agree to be my wife."

"Henry..." she began, her voice breaking.

He dropped her hand and reached for her, pulling her body against his in a desperate, fierce embrace. And then, almost instantly, his arms stiffened and his eyes flew to hers. His head, which had rested for a brief, unmistakable moment against her belly, shot back as if it had been burned. He stood and took a step away from her, as if he needed distance to grasp this new information. As if her body now disgusted him.

"Henry," she said softly.

"Aw, Lyd." Henry's shoulders slumped, and

all traces of the mature man he'd become disappeared. He was a lost boy once again.

"Please, I'm so sorry," Lydia said, taking a step toward him. "I didn't want you to find out. Not this way."

He looked directly at her then, a gaze she couldn't avoid. "What happened?" he asked.

With those simple words, Lydia found the strength to tell the whole story, the series of events she'd never confided in anyone, from her innocent crush to the party and her humiliation in that darkened room. Her agony on learning she was pregnant, her desperation to keep her shame hidden. The words poured out of her, hardly allowing her pause for breath, tears trickling down her cheeks.

"The baby's going to a good home," she concluded. "Mrs. Weatherly, the woman who runs this place, is taking care of that."

"What about the guy—the guy who did this to you?"

Lydia sighed. "I haven't talked to him since I told him I was pregnant. And believe me, it was over well before then. I couldn't…" She teared up again. "I thought I was flirting, that's all. I never meant things to go so far...." She stared down at the floor, miserable at having caused Henry such hurt.

But just then, when Lydia thought the worst had come to pass, Henry did the last thing she expected. He leaned over and touched her stomach, resting his hand lightly.

"My poor city girl," he said quietly. "Going through this all by yourself."

Relief flooded through Lydia like a drug, relaxing all her muscles and leaving her dizzy. She swayed toward Henry and he caught her, his arms circling and his hands pressing firmly against her back. They kissed with a tenderness born of a love that had survived everything that had come between them. They kissed as two people intimately familiar with each other, with no secrets to protect or pretenses to maintain.

When they finally separated, Henry led Lydia to the sofa. He pulled her down next to him, one arm wrapped around her shoulders, and she leaned her head into the warm refuge of his chest.

"So, the proposal..." Lydia began.

"I've been wanting to ask you that question since I got on the train at Urbana," Henry said. "The baby doesn't change that."

"But the baby—it's not yours."

"It's yours," Henry said. "That's all that matters. If you and I raise it, I'll be the baby's father. No one needs to know."

Lydia raised his hand and kissed his palm, her gesture expressing the love she couldn't put into words. Henry reached into his pocket with his other hand and pulled out a ring. It got stuck halfway down Lydia's pregnancy-swollen finger, but she grinned all the same, holding up the simple gold band to admire it in the light. She turned around to face Henry and kissed him, the taste of his lips making her hungry for more.

"Mrs. Weatherly will not approve," Lydia whispered, "but maybe you should come up to my room."

They tiptoed up the stairs, giggling like children sneaking away from their parents. If any of the guests complained about the squeaky bed frame that night, Mrs. Weatherly did not acknowledge it the next morning. When faced with a freshly bathed Henry and a beaming Lydia, the engagement ring still stuck on her finger, she smiled and kissed them both.

"All's well that ends well, then," she said.

"I'm glad you came to your senses, young man."

Lydia started to explain that Henry wasn't the one who got her into trouble, but he shot her a quick glance.

"Yes, Mrs. Weatherly," he said. "I plan on spending my whole life making it up to her."

But you're the one who saved me, Lydia wanted to say. And many years later, when she thought her life was ruined beyond repair, he would do it again.

Chapter 13

Cassie

The envelope was placed carefully in the center of Cassie's pillow, and the neat letters of her name looked so different from Cooper's usual careless handwriting that it took her a moment to figure out it was from him. She'd hoped to see him after she returned from her grandparents' house, but then remembered he'd still be in the office fine-tuning contracts from the London trip. Yet another working Sunday.

Usually, Cassie would have turned on her laptop and got to work herself—or rushed off to her own office. She'd spent an hour or so that morning halfheartedly reviewing the documents she'd promised to deliver to Jeffrey on Monday, but the idea of getting them out exhausted her. She knew they were good enough. Once, that wouldn't have been acceptable. Her notes had to be the most detailed, her memos covering every possible contingency. But a few days away from work had given Cassie a new sense of peace. Good enough would be fine.

She walked to the bedroom to change into sweatpants. That was when she saw the envelope.

She sat down on the side of the bed and took out a one-page letter.

Dear Cassie,

I've never done this before, so I hope I get it right. If I'd known you needed a love letter, I would've written one years ago. It seems so hard to find time to talk when one of us isn't tired or angry. So I'm going to spell it out here, in writing, and hope it works.

1) I love you. I always have, even during those years when we were just

friends. Never doubt my love for you. Through everything, it's always been there.

2) I want to marry you because you're also my best friend. I know we could live happily together. But you're right, things aren't working right now. I guess some of that's my fault. I didn't know how to make you happy. So, from now on, tell me and I promise I'll listen. If taking that job in San Francisco is what you want, I'll go with you. If you want to wait before getting married, that's fine, too. What scares me is the thought that you couldn't trust me enough to tell me the truth.

I have a horrible feeling this reads like a legal document rather than a love letter. I did my best. Cassie—I don't know how else to say it. You are the love of my life, my darling, my heart's desire, my best friend. Is that more like it?
I love you,
Cooper

Cassie lay back on the bed and held the letter up above her, reading and rereading the sentences with a growing smile. Okay, so Cooper would never win any prizes for romantic poetry. But that was what she loved about him—he didn't put on airs or try to be what he wasn't. He did the best he could, despite his obvious squeamishness about putting his feelings on paper.

She was still clutching the page when she heard the front door open. Cassie rushed out to the living room, where Cooper was putting down his briefcase. He looked up when he heard her, then saw the letter in her hand.

"So…" he began.

Cassie threw herself into his arms and hugged him. "It's perfect," she said.

Cooper sighed and ran his fingers through her hair. "Oh, God, I couldn't concentrate on work today. All I could think about was you reading this. Who knows what's in some of the clauses I approved.…"

"Who cares?" Cassie laughed.

"Was it okay?" he asked, drawing his head back so he could look at her. "Was it what you wanted?"

"Yes," Cassie said. "And this." She ran her hands up and down his sides, suddenly aroused by his vulnerability. She couldn't re-

member the last time she'd seen Cooper unsure of himself.

Despite her matted hair and unflattering
outfit, Cassie felt sexier than she had in a
long time. The unassailable fact of his love
for her—something she'd taken for granted
so long—brought on a rush of gratitude and
comfort. She and Cooper had always pushed
each other to be better, whether it was getting
top scores on their law-school exams or working with high-profile clients at their firms.
Now she saw that none of that professional
success truly mattered. Cooper didn't expect
her to be a superstar lawyer. He wanted her
to be herself.

"So, you said you wanted to make me
happy," Cassie murmured.

"Yes."

"Well, I had an idea," she said, leading him
to the couch. She pushed against his chest,
forcing him to sit as she climbed into his lap,
her legs curled up on either side. Straddling
him, she gently unbuttoned his shirt, rubbing her hands along his chest, reveling in
the tickle from the light dusting of hair.

When they'd made the jump from friends
to lovers—literally, by throwing themselves

on the narrow single bed in Cooper's law-school dorm room—sex had been a giggly, joking affair, as if they couldn't quite believe their friendship had taken this physical turn. Over the years, their bedroom interactions had become shorter and to the point, one more thing to check off their to-do lists. That didn't make it any less satisfying—they both knew how and where to touch each other to produce the desired effect. But lately, even these time-efficient sessions had become less frequent. Any extra minutes devoted to sex would mean that many fewer minutes of valuable sleep. Sleep usually won out.

Now, Cassie cleared her mind of deadlines and upcoming conference calls and wedding duties. She focused on Cooper's body beneath hers, his hands reaching under her sweat-shirt and massaging her back. They kissed slowly, tenderly, as if they had all the time in the world. As if kissing was an end in itself, rather than a step on the way to the next level.

Cassie tugged her sweatshirt over her head. She wasn't wearing a bra, leaving her breasts exposed and ready for Cooper's tender kisses. And then it became harder to wait. They were tearing at each other's clothes, falling off the couch onto the rug, pressing their bodies together. Cassie watched Cooper's transported expression. Then, as they began moaning with need, he looked back at her. Their eyes locked, and for once looking at each other during sex didn't bring on a fit of giggles. They focused on each other as their bodies moved together in an urgent rhythm and even afterward as they separated.

They lay there silently for a few minutes, their fingers still exploring each other tenderly. Cassie reached up to the couch and pulled down a fleece throw, wrapping them together.

Usually, this would be the time for a joke to diffuse the tension of their intense lovemaking. Words that would put them back on the solid ground of friendship. But this time, Cassie couldn't think of what to say. She didn't want to lose the connection she felt, the sense that they'd bonded on a deeper emotional level.

"So, the letter?" Cooper asked.

"Yeah, it worked," Cassie said with a smile. He had bared his heart to her. Now it was her turn, no matter how scary. She would make the leap and let logic come later.

"About San Francisco," she began. "I don't think I'm going to take the job."

"Are you sure?" Cooper asked. "Because I meant what I wrote..."

"I know. And it's incredible that you'd be willing to give up your job for me. But, the thing is, I don't know if I even want to be at the firm anymore. I don't know how long I'll last, anyway, once I turn down the promotion. I'll be the in-house slacker."

"Not necessarily," Cooper said. "They love you."

"These past few days, not being at work— it's been fantastic. I haven't missed it at all. I mean, I don't want to quit working—I still love being challenged—but I want a normal life. I think I could find a position with more reasonable hours."

"You're positive?"

Cassie nodded. "You love your job, right?"

"Yeah."

"So you should stay there," Cassie said. "I was thinking of calling Kristen. Remember, she's in that family-law practice? Maybe see if they've got an opening. It's not my specialty, but I do know my way around a contract...."

"You'd be great," Cooper said.

Cassie imagined walking into the office tomorrow and announcing to Jeffrey that she was leaving the firm. She was nervous about it, yes, but also relieved. It was surprisingly easy to picture.

"I'm sure."

Cooper pushed a lock of hair back off Cassie's forehead. Cassie grabbed his hand and pressed it against her cheek.

"There's one more thing I have to ask," she said. "Cooper Lynch, will you marry me?"

Cooper smiled and looked up at the ceiling, pretending to consider her offer.

"I think after your performance here today, I'd be a fool not to," he said.

"Then let's do it," Cassie said. "No more visits to hotel ballrooms and overpriced bridal salons. I don't care about all that. Our life is hectic enough. What would you say to making it small, maybe at my grandparents' place?"

"Okay," Cooper said.

"Your parents wouldn't freak?" Cassie asked.

"After the circus of my sister's wedding, they'd be relieved," he said. "So, you're thinking…soon?"

"Why not?" Cassie said. "I suspect that one

of the reasons I kept putting off planning the wedding was that it seemed too overwhelming. I couldn't deal with it. But if it was more like a family party, I'd actually look forward to it."

"Listen, I meant what I said," Cooper said. "I want to make you happy. Just ask."

"Well, there is one more thing."

"Yeah?"

"What do you think about…ice cream?"

Cooper laughed and wrapped Cassie in his arms. Then they dressed and went to investigate the freezer.

Later, as the last of the late-afternoon sunshine flooded the apartment, Cassie called her grandmother to ask about having the wedding at her house.

"Of course," said Lydia, obviously delighted. "I would have offered earlier if I'd thought it was a possibility."

"Cooper and I had a long talk," Cassie told her. "A really good talk. We decided we want a small gathering, with just family and close friends. We think your yard would be beautiful for an outdoor ceremony, and the rooms are big enough that we could have the reception inside if it rains."

"When did you want to do it?" Lydia asked.

"Soon," Cassie said. "It'll depend on when Cooper can get time off work, but probably in a few months. July, maybe?"

"Oh, July would be lovely," Lydia said. "The clematis will be blooming by then."

"Now, I don't want you to worry about anything," Cassie asserted. "I know there are caterers in Fentonville, so let me take care of all the details."

"Oh, I could put together some casseroles…."

"No!" Cassie laughed. "You are not spending days cooking! I want you to relax and enjoy yourself."

"Oh." Lydia sighed. "I've never helped plan a wedding before."

Cassie thought about the other marriages in Lydia's life. She and Henry had said their vows in some government office in Paris; her own son had eloped to Las Vegas.

"Well, I want you to be a part of it all," Cassie said. "I'll come out next Sunday and we'll talk about it, okay?"

"That sounds perfect," Lydia said. "Oh, I'm so happy for you."

"I'm happy for me, too." Cassie couldn't help smiling as she spoke.

"I can see the difference, you know," Lydia said. "Lately—well, I knew you were happy to be marrying Cooper, but you seemed so cool about it. I wasn't convinced you'd go through with it. And that would've been a shame, because Cooper is wonderful."

"I know."

"The two of you are going to be so happy," Lydia commented. "I know, because you were friends first. That's the way it was with your grandfather and me. Once you have that foundation, you can rely on it when the marriage hits its bumps."

Bumps. Cassie thought back to her meeting with Victor DiStefano. Henry married Lydia knowing she carried another man's child. Paul's dark hair and eyes were so different from his own light-haired Scottish stock. Did Henry—always even-keeled and unruffled—ever get angry about being confronted with such obvious proof of Lydia's infidelity?

"Would you say Grandpa's your best friend?" Cassie asked.

"Oh, yes. Without a doubt." Lydia didn't hesitate.

"Cooper's my best friend, too," Cassie said. "I guess I always took that for granted. He offered to move to San Francisco with me, give up his job, if that's what I want. But it's not."

"So—the promotion?" Lydia asked.

"I'm turning it down. I'm staying. Probably going to look for a new job."

Cassie knew Lydia was smiling. But Lydia had never been the type for emotional displays.

"Oh, that's good news," Lydia said. "You know I would've supported you, no matter what you did, but I'm so glad you'll still be nearby."

"Me, too," Cassie said.

"How about dinner at Moody's?" Cooper suggested after Cassie and Lydia had said their goodbyes. "Bleu cheeseburger? Sound good?"

"Oh, yeah," Cassie said. "Just give me a minute." She reached into her purse to get her lipstick, and her fingers brushed against an envelope her grandfather had handed her as she was leaving the house that afternoon. She opened it and pulled out a note on Henry's company stationery, wrapped around a check for three hundred dollars. The words were written neatly and meticulously, as if each had been chosen as carefully as her grandfather spoke.

Cassie—
I know you're an independent career girl, but it's my sacred duty as a grandfather to help you with wedding expenses. Please use the enclosed check for whatever you deem necessary. I would be happy to advise you on flowers, if the opinion of an old man is of any use to you. Florists are notorious for overcharging clients. Best check with me before signing anything. You may be almost a married woman, but I still reserve the right to look out for you.
Love,
Grandpa

Cassie smiled. In some ways, nothing had changed since she was a little girl, when Henry would dole out her weekly allowance.

"What's that?" Cooper asked.

"A note from my grandfather." Cassie scanned the paper again, nagged by a vague sense that she was missing some important information.

Florists are notorious… Best check with me…

The straight line of the *F* extended far below the rest of the text. So did the bottom of the *B,* as if the writer emphasized the first motion he made when writing.

It was a distinctive flourish. And it was one she'd seen before. Now, she remembered where: Lydia's love letter. The *F.B.* signed at the end had this same flourish, with the first stroke of the letters stretching downward.

Henry had written the letter. Henry was the one who'd loved Lydia all along. Suddenly, the pieces of the puzzle came together. Lydia had escaped to Europe after getting pregnant, and Henry had written to her, wondering why she'd left and how he could get her back. It had always been Henry, never Victor. No wonder Lydia had treasured the letter all these years.

But why had he signed it F.B.? And one final riddle still nagged her. Lydia had referred to bumps in her marriage. But surely, all the difficulties had come before they were married? Once they'd returned from Europe, they had been content, from everything Lydia had told her. But maybe the happy ending had been more complicated than Cassie knew.

Chapter 14

Lydia

The day after Henry arrived in Paris, he spotted the letter on Lydia's bedside table and picked it up.

> Dearest Lydia, my darling,
> This is my last hope, because I am desperate, desperately in love with you…

"What did you keep this for?" he asked with an embarrassed smile. "I was pretty shook up when I wrote it—it probably doesn't even make sense."

Lydia snatched the letter from his hands and held it to her chest.

"This is the most wonderful letter I've ever received in my life. When I read it..." Her eyes filled as she remembered when the letter had arrived, sitting in the pile of mail in Mrs. Weatherly's front hall. It was the day after she'd heard from Nell that Henry was still thinking about her. The scrawl on the envelope was so different from Henry's usual careful penmanship that she didn't realize it was from him until she checked the return address. She'd read his words, with their panicked explosion of feeling, and was torn between love and wrenching guilt. She wrote him back with the same honesty, finally acknowledging her true feelings for him but also leaving him in no doubt of her betrayal. Offering him the chance to give up on her with no regrets. Then she waited, wondering if he would.

"Anyway, I'm saving it." She carefully folded up the page. "When I'm a shriveled old lady, I'll want to read it and relive my passionate youth."

Henry laughed, but his smile told Lydia that even he had been swept away by the excitement of their new life. Mrs. Weatherly had relaxed her rules, allowing Henry to move into Lydia's room while they applied for a marriage license. Mrs. Weatherly hinted that she "knew the right people" to get the paperwork pushed through in a hurry. They were young and they were together. They were invincible.

"You know, I saved your letter, too," Henry admitted, taking a creased sheet of paper from his wallet. "I read it over and over on the ship, to keep my spirits up." Lydia took the page from him and read the opening lines.

Dear, dear Henry,
I received your letter today. You say you love me more than I know, but I do know. Deep down, I always have. What I couldn't admit until now was how much I love you back…

Although she'd written it only a few weeks before, it already seemed like a distant memory. Lydia folded the letters together and slipped them in the side pocket of the compact traveling bag she used as a purse.

"I'll keep them both," she said. "Who knows when I'll get another love letter?"

Henry's letter had saved them. Had he not revealed the deep, urgent feelings hidden beneath his calm exterior, she might have let him slip away forever. But even as she tucked the pages out of sight, she'd no idea that Henry's letter would save her again in the years to come.

The bag—and the letters—went with Lydia and Henry to the dingy magistrate's office where they spoke their vows in halting French, with Mrs. Weatherly whispering the English translations behind them. Lydia reread the letters during their honeymoon in a small fishing village in the south of France, a place Mrs. Weatherly had told them about, insisting they treat themselves to a honeymoon.

"Oh, put those away," Henry had said, swatting at the papers in her hand.

"Don't touch them!" Lydia protested with mock anger. "Our grandchildren will want to read them someday."

"You wouldn't dare!" Henry laughed. The pages fell to the floor as he drew Lydia toward him on the bed, the two of them laughing as the rusty springs groaned with the weight of their bodies. They'd spent two weeks there, rediscovering each other's bodies in that musty, sagging bed, Henry touching her stomach tentatively at first, then adapting to her new shape in his hunger to feel her body next to his once more. Sitting with their feet in the sand while they watched the fishermen bring in their catch. Sipping coffee at a sidewalk café and writing postcards to their parents, telling the tale of their elopement in a few cheerful lines. Returning to Paris with sun-browned skin and an ease with each other that signaled to the world that they were now truly married.

The letters had gone with Lydia to the hospital the day she gave birth to Paul, a hazy stretch of hours filled with pain and anticipation and Mrs. Weatherly's authoritative voice, translating the doctor's instructions. Lydia's only clear memory of that day was her first sight of the baby. The crushing disappointment as she took in the dark hair covering his head, the black eyes peering at her. Her fear that Henry couldn't possibly love a child so obviously not his. And then her relief, the tears streaming down her cheeks, as Henry cradled the baby and looked at Lydia with awestruck tenderness.

"We're a family now," he said. "A family."

The letters went with Lydia and her family six months later as they boarded the ship to America, to a new life. Lydia and Henry might have appalled their parents with their sudden marriage—followed by the even-more-unexpected announcement that they'd had a "honeymoon baby"—but they redeemed themselves as soon as they arrived home with a grandchild in their arms. If Lydia's father thought Paul looked suspiciously large for a four-month-old baby, or if her mother was struck by his dark hair and eyes, neither said a word. From the beginning, they doted on their grandson, finding any excuse to take him out and parade him proudly around town. The baby formed an immediate bond between Lydia's and Henry's parents, bringing joy to a house that had previously been filled with sadness.

Lydia read both letters one more time after they'd settled in their tiny apartment near the University of Illinois campus, while Henry finished his last year of school. She then folded the pages and put them in the bottom drawer of an old dressing table Mother had given her, neatly stacked with the other mementos of her time in France: her marriage certificate, her sketches, a goodbye card from Mrs. Weatherly. The letters sat there, undisturbed, for years, as Henry and Lydia moved to a small house in Fentonville and Paul grew from a rambunctious toddler eager to make her smile to a moody teenager, apt to storm out the door if she tried to discipline him.

The dressing table—with the letters still inside—finally went back to its original home, when Lydia and Henry moved in with Mother after Father's death. Mother insisted that Lydia and Henry take the master bedroom, so their roles were reversed. Lydia now slept in the largest room in the house, while her mother spent most of her time surrounded by girlish pink wallpaper. Henry, once an unwelcome visitor, was now head of the household, with Mother deferring to his wishes and flattering him at every opportunity.

But in the end, all that love wasn't enough to make Paul happy. Perhaps, if there'd been more children in the house, he would've learned how to adapt to others. His outsize personality would've been reined in. But despite years of trying and hoping, Lydia was never able to get pregnant again. Even as she mourned the loss of those never born, the guilt that had haunted her for years slowly faded. If that night with Victor hadn't happened, she and Henry would have no children at all. Paul might have started life as a mistake, but his arrival had been an unexpected blessing.

Lydia tried to take comfort in that as Paul grew up, disappointing her again and again—dropping out of college, refusing to hold a steady job, racking up speeding tickets, getting involved with Shelly. Eventually, Lydia found herself relinquishing control. If Paul was difficult, it was no surprise, given who his real father was. It was in his blood; she'd been foolish to think he could turn out any other way.

It was only years later, as she raised Cassie and reviewed past mistakes, that she discovered Paul was more like her than she'd ever known. Like her, he'd been bored by Knox Junction, unchallenged at school, longing for a more exciting life. But rather than retreating into books—as Lydia had—he'd found increasingly dangerous ways to escape. The years when Paul needed his parents most, those middle-school years when he was unsure of himself and his place in the world, were the years Henry's business had boomed. Henry often worked from early morning to well past sunset, and Lydia helped shoulder the burden. She met with prospective clients, sketching detailed layouts of plant beds and backyards. Working with her husband—while bringing art into her life again—was a dream come true. Lydia and Henry's partnership, in life and business, had only deepened with the years. But there wasn't enough space in that partnership for Paul. Henry—the ultimate dutiful son—was clearly mystified by Paul's willfulness, and Lydia watched, heartbroken, as father and son drifted further apart.

Lydia had always hoped the love of a good woman would turn Paul's life around. But when that woman did come along, Lydia was completely unprepared. She'd tried to be kind when she first met Shelly. Lydia could still remember vividly the pain she felt when her parents disparaged Henry. But Lydia found little to admire in Shelly, a sweet but silly girl who'd grown up in a trailer park and whose idea of great literature was *Jonathon*

Livingston Seagull. A girl who considered daisy chains a major artistic achievement and seemed to have no goals other than a vague desire for world peace. Shelly let life carry her along, never planning ahead, confident that her beauty and sweetness were all she needed.

Shelly had seemed so obviously temporary—the sort of girl a boy could have fun with and then move on—that Lydia had trouble accepting Paul's words when he told her they'd gotten married.

Lydia asked if Shelly was pregnant.

"No!" Paul protested. "Why would you say that?"

Personal experience, Lydia thought. But she said nothing.

"Can't you be happy for me? For once?" Paul asked.

"Of course I'm happy for you," Lydia said. But even she could hear the insincerity in her voice. The judgment. The disapproval.

"Sorry to be such a disappointment," Paul said sarcastically. "Again."

Before Lydia could argue, he'd stormed off, his anger flaring.

"It's time we went easier on him," Henry said that evening. "Paul may not be the perfect son, but we were never the perfect parents. I want to make peace with him, and maybe Shelly can help us do that. She's good for him."

"How?" Lydia asked. "Because she'll teach him how to read his horoscope?"

"Because she's kind," Henry said gently. "And she loves him." He smiled. "Haven't you noticed the way she looks at him?"

A few days later, at the hastily arranged congratulatory barbecue Lydia had organized in the backyard, she watched Paul and Shelly walking hand in hand. Even as Lydia cringed at the sight of Shelly's white-trash relatives—that mother of hers, who practically breathed cigarette smoke!—she had to admit that Shelly herself showed a grace that belied her upbringing. She greeted everyone with a smile of delight. She patted shoulders and grabbed hands during conversations, charming touches that drew people toward her. And she gazed at Paul as if he was a special prize, a gift she didn't quite deserve. It came to Lydia that *she* hadn't looked at Paul like that in years—as if he was already perfect, rather than a work in progress.

As the party wound down, Lydia asked

Paul to help her carry some of the dishes into the kitchen. When they were alone inside, she reached out and touched his arm. "I'm sorry about my reaction when you told me you'd gotten married. I was surprised, that's all."

Paul shrugged.

"I wanted to tell you I like Shelly," Lydia went on. "Very much. She's a lovely person."

Paul turned to face her as if he'd just started listening. "Oh," he said, a little shocked. "Thanks."

"I know you'll be very happy together," Lydia said.

Paul smiled, a real smile, like the ones he used to give her when he was three years old and she'd sneak him a cookie after lunch. When it was just the two of them, with their own private language and jokes.

"The thing about Shelly," Paul began, then paused as he searched for the right words. "She makes me want to be a better person."

Lydia smiled. "That's how I felt about your father," she said. "Still do."

They hugged then, as they hadn't in years. Lydia sensed that they'd turned a corner. Maybe they would no longer be opponents. From now on, they could be on the same side.

And Shelly did bring a new ease to the family. But it wasn't until Cassie was born, a little more than a year later, that Lydia finally saw her deeper qualities, the strengths Paul had seen from the very beginning. Because despite Shelly's flightiness and giddiness and unpredictability, she was an excellent mother. It was obvious in the way she doted on her daughter, the way Cassie grew up curious about the world and its possibilities. Much as her own parents had grown to love Henry for the happiness he brought Lydia, so Lydia began to appreciate the way Shelly helped calm her restless son. How could she not be grateful?

Those had been idyllic years, with Paul working steadily in home construction, and Henry expanding his business and building the greenhouse out back. Shelly and little Cassie stopped by regularly for lunch or backyard picnics. Lydia was happy. Her family was happy. Then tragedy struck—and she became tormented by the belief that it was all her fault.

Henry had been talking to Paul about the benefits of owning his own business rather than being at the beck and call of others. With

Shelly's encouragement, Paul had looked into starting his own painting company. "There's enough work out there, and it's what I like doing," he told Lydia. "Taking plain white walls and turning them into something special."

Lydia understood. He'd always shown an interest in paint and color, just like her. And like his biological father. But he'd never had the discipline to apply himself, abandoning the paint set she'd given him for Christmas one year by mid-January. Quitting art classes she signed him up for after just a few sessions. Refusing to sit still when she tried to show him how to use pastels.

"The thing is, I've got to get licensed," Paul continued. "There's all kinds of paperwork, so it's a hassle. I've got to send in a copy of my birth certificate. Do you have it?"

For years afterward, Lydia would wonder why she hadn't simply handed it over. Yes, Paul would have noticed that the date on the certificate was different from the day they'd always celebrated as his birthday. His actual birth date, imprinted forever on that French certificate, was a mere five months after Lydia and Henry's marriage. It had been easy enough once they returned to America to tell everyone that Paul had been born exactly nine months later. He'd been a small baby, thank goodness, and no one seemed to notice Lydia's deception. Over time, she'd actually forgotten his real birthday. But it was printed on that paper.

A secret kept this long couldn't be revealed this casually on a Sunday afternoon. So she stalled. And Paul saw the fear in her eyes.

"I'm adopted," he said quietly.

"What?"

"I've always known I was different," Paul said. "I don't look like you or Dad. I didn't turn out anything like you. I guessed ages ago."

She could have nodded. Or simply stuck with the lie she'd been telling for so long. But the weight of her secret became too much. This was her son, her blood. He deserved the truth.

So she told Paul the whole story—about Victor, and the escape to Paris, and Henry's forgiveness. How she and Henry had never thought of Paul as anything other than their son.

Paul stared at her blankly as she spoke, but

Lydia could hear his quick intakes of breath. After she finished, he struggled for words.

"So my real father…"

"Your dad is your real father," said Lydia firmly. "The man—the man who got me pregnant has no place in our life. I haven't talked to him since I left for France. I have no idea where he is and no interest in knowing."

"But…" Paul hesitated. "How could you not have told me?"

"What would be the point?" Lydia exclaimed. "To hurt your father's feelings? To remind me of a time I was miserable?"

"Just what every son dreams of hearing," Paul said bitterly. "That he was a mistake."

"Paul, that's not what I meant." Lydia tried to reach out to Paul, but he brushed her away.

"Forget it," he snapped. "Just forget it. Geez, Mom, I can't believe that after all these years, you choose *now* to tell me this. I mean—damn it, I always knew something was wrong. I just never imagined this."

"You didn't think I was your real mother?"

"I wondered about it," Paul said, finally meeting her eyes. "It sure seemed like you didn't want to be."

At least they were being honest, Lydia told

herself later. But in that instant, all she could feel was a searing disappointment that the truth was only pushing them further apart.

"I gotta go," Paul said, turning and heading for the door. "Eve is expecting us for dinner."

"Paul," Lydia began.

"Later, Mom," Paul said. "We can have more family revelations later. Right now, I need to figure this out." And he'd left, letting the screen door slam behind him.

That was the last time she saw him. That evening, he took Shelly and Cassie to Eve's trailer, where he drowned his sorrows in beer. And later, he got behind the wheel of his car and drove to his death. She'd found out in the middle of the night, when Eve called, hysterical and slurring her words, and Lydia—half-asleep and still disoriented—couldn't understand what she was saying, let alone determine what needed to be done. It was Henry who'd rushed off to the hospital to identify the bodies, Henry who'd picked up Cassie from the police station and brought her home. Lydia had stayed in bed, unable to move, unable to speak. Unable to think about anything but the fact that her son was dead and it was her fault. If she'd kept the secret she'd hidden for so long, Paul wouldn't have been angry, wouldn't have gotten drunk, wouldn't have crashed the car. The guilt filled her body with leaden weight, so heavy that she thought she would die, too.

Sometimes, salvation comes from the unexpected people. Just as Shelly had been Paul's unlikely angel, Nell was the one who finally convinced Lydia to leave her bed. Henry, his own face lined with grief, tried unsuccessfully to coax her to come downstairs, to sit on the porch and feel the soft spring breeze. He brought Cassie up to the bedroom telling her she couldn't stay long because Grandma was sick. When Cassie asked when she'd be ready to come down and play, Lydia would pretend to cough to cover a sob. "Soon, sweetie," she'd say, patting Cassie's tangled blond hair. "Soon."

But soon never came, and as the days stretched into weeks, Lydia had scarcely enough strength to drag herself to the bathtub. The tears flowed without end, as though pouring from a bottomless well. Some days, she allowed herself to wail with grief, holding a pillow against her mouth to muffle the sound, hoping if she let the wracking sobs come hard and loud she could somehow be cleansed. But each new day brought a fresh supply of tears and hopelessness.

And then Nell arrived.

She was in her artistic phase, living in a commune out west, without electricity, running water or a phone. It had taken time for word of Paul's death to reach her. Lydia wondered who had written. Henry, probably. It would be like him to pore through her address book, making sure the right people knew, finding a way to put down on paper the enormity of what had happened.

"What are you doing in Mother's room?" a voice called out in mock horror. Lydia lifted her head slightly from the pillow to take in the sight of her sister, clad in a hand-knit sweater and paint-smeared jeans.

Nell swept in, still talking, unfazed by the room's disheveled state and her sister's lethargy. "I can't think of this as your room, you know?" she said, jerking back the curtains and opening a window. "Remember when we were sick and Mother would let us lie here while she read to us?"

Lydia nodded, unable to speak.

"It's amazing how different things are here," Nell continued. "The light in New Mexico is so clear. Wonderful for painting. You have to come out there. It'll change your life."

Lydia stared, torn between annoyance at Nell's self-centeredness—how like her, to focus only on herself!—and shock that her sister could be treating her like a normal person. Suggesting a trip to New Mexico when Lydia hadn't been in her own kitchen in weeks.

"Do you know the best part of living at an artists' colony?" Nell asked, then went on without waiting for an answer. "I'm constantly being inspired by others. I went there intending to work on my sculpture—you know, exploring how the female form influences our role in society—but now, after meeting Lottie, this fabric artist, I'm looking at traditional women's needlework in a whole new way. How it can completely subvert the patriarchal establishment."

Lydia's head was spinning. But as Nell talked on, babbling about her flaky artist friends and her creative growth, Lydia's mind drifted along with her. For a few minutes, she escaped to the New Mexico desert, where the air was clean and the sun burned brighter. Nell brought her, however briefly, to a place without memories of Paul.

"...so I've got it all in a bag downstairs," Nell was saying. "I thought we could set up in the dining room."

"Set what up?" Lydia asked.

"The quilting!" Nell laughed. "Weren't you listening?"

"I'm not sure..." Lydia began.

"C'mon," said Nell. "I dragged all this stuff halfway across the country. The least you can do is look at it." She didn't ask Lydia to come, in the tentative, worried manner Henry did. Nell *expected* her to. Lydia was reminded then of her mother's rigid sense of right and wrong. Things must be done a certain way, no arguments permitted. Nell had spent her life rebelling against Mother's dictates, but now Lydia saw that she shared the same determination.

"How about this?" Nell asked, pulling a cotton dress out of the closet.

"Oh, I don't know if it's clean...." Lydia tried to stall.

"It's cleaner than that," Nell said, gesturing

to Lydia's wrinkled nightgown. She tossed the dress on the bed. "Go change in the bathroom if you want. Some of us have moved past our hang-ups about our bodies, but I don't expect you have!" Nell stood expectantly. If she'd left the room, Lydia could've climbed back into bed, and burrowed under the covers like she did every other day. But Nell was watching. Nell was waiting. And for some reason—the reminder of her own mother?—Lydia didn't want to disappoint her.

"Give me a minute," Lydia said. And a minute was all it took to put on the dress, splash water on her face, brush her teeth and then walk slowly down the stairs.

Nell's quilting was the first step; it got her out of the bedroom and filled her days. Nell showed her that quilts could take any form imaginable. They didn't have to be neatly ordered, grandmotherly projects. They could be bold, with bright colors and jagged shapes. Lydia stared at the scraps of fabric the same way she used to assess paints—sorting out the colors that moved her, holding pieces together as she searched for a combination that worked. The dining room table became her canvas, scattered with bright colors and abstract patterns.

Painting no longer appealed, Nell had intuited that. Painting required hours of sitting and thinking. Lydia needed to be active, to keep her hands occupied at all times. The movement of stitches across a seam could distract her—even if only temporarily—from her shattered life.

Quilting also gave Lydia a way to relate to Cassie. The two of them would sort fabric scraps by color, and Cassie would pretend to make clothes for her dolls as Lydia pinned her next project. Quilting brought Lydia back into the life of the house. But still, she moved through it like a shadow, all emotions deadened. She smiled at Cassie without feeling joy, kissed Henry good-night without feeling love.

It was as she planned her third quilt that she rediscovered the letter. She was trying to recall a color combination she'd seen on an old bracelet of her mother's, shades of red and deep yellow that she remembered as particularly glamorous. Wanting to re-create that look in fabric, she searched the drawers of her dressing table, trying to find the bracelet. Finally, there was only one drawer unopened.

The drawer where she stored her memories of France. Her memories of Paul as a baby.

She'd avoided that drawer for months, for the same reason she avoided the closed door of Paul's old bedroom. Facing physical proof of his loss had been unbearable. But now, looking at the drawer, she felt like a diver perched miles above a swimming pool. Jumping in might kill her. But she was teetering on the edge, and with a reach toward the handle, she gave in.

The bracelet was there, in Mother's old silk carrying case. Beneath it were old papers. Lydia spread them all out on the dressing table. There were sketches of Knox Junction, some of them rough drafts of paintings that now hung downstairs. Christmas cards from Mrs. Weatherly, which had arrived for years, until a note from her niece informed them that she'd died in her sleep. Paul's impossibly tiny handprint and footprint on a hospital document. Their first family photo, taken in a Parisian studio. Lydia began to cry then, but these were silent tears now, trickling down her cheeks as she looked at her much younger self, clutching Paul's blanket protectively, Henry with one arm around her and one hand at Paul's feet. And their precious baby, his face contorted with a yawn, his dark hair like a helmet.

Then, under the photo, Lydia saw it. A folded page, slightly yellowed. The paper was stiff, and she loosened the folds carefully to avoid breaking it.

Dearest Lydia, my darling...

She read it through, then immediately reread it, her heart racing. This page, which she'd vaguely remembered as a sweet love letter, carried her back to the pain and urgency of those days. And once again, she was weakened by the force of Henry's love for her. The everyday routine of decades had softened those emotions. The passion they had once shared had long since given way to a quieter, more tender appreciation. But Henry's words still retained their power.

I would do anything to make you happy.

She reflected on the past few months, endless hours she'd spent in bed, hovering between sleep and unwanted consciousness. Hours that Henry had tended to her, washed clothes, bought groceries, taken care of Cassie, tried to help Lydia come to terms with her grief. He'd promised, all those years ago, to make her happy. And he hadn't stopped trying.

Lydia pushed the papers back into the drawer, moving with a sudden impatience. She rushed down the stairs, calling out his name, but no one answered. She peered out the front windows and saw his car parked in front, then she checked the backyard. In the distance, the greenhouse door was open.

Lydia walked briskly down the backyard path. She was like a giddy teenager again, simultaneously excited and nervous about seeing the boy she liked. Filled with anticipation about what would happen when she finally told him how she felt.

Henry stood at the other side of the greenhouse, holding Cassie so she could look at a row of seedlings. Lydia paused, watching his strong arms support his granddaughter, listening to his calm voice explain how the plants were growing. His fingers brushed gently along a tiny leaf, then he took Cassie's hand in his and helped her touch. Cassie stared silently, utterly caught up in Henry's spell. Lydia remembered what that was like, being the object of Henry's attention. The sense that you were the most important person in the world.

Lydia started walking toward them. Cassie saw her first, crying out, "Grandma!" and wriggling to make Henry put her down. Lydia bent and hugged Cassie, kissing her cheeks until Cassie pulled away in a fit of giggles. Henry was striding toward her now, concern in his eyes. When had the sight of his wife made him so wary?

Lydia flew into his arms, the impact of her body making him step back in surprise. Then he straightened and he held her with a strength and warmth that transported her to the years they were teenagers, when they clung to each other as if letting go would make them wither away. Lydia's shoulders were shaking, and Henry reached down to wipe her tears, but her face was dry—she was laughing, laughing for the first time in months. Cassie heard her and joined in, her light, musical voice echoing through the greenhouse.

"Henry, I found the letter." Lydia knew she didn't have to explain. He would understand.

"Oh, that," he said.

"The…the things you said—I'd forgotten,"

Lydia stammered. "I'd forgotten how much I love you."

"You never forgot," Henry reassured her. "I know that."

"You've rescued me so many times," Lydia said. "And I kept forgetting. I kept taking you for granted...."

"You've rescued me just as many times," Henry said. "When Timothy died, I thought I would, too. I know what it's like to go through this kind of grief. I know it takes time. Without you back then, I wouldn't have made it."

Lydia cried then, tears for Timothy, tears for Henry as a young man, so sad and so alone.

"How do you get through it?" Lydia whispered. "How do you get over this?"

"You don't," Henry said. "You survive, that's all. Make what you can out of the rest of your life. Honor the person who died by not giving up."

"Grandpa! Look!" Cassie tugged at Henry's trousers, holding up a tiny flower she'd plucked from one of the pallets.

"Cass!" Lydia began to scold, but Henry shushed her.

"Next time," he said to Cassie, "ask me before you pick something, okay, honey? But that's a real pretty flower you've got there. What do you say we bring it inside and put it in your room?"

Cassie smiled delightedly and skipped toward the door. Henry put his arm around Lydia's shoulders and they walked out behind her.

"It's not over, don't you see?" Henry said. "We still have to be parents."

It wasn't over. Her own child might be gone, but Lydia had been given a second chance. A chance to raise Cassie the way she wished she'd raised Paul—with love and acceptance rather than unreasonable expectations. Cassie, a little girl who'd lost both her parents, whose own grief Lydia had overlooked.

"Is Shelly's mother still trying to get custody?" Lydia asked.

"Looks like it," Henry replied. "We'll know for sure in a few weeks."

"I won't let her take Cassie."

"Let's cross that bridge when we come to it," Henry said. "No one's coming for Cassie anytime soon."

Lydia walked back to the house that day with a determination stronger than her grief. She, Henry and Cassie were a family. She would do whatever she had to do to make them a happy one. She still cried for Paul, late at night or at times when she'd the house to herself. As Henry had predicted, she never got over his loss. But she transformed her sadness and guilt into strength—whatever she hadn't been able to give Paul, she would give Cassie. She would encourage Cassie's interests, support her dreams, remind her that she was deeply loved.

And Cassie would never, ever, find out the truth of her father's birth. Some secrets were meant to stay buried.

Chapter 15

Cassie

Cassie folded Cooper's letter and slipped it between the towels in the linen closet. She liked knowing it was there, available whenever she needed it. She'd contemplated bringing it to Lydia's, to show her grandmother how her life with Cooper had changed, then decided against it. This was personal. It deserved to be savored privately.

"You ready?" Cooper called from the front hall. He'd gotten up at six that morning to finish a contract so he could come to Lydia and Henry's for lunch. If they were going to be married the Fourth of July weekend, these planning sessions were critical.

The highway was busier than usual. The arrival of warm weather had apparently encouraged more people to leave home. But Cooper didn't seem stressed by the stop-and-go traffic. He put on his sunglasses and turned up the radio, making Cassie laugh at his attempts to play air drums on the steering wheel. Quitting her job had been good for them both. Cooper still worked hard, but he was able to leave work behind during his precious time off. Cassie's new ease was rubbing off on him.

"So how was your last day?" Lydia asked Cassie, after greeting them both with hugs and kisses.

"Not bad," Cassie said. "I spent the morning cleaning out my desk, then my group treated me to lunch. Jeffrey even took me aside to tell me I'd always have a place at the firm."

"He's convinced Cassie will come to her senses and beg for her job back in a few weeks," Cooper said with a smile.

"Not likely," Cassie said. "I was so relieved

to walk out of that building—honestly, it was like being released from a life sentence."

"This giving you any ideas, Coop?" Henry laughed.

"Not yet," Cooper said. "At least one of us has to be gainfully employed, you know. Mortgage and all."

Cassie slapped Cooper lightly on the arm. "Grandpa, did Grandma tell you about the interview I've got next week? It sounds like a great opportunity...."

They gathered at the dining room table, chatting and joking like old friends. Cooper, she noticed, no longer talked to her grandparents with careful respect. He teased Lydia and traded knowing glances with Henry—he was part of the family. It felt right to have him here. They were finally in balance.

She considered telling her grandmother what she and Cooper had talked about on the drive down, how they'd passed the suburbs just outside the city and discussed where they'd move when they had children. Not Knox Junction—they agreed it was a little too far from downtown. But maybe a town in between, a place Lydia and Henry could easily drive when they wanted to see their great-grandchildren. When get-togethers would be more than just Sunday lunch.

Probably wouldn't happen for a few years. Not until Cassie got a new job, and worked for a year or two. But for the first time, Cassie could clearly see a future unfolding before her. A future full of promise and purpose. One she'd chosen for herself.

"If you're all finished," Lydia said, picking up her plate and reaching for Henry's, "I've got a list of wedding questions to go over with Cassie."

"That's my cue," Henry said. "Why don't you let me and Cooper clean up? You go off and have your girl talk."

Lydia kissed him on the cheek, and Cassie smiled at Cooper's grateful expression. "Saved!" he whispered in her ear.

Cassie followed Lydia into the living room. After confirming that she did want a buffet rather than a sit-down lunch, and that alcohol would definitely be served, Cassie peered at the next item on the list. Invitations.

"Are you sure you want to send them yourselves?" Lydia asked. "I believe it's proper etiquette, if I'm hosting…"

Cassie shrugged. "If you really want them

to go out in your name, that's fine with me. Just promise you'll put Cooper's somewhere on there too."

Lydia smiled happily. "I'm sure there's a right way to do it. I'll ask Doris—her niece got married last year." She added a check mark to the paper.

"I've got all the addresses," Cassie said. "I'll bring them next time I come." She paused, unsure how to broach unwelcome news. "Actually, I've been meaning to talk to you about that. I want to invite my mom's mother." She still couldn't think of the woman as her grandmother. That title was reserved for Lydia. "Eve."

Lydia stared at her, shocked. "Eve?" she said, her voice tinged with disgust. "But... you haven't seen her for years!"

"Um, actually, I saw her a few weeks ago," Cassie admitted. "She's changed—you wouldn't believe it. She stopped drinking a while ago, and she's really straightened herself out."

"She sent me a note a while ago," Lydia said, "claiming she had undergone some sort of treatment and wanted to right past wrongs. But I didn't believe her."

"Please, Grandma," Cassie said. "I want someone from my mother's family to be there. And Eve—she's not a bad person."

Lydia sat silently.

"I know it's hard to forgive her for the accident," Cassie said. "I talked to her about that night. You know what she told me? That my dad and mom were celebrating. She blames herself for letting them drink too much. She always will, I think—"

"Wait," Lydia interrupted. "What did she say about Paul?"

"That when my dad came to her house that night, he said he'd worked things out with you and he felt like a new person. She said he was happier than she'd ever seen him."

Cassie watched Lydia's face crumple as she spoke. She'd hoped these words would bring her grandmother some comfort, but the opposite seemed to be happening. Lydia's lips trembled and tears spilled from her eyes down her cheeks.

"Grandma!" Cassie exclaimed, reaching over to grab her hands. Lydia's fingers gripped hers tightly, and a smile curled the edges of her mouth.

"Oh, honey." Lydia was obviously struggling to keep her voice level. "All these years, I thought…"

"It's okay," Cassie said, stroking her grandmother's hands.

"The last time I saw Paul, we had a fight," Lydia explained. "At least, I thought it was a fight. He left the house so angry. And I never spoke to him again. That was my last memory—him storming out of the house…"

"Well, whatever it was, it sounds as though he got over it," Cassie said. "Eve says he was happy. He talked about you to her, and he was happy, all right?"

Lydia nodded, the tears still falling despite her smile. "Bless you for telling me," she said.

"You can thank Eve," Cassie said. "That is, if you invite her to the wedding."

"Cassie." Lydia jerked to attention. "Did Paul tell Eve what he'd worked out with me?"

"Eve didn't mention anything specific. I think she assumed it was the usual mother-son stuff. You and my dad butted heads a lot, didn't you?"

"Yes, the usual mother-son stuff, as you say. Nothing more than that." But Lydia wouldn't meet Cassie's eyes. Cassie waited, wondering if Lydia was finally going to confide in her.

Lydia stood up suddenly, wiping her face briskly with the back of her hands. "You know, I almost forgot. I've got something to show you downstairs."

Cassie followed her to her basement workroom, where the quilting table was covered with bolts of cloth. But in contrast to the vibrant colors Lydia usually favored, these fabrics were shades of cream and light green, like a beachscape on a cloudy day. Cassie ran her hand over them, feeling the comforting softness.

"What do you think?" Lydia asked. "For your quilt."

Cassie smiled. "It's perfect, Grandma."

"Don't worry—I've got a very conservative pattern in mind," Lydia said. "I have a sketch here somewhere...." She began pushing fabric aside, then peered around the room, eventually settling on a box in one corner. "Here it is," she said, and as she turned, she noticed Cassie still staring at the box. The box where she'd found Henry's letter.

The silence hung heavily between them. Lydia had every opportunity to change the subject, but she didn't. She waited for Cassie to speak.

"Grandma," Cassie said hesitantly, "when I was here before, I did look in that box. I found the letter."

Lydia watched her.

"It's from Grandpa, isn't it?" Cassie asked. "Even though it's signed F.B.?"

Lydia smiled. "Farm Boy. It's a nickname I used to have for him."

Cassie was ready to tell her grandmother the whole story—how she'd searched for the truth, and found peace in her own life. But how much did Lydia really need to know? Did she need to hear that Victor DiStefano was still disparaging her, more than fifty years later? That he had no interest in learning about his son's life?

Cassie decided to tell Lydia only the part that mattered. The information that would make her happy.

"After reading it…" Cassie hesitated, embarrassed. "Well, I was really touched. I've never gotten a letter like that in my life. Cooper and I were having some problems—as you probably guessed—and I told him about it. Not what was in the letter, exactly—I know that's private. But he could tell I needed some romance, even if I didn't know it myself. So he wrote me a love letter. Put down on paper how much he loves me, how he wants to work everything out… Now we're closer than ever, and it never would've happened if I hadn't seen your letter."

Lydia reached out and hugged her granddaughter. She brushed her hand against Cassie's cheek, in a way she hadn't done since Cassie was a child.

"These men can surprise us, can't they?" she said. "I hope you saved it."

"The letter?" asked Cassie. "Oh, yes. It's in a safe place."

"You know," Lydia began, "a woman in my quilting group once told me it's good luck to sew a love letter into a quilt."

"Why?" Cassie asked.

"It sounds like the kind of nonsense your aunt Nell would come up with, doesn't it, along with crystals and all that rubbish." Lydia smiled at the idea. "But I've always believed it. If a letter was written with love, perhaps that spirit can be sewn into the fabric. Then you can wrap yourself in it whenever you need comforting."

Cassie laughed. "It's a nice idea," she said, "but I want my letter accessible. If Cooper's really getting on my nerves, I want to be able to take it out and remind myself why I married him."

"I understand," Lydia said. "I don't have to read Henry's letter anymore. I memorized it years ago." She smoothed the pieces of fabric on the table. "I might find another use for it soon." Cassie watched her grandmother's hands move through the cloth, already gauging how the quilt squares would fit together. And she could picture what would happen next: those same hands smoothing the yellowed paper between two pieces of fabric, stitching the letter into Cassie's marriage quilt. A bond of love enveloping the next generation.

"But your letter…" Cassie began.

"I don't need it anymore," Lydia said. "It's served its purpose."

That night, as she slipped into bed, Lydia told Henry that Cassie had discovered his letter.

"You should've thrown it away years ago," Henry muttered in mock disgust.

Lydia rubbed his shoulder. "I wish you'd

seen her face, Henry. She's happy. Really happy."

"I know," he said. "Cooper, too."

Lydia pressed her stomach against Henry's back, her legs next to his, tucked together in a curve formed naturally from years of experience. Her hand stroked Henry's arm and his feet intertwined with hers.

"Cold?" she asked.

"A little."

Lydia reached down and pulled up the quilt, a riot of bright oranges and reds and yellows. As she tugged, her fingers traced the outline of the paper within, the page she'd sewn inside years ago.

Dear, dear Henry,
I received your letter today. You say you love me more than I know, but I do know. Deep down, I always have. What I couldn't admit until now was how much I love you back. I've done everything I could to deny my feelings, hurting you in the process. I've put myself first, always. Yet you continue to love me. I see now, too late, what I left behind.

Henry, something terrible has happened. Something unforgivable. I've made a horrible mistake for which I alone must bear the consequences. That's why I ran off to Europe so suddenly— because of my own shame and regret. Not because of you.

I wish I could write that I don't love you. Then you could forget me and start a new life. That would be the right thing to do. But you see, I must tell you the truth, or as much as I dare. I do still love you. I miss you desperately. At night, I think of your arms holding me. I relive that night in the apple orchard, the night I once tried so hard to forget. If you can forgive me, there may be hope for us. Right now, I need time to sort it all out. But I will come back, and when I do, I'll return to you if you want me. The choice is yours.

I love you. I always will.

Your Lydia

* * * * *

ReaderService.com

Manage your account online!

- Review your order history
- Manage your payments
- Update your address

---

*We've designed
the Harlequin® Reader Service
website just for you.*

Enjoy all the features!

- Reader excerpts from any series
- Respond to mailings and
  special monthly offers
- Discover new series available to you
- Browse the Bonus Bucks catalog
- Share your feedback

Visit us at:

ReaderService.com

REQUEST YOUR FREE BOOKS!
2 FREE NOVELS PLUS 2 FREE GIFTS!

HARLEQUIN®

super romance®

More Story...More Romance

YES! Please send me 2 FREE Harlequin® Superromance® novels and my 2 FREE gifts (gifts are worth about $10). After receiving them, if I don't wish to receive any more books, I can return the shipping statement marked "cancel." If I don't cancel, I will receive 6 brand-new novels every month and be billed just $4.94 per book in the U.S. or $5.24 per book in Canada. That's a savings of at least 14% off the cover price! It's quite a bargain! Shipping and handling is just 50¢ per book in the U.S. and 75¢ per book in Canada.* I understand that accepting the 2 free books and gifts places me under no obligation to buy anything. I can always return a shipment and cancel at any time. Even if I never buy another book, the two free books and gifts are mine to keep forever.

135/336 HDN F47C

Name	(PLEASE PRINT)	

Address		Apt. #

City	State/Prov.	Zip/Postal Code

Signature (if under 18, a parent or guardian must sign)

Mail to the **Harlequin® Reader Service:**
IN U.S.A.: P.O. Box 1867, Buffalo, NY 14240-1867
IN CANADA: P.O. Box 609, Fort Erie, Ontario L2A 5X3

**Are you a current subscriber to Harlequin Superromance books
and want to receive the larger-print edition?
Call 1-800-873-8635 or visit www.ReaderService.com.**

* Terms and prices subject to change without notice. Prices do not include applicable taxes. Sales tax applicable in N.Y. Canadian residents will be charged applicable taxes. Offer not valid in Quebec. This offer is limited to one order per household. Not valid for current subscribers to Harlequin Superromance books. All orders subject to credit approval. Credit or debit balances in a customer's account(s) may be offset by any other outstanding balance owed by or to the customer. Please allow 4 to 6 weeks for delivery. Offer available while quantities last.

Your Privacy—The Harlequin® Reader Service is committed to protecting your privacy. Our Privacy Policy is available online at www.ReaderService.com or upon request from the Harlequin Reader Service.

We make a portion of our mailing list available to reputable third parties that offer products we believe may interest you. If you prefer that we not exchange your name with third parties, or if you wish to clarify or modify your communication preferences, please visit us at www.ReaderService.com/consumerchoice or write to us at Harlequin Reader Service Preference Service, P.O. Box 9062, Buffalo, NY 14269. Include your complete name and address.

REQUEST YOUR FREE BOOKS!
2 FREE NOVELS PLUS 2 FREE GIFTS!

♦HARLEQUIN®

SPECIAL EDITION
Life, Love & Family

YES! Please send me 2 FREE Harlequin® Special Edition novels and my 2 FREE gifts (gifts are worth about $10). After receiving them, if I don't wish to receive any more books, I can return the shipping statement marked "cancel." If I don't cancel, I will receive 6 brand-new novels every month and be billed just $4.74 per book in the U.S. or $5.24 per book in Canada. That's a savings of at least 14% off the cover price! It's quite a bargain! Shipping and handling is just 50¢ per book in the U.S. and 75¢ per book in Canada.* I understand that accepting the 2 free books and gifts places me under no obligation to buy anything. I can always return a shipment and cancel at any time. Even if I never buy another book, the two free books and gifts are mine to keep forever.

235/335 HDN F46C

Name	(PLEASE PRINT)	

Address	Apt. #

City	State/Prov.	Zip/Postal Code

Signature (if under 18, a parent or guardian must sign)

Mail to the Harlequin® Reader Service:
IN U.S.A.: P.O. Box 1867, Buffalo, NY 14240-1867
IN CANADA: P.O. Box 609, Fort Erie, Ontario L2A 5X3

Want to try two free books from another line?
Call 1-800-873-8635 or visit www.ReaderService.com.

* Terms and prices subject to change without notice. Prices do not include applicable taxes. Sales tax applicable in N.Y. Canadian residents will be charged applicable taxes. Offer not valid in Quebec. This offer is limited to one order per household. Not valid for current subscribers to Harlequin Special Edition books. All orders subject to credit approval. Credit or debit balances in a customer's account(s) may be offset by any other outstanding balance owed by or to the customer. Please allow 4 to 6 weeks for delivery. Offer available while quantities last.

Your Privacy—The Harlequin® Reader Service is committed to protecting your privacy. Our Privacy Policy is available online at www.ReaderService.com or upon request from the Harlequin Reader Service.

We make a portion of our mailing list available to reputable third parties that offer products we believe may interest you. If you prefer that we not exchange your name with third parties, or if you wish to clarify or modify your communication preferences, please visit us at www.ReaderService.com/consumerschoice or write to us at Harlequin Reader Service Preference Service, P.O. Box 9062, Buffalo, NY 14269. Include your complete name and address.

REQUEST YOUR FREE BOOKS!

 HARLEQUIN® HISTORICAL:
Where love is timeless

2 FREE NOVELS PLUS 2 **FREE GIFTS!**

YES! Please send me 2 FREE Harlequin® Historical novels and my 2 FREE gifts (gifts are worth about $10). After receiving them, if I don't wish to receive any more books, I can return the shipping statement marked "cancel." If I don't cancel, I will receive 6 brand-new novels every month and be billed just $5.44 per book in the U.S. or $5.74 per book in Canada. That's a savings of at least 16% off the cover price! It's quite a bargain! Shipping and handling is just 50¢ per book in the U.S. and 75¢ per book in Canada.* I understand that accepting the 2 free books and gifts places me under no obligation to buy anything. I can always return a shipment and cancel at any time. Even if I never buy another book, the two free books and gifts are mine to keep forever.

246/349 HDN F42C

Name	(PLEASE PRINT)	
Address		Apt. #
City	State/Prov.	Zip/Postal Code

Signature (if under 18, a parent or guardian must sign)

Mail to the **Harlequin® Reader Service:**
IN U.S.A.: P.O. Box 1867, Buffalo, NY 14240-1867
IN CANADA: P.O. Box 609, Fort Erie, Ontario L2A 5X3

Want to try two free books from another line?
Call 1-800-873-8635 or visit www.ReaderService.com.

* Terms and prices subject to change without notice. Prices do not include applicable taxes. Sales tax applicable in N.Y. Canadian residents will be charged applicable taxes. Offer not valid in Quebec. This offer is limited to one order per household. Not valid for current subscribers to Harlequin Historical books. All orders subject to credit approval. Credit or debit balances in a customer's account(s) may be offset by any other outstanding balance owed by or to the customer. Please allow 4 to 6 weeks for delivery. Offer available while quantities last.

Your Privacy—The Harlequin® Reader Service is committed to protecting your privacy. Our Privacy Policy is available online at www.ReaderService.com or upon request from the Harlequin Reader Service.

We make a portion of our mailing list available to reputable third parties that offer products we believe may interest you. If you prefer that we not exchange your name with third parties, or if you wish to clarify or modify your communication preferences, please visit us at www.ReaderService.com/consumerschoice or write to us at Harlequin Reader Service Preference Service, P.O. Box 9062, Buffalo, NY 14269. Include your complete name and address.

HHDIR13R